FINDING BUCKY

C.J. PETIT

TABLE OF CONTENTS

PROLOGUE

April 5, 1851
Southfield, Michigan

"Hey, Piggy. Maybe you and Bucky should get married. Then your kids would look like pigs with teeth!" yelled Billy Riggs to a loud chorus of laughter and pig sounds.

Stanley tried to act like the daily teasing didn't hurt, but it did. He knew that he should try and stand up to them, but knew he was no match for those big fifth graders or even the third years, for that matter. So, rather than take another beating, he turned and walked away, ashamed at his cowardice.

"There goes Piggy, just waddling off. Oink! Oink! Sooeeee! Pig!" shouted Hank Thornton, the biggest of the fifth graders and probably Stanley's biggest tormentor.

Stanley continued to walk away, wishing that he could stand up to them and give it back, *but what could he do?* He'd just get teased again, or worse. Sometimes, the boys would get around him in a circle then play 'Push Piggy' and just keep shoving him back and forth until he fell before circling around him and shouting, "Pig in a poke!"

FINDING BUCKY

Once he was clear of the boys, he walked to the school entrance and sat on the steps. He was all too aware of his fat body that had instigated the teasing and bullying for long as he could remember. He tried not to eat so much, but it never seemed to make a difference. Being ten years old and being fat wasn't any fun, and he didn't think being fat and eleven would be any better.

As he was sitting, he heard the same group of boys turn their attention to his female counterpart, Ellie McCormick, known to the boys and girls alike as Bucky. Looking at Ellie from behind, she looked like any other girl, but when she turned to face you, the origin of her nickname was plainly visible. Her front teeth were enormously out of proportion. Add the apparent absence of eyebrows to her overly large incisors, and Ellie was the other freak in the school worthy of derision. Ellie was only nine, and despite her prowess in the classroom, was shunned by everyone, everyone but her fellow outcast, Piggy Murray.

Stan and Ellie, even though they were in different years, sat together in the classroom, mainly because no one else wanted to sit with them. Both did well in class, but failed miserably with their social skills, at least with the other students. Yet soon after they had been forced to be together, they found solace on that same bench. They discovered a strong kinship that only outcasts could understand. On that bench seat they were Stan and Ellie, not Piggy and Bucky.

Stan may not have defended himself against the cruel treatment from the other students, but he would try to protect Ellie, even though it meant opening himself up for more ridicule and abuse. It was after one of those interventions that Stan began getting linked with Ellie as a future husband and breeder of buck-toothed pigs. It was now a standard taunt, and both he and Ellie were subjected to it. The girls were just as bad as the boys when it came to attacking Ellie, but they usually left it to the boys to harass Stan.

Ellie was on the other side of the schoolyard when she heard the taunts, then spotted Stan, walked over to the steps and sat next to him.

He looked over at her, smiled and said, "Hello, Ellie."

Ellie didn't smile but replied, "Hi, Stan. Are you all right?"

"I guess."

"Can you help me with my arithmetic later?"

Stan nodded and replied, "I'll always help you, Ellie."

Ellie smiled at Stan, a rare occurrence as she tried desperately to hide her big teeth, and her sparkling eyes made Stan smile back. Ellie always made Stan smile, whether she smiled or not.

It had been like that between Stan and Ellie since Ellie first arrived at school, her prominent teeth almost instantly earning her the 'Bucky' nickname. Stan, who had been the sole brunt of their taunts for his entire first year, was sympathetic to the first-year student. There were times, especially in that first year, when Ellie would burst into tears, and Stan would be there to console her. He'd tell her that she was smart and a good person, and that her attackers were stupid and stinky, too. He was able to turn her tears into hidden smiles with his humor and kind words. He was always there to let her know that she was better than they were, but helping Ellie made Stan feel better, too. It made him feel as if he was her protector, her armored knight deflecting the dragon's flaming breath.

FINDING BUCKY

At first, they used each other as shields to help ward off the barbs of their schoolmates, but it soon grew into a deep friendship, each confiding hidden feelings and thoughts that they would tell no others, not even their parents...especially not their parents. What was unusual was that both Ellie and Stan were only children. Every other student in the school had at least two other siblings. Of course, this added ammunition to the verbal bullying.

Ellie's parents always told her that she would change and soon be a pretty girl that all the boys would like, but she didn't believe them.

Stan's mother tried to tell him that he'd change as well, but his father was embarrassed and ashamed of his only son and made him work even harder to try and burn off the fat, but to no avail. No matter how much work Stan did or how well he did in school, his father never gave him any praise.

While his father never called him 'Piggy', he did have another whole dictionary of insulting nicknames for his son. Stan could have hated his father but instead, vowed that he would try to prove him wrong and worked even harder to make that happen.

Stan and Ellie may have had different home lives, but ever since those first few days on the same school bench seat, they found comfort in each other's company. They had no one else, yet each felt that they needed no one else.

———

May 22, 1857

Stan and Ellie sat on the steps of the empty schoolhouse. The school year was over, and both had already graduated, but it remained one of the places where they would talk.

They needed the privacy even with the school closed as Ellie's parents had forbidden her to see Stan for some unknown reason. Neither had spoken for five minutes as they each tried to find a solution to their pending separation.

Stan finally asked, "Ellie, can't you stay with your grandparents or something?"

Elli shook her head and replied, "I asked my father if I could and he said we were all going and that's all he wanted to hear about it."

"But it's so far away, Ellie."

"I know. But I'll write to you, Stan. I promise."

"I know you will, Ellie. And I'll write to you, but it's just not the same," he said, then after a short pause, asked, "So, you're leaving on Saturday?"

She nodded and said, "I'm going to miss you terribly, Piggy."

He grinned at her whenever she called him Piggy because it was meant to remind him of their long-term friendship. It wasn't the same, mean-spirited taunt that he still heard from others.

"And I'll miss you more, Bucky," he replied.

She gave him a big smile before saying, "At least when we get there, no one will ever call me that."

"You're too pretty to be called anything but beautiful, Ellie."

Ellie glanced around the empty schoolyard, and quickly kissed Stan on the cheek.

"Ellie," Stan said quietly, "when you get there, you know you'll be very popular with boys. You're pretty and smart and so nice.

I'd understand if you found someone better. Heck, anyone is better than me."

Ellie sat up straight, glared at him and snapped, "Stanley Murray, I'm ashamed of you! You insulted me by making me sound like some shallow tart who thinks that looks are all that are important."

Stan put his palms out before him as he shook his head and quickly said, "No, Ellie. I'm sorry. That came out all mixed up. It's just that we're going to be so far apart, and I want you to be happy."

Ellie's glare evaporated and her face softened as she said quietly, "You make me happy, Stan. No one else can ever make me any happier."

"But we're still kids, Ellie. You're going to grow up to be a really beautiful woman and I'll always be a fat slob."

Ellie wanted to slap him for that remark, but she knew why he felt that way. Until she was twelve, her teeth had marked her as Bucky. Then after the end of her fifth year, the sudden change that her parents had hoped would come finally arrived. It was the same summer she started having her monthlies that she began to undergo a physical transformation that made a momentous change in her appearance. By the time she returned to school, the changes were evident and suddenly, she was no longer Bucky and drew the attention of the other boys. Stan had gotten taller, but still carried too much weight. He was still 'Piggy' and now the lone member of the outcasts.

Yet, Ellie continued to sit with Stan and ignore those boys who had taunted her when all they noticed was her teeth. Even though Stan hadn't had to defend Ellie any longer, being the only object of derision kept the taunts and abuse at constant levels.

Instead of slapping him, she said quietly, "Stan, it doesn't matter to me. Only you matter."

Stan looked at Ellie, smiled and said, "You're the nicest person I ever met, Ellie. Don't ever change."

———

Three days later, Stan waved at a despondent Ellie as she sat on the back of their Conestoga wagon. She was still teary-eyed but waved back. Stan was miserable but hoped that Ellie would be happy in her new home in Wyoming.

He stood watching the line of wagons rolling west and remained staring for another forty minutes before it disappeared around Parson's Hill. He exhaled, then turned and walked slowly back to his parents' house.

When he was in his room that night, he sat at his small desk and began to write a letter to Ellie. He'd write letters to her every day until he received her first. Once he had an address, he'd mail the whole bunch. He guessed he'd have over sixty before he knew where to send them.

The stack was almost eighteen inches deep before he stopped adding to the pile. He had never received a letter from Ellie, yet he was convinced that it wasn't Ellie's decision not to write. Her parents hated him, and he didn't doubt for a moment that they had somehow kept her from writing.

———

August 20, 1861

Stan stood in line with the other recruits. He was already wearing his uniform and was anxious to receive his weapons issue. He'd be assigned a forty-inch saber and one of the new

FINDING BUCKY

Spencer carbines that had really impressed him. The Michigan Brigade was among the first to be equipped with the weapon, and he really wanted to try the gun, but knew he'd have to do it under the watchful eye of Sgt. Harper. Most cavalry units were being issued the Burnside carbine. It was a good gun but was a single shot breech-loader that needed percussion caps. The Spencer was a significant improvement in his opinion and those of his fellow Wolverines. A seven-shot repeating carbine that used brass cartridges loaded into a tube in the stock. It had a good range, too.

He finally reached the front of the line, received his issue saber and then his Spencer, serial number 6100992. He signed for both weapons and was handed a box of cartridges for the carbine, then walked back to his tent and sat down, waiting for Jim to return with his weapons. While he waited, he removed the big cartridges from the box and slid them into his cartridge pouch.

Now, he just needed his horse. He loved horses, like most boys did. His only horse that he was able to call his own before joining the cavalry was a tired mare that couldn't do more than trot, and even that was an adventure. He was convinced that his new horse would be much better.

Jim Franklin came walking toward him with a big grin on his face and his sword, carbine and ammunition in his hands.

"Stan, did you ever see anything so beautiful as this carbine?"

"Yeah, but she's gone to Wyoming."

Jim shook his head, laughed and said, "Stan, you are a hoot. Your girl left four years ago and you're still mooning over her."

He sat down across from Stan in their dog tent, set down his saber and began admiring the carbine.

"You know she was never really my girl, Jim. I told you that. She was just always nice to me when no one else was."

"Why weren't they nice to you?"

"Because I was so fat."

"You were fat? Really?" he asked as he pried his eyes from the Spencer and looked at his friend.

"As fat as a pig. All the other kids called me Piggy."

"When did you lose all the weight?"

"Right after she left, I sort of apprenticed myself to a blacksmith."

"How can you be 'sort of' apprenticed?"

"It wasn't official. You know, he didn't come asking for me or anything. He needed some help, so I offered to work for free. At first, he thought I was kidding, with me being fat and all. But, after two months, he began to pay me. I was finally able to move out of my family home and I worked as a blacksmith until last month."

"The blacksmith part I can see, but I still can't believe you were fat."

"Trust me, I was. Didn't you have any fat kids in your school?"

"Yeah. Fatty Schumer. We ran him ragged."

"Now you know what it was like for me, but I was on the receiving end."

12

"I'll bet that none of those kids would mess with you now."

"I don't care anymore, Jim. I just want to get on with my life, you know?"

Jim didn't understand, but nodded and asked, "How long do you think this war's gonna last?"

"I think those Rebs are serious, Jim. They're mighty unhappy with us Yankees."

"Well, I ain't all that happy with them, neither."

"They're the ones that started it, Jim. It may take a while, but we're gonna lick 'em."

"It won't take that long, Stan. You'll see."

Stan looked at Jim, then opened his Spencer's breech as he replied, "I hope you're right, Jim. I really do."

———

July 3, 1863

First Sergeant Stan Murray sat astride his anonymous dark brown gelding next to First Lieutenant Fritz Anderson as sounds of sporadic cannon and gunfire rolled across the ground from the south near Culp's Hill. It sounded like the rebels were making another push over there, but his attention was to the west, as it was for every man in the Michigan Brigade.

Lieutenant Anderson pointed to the west and said loudly, "That's Jeb Stuart down there, Sergeant Murray. We're outnumbered, but we're gonna stop those rebel bastards,"

"Yes, sir. The men are ready. We'll take it to 'em."

"You're damned straight."

Stan sat with his new Spencer carbine in its scabbard, but it wasn't going to be needed in this action. This was going to be an old-fashioned saber charge. They wouldn't be using any of the long guns today, but maybe some would put their pistols to use once they closed on the enemy. He glanced behind him at the men, and found all of their eyes staring forward, anxious to get into the fight. All the other battles and skirmishes they had survived paled in comparison to the one that awaited them just minutes away.

This one was the Big One, the important fight that would make a difference in the battle and maybe the war itself. They had to stop that rebel cavalry from flanking the right of the Union forces.

If that large mounted force made it to the rear of the Union lines, the whole defense would collapse, especially if Bobby Lee threw his infantry at the front. He suspected that was exactly what he was planning on doing because the first two days at Gettysburg hadn't gone his way. It looked like he was going all out for one more push, and Stan felt that this would be the last day of this costly battle. He knew that the infantry had taken the biggest hits, but this was their time.

They had to stop J.E.B. Stuart's cavalry from turning a Confederate defeat into a rebel victory. They had to keep General Meade's Army of the Potomac from being sent scurrying back to Washington in tatters.

He could see General Custer up front watching the oncoming rebel cavalry for the right moment to launch the attack. He was only a couple of years older than Stan but already wore the stars of a general officer. He may have been flashy, but the man could fight, and every one of his men wanted to follow him into this fight.

FINDING BUCKY

The general suddenly waved his saber, the bugle sounded and hundreds of Union cavalry charged across the lush grass of the Pennsylvania countryside, throwing thousands of clumps of grass into the air as the iron shoes smashed into the turf. It began from the front as the men in the back waited for the rider before him to move. It was like a giant squeeze box as it began to suck in air before playing its first note. Then, it became a wave of blue as the Wolverines thundered down into the long valley.

Stan didn't think of anything other than maintaining his position until contact was made with the Confederate cavalry as his horse galloped beneath him and his saber rested on his right shoulder until it was needed.

Stuart's large column halted at the surprising sight of the oncoming Yankee charge, drew their sabers and moved to meet the attack. The Confederates greatly outnumbered the Yankee horsemen, but the Wolverines were determined and only had to stop Stuart to secure the victory. Stuart had to get through and to do that, his men would have to kill almost every one of those boys in blue from Michigan.

The two groups collided in a swarm of flashing steel, as horses screamed, and the rebels yelled. The amount of clashing metal sounded like a continuous ringing buzz interspersed with pistol shots and scream of dying men and horses. There was no order anymore as chaos reigned, and Stan was in the middle of it.

He was desperately trying to keep from being sliced or stabbed by the Confederate trooper he was dueling, and after three successful parries, Stan was able to slide his saber across his adversary's weapon and then slam the tip home into his chest. The man fell, and his saber dropped to the ground beside him. Stan pulled his mount away and turned to engage another cavalryman. This man was more skilled in his use of the blade.

He was a captain and Stan thought he may have learned his skills at the Military Academy at West Point. Their sabers crashed together almost a dozen times before Stan gained a critical edge, the strength of his arm was far more than the captain's. He could feel the man's strength ebbing, and after two more strikes the captain simply lost control of his saber, the weapon flying when his grip failed.

Stan could have sliced him in half but didn't. He didn't know why he didn't, but he just turned to take on another foe. The captain just watched him leave, wondering why he wasn't dead. He could have pulled his pistol and shot Stan in the back, but he was, after all, a gentleman, and instead, in an incredible sight on the still very active battlefield, dismounted and recovered his saber before quickly stepping back into the saddle.

The entire clash seemed to have gone on for hours, but probably lasted less than thirty minutes. It suddenly ended when the Rebel bugler sounded the recover call and the rebels began an orderly retreat. The two groups broke apart and the Confederates returned the way they had come. Losses were about the same on both sides, but the Union cavalry had done what they needed to do. They had protected the flank, even as the rebel infantry led by Pickett was making a last desperate charge across the killing fields of Gettysburg and would pay the price for the Yankee cavalry's effort.

The Michigan Brigade had done its job, and the men reformed. First Sgt. Stan Murray found his company and began doing a count of missing, dead and wounded. It hadn't been as costly as he had anticipated after talking to the men to confirm those who were killed. There were none missing but they had suffered four dead and eleven wounded. In a charge of desperation that they had just mounted, he had expected much worse. He took the names of the dead and wounded and looked around for Lieutenant Anderson but didn't see him anywhere.

FINDING BUCKY

He got the men situated and then set his horse to a trot toward a group of officers sitting on their horses in conference. He spotted Captain Arbuckle, the company commander among them, then after drawing close, waited for the captain to notice him.

Finally, the captain glanced his way, caught his eye and waved Stan over.

With no fanfare or embellishment, the captain said, "Sergeant Murray, Lieutenant Anderson died in the initial part of the engagement. The colonel has commissioned you as a second lieutenant. You'll be taking Lieutenant Pruitt's spot. Lieutenant Pruitt is now a first lieutenant. Tell Sergeant Hancock that he is now the first sergeant and Corporal Riley will replace him as sergeant. Tell him to make his recommendation for corporal to me."

Stan didn't even blink as he replied, "Yes, sir. Did you want the casualty report?"

"Yes, how many?"

"I have the names here, sir. We lost four dead and eleven wounded, four of them serious. The other seven should be back to duty in a day or two."

"Very good," he answered as Stan handed him the list before wheeling his mount away.

He trotted his horse back to the still waiting troopers, who were formed into a rough standard formation.

He pulled his horse to a stop before them and in the same manner as the captain had used to give him the news, Stan said, "Lieutenant Anderson was killed in the initial contact with the rebels. Lieutenant Pruitt is now a first lieutenant and will take

17

his place. I will take Lieutenant's Pruitt position. Sergeant Hancock, you will be the new company first sergeant and Corporal Riley will take your position. I'll need you to give me the name of the new corporal as soon as possible."

Sgt. Richard Hancock trotted over and saluted, then Stan returned his first salute as an officer.

"I'll let you know…Sir," he said but spoiled the effect somewhat with a grin.

Stan kept his own grin to himself, and replied, "Very well…Sergeant."

———

After Gettysburg, the unit was involved in other battles and skirmishes, the major ones being the Battle of the Wilderness and Yellow Tavern, but Stan knew that Gettysburg was a crushing defeat for Lee and from that battle on, the Union army would control the flow of the war. Even though both sides lost about the same number at Gettysburg, the Confederates lost a third of their army, men that would be hard to replace, and just as importantly, it was Lee's first major defeat and a terrific morale booster for the Army of the Potomac. Now, it would just be a grinding, man-chewing fight to the finish, and they found just the general to do it, too.

After Gettysburg and General Meade's much criticized decision not to pursue Lee's retreating army, President Lincoln brought in a general from the western battlefields who understood the realities of war and the huge advantage the North had in manpower and material.

General Grant was a Westerner, as Stan was, with no spit and polish. He was a fighter, not a politician. He would press the attack, and Stan just hoped that General Robert E. Lee would have the common sense to surrender when it became obvious, even to the most dedicated rebel that they couldn't win on the battlefield. Stan knew it would take more than just common sense, it would take a deep understanding of the consequences for the North and the South alike if Bobby Lee gave in to the strident voices calling for him and the other generals to release their soldiers to undertake an extended guerilla war. It would take an enormous amount of moral courage to ignore those voices and to do what was best for both his men and the country.

When he did surrender at Appomattox Courthouse, Captain Stanley Murray's company was on hand to accept the surrender of the army of Virginia. Immediately after the surrender, the Brigade was dispatched to assist General Sherman in North Carolina with Joe Johnston's army, but his army surrendered before they arrived.

Even though there was still fighting in parts of the South, victory was declared, and the brigade, along with most of the armies went to Washington City to attend the Grand Review of the Armies in May of 1865. Stan had never seen anything like it and doubted if anyone else had, either. It was much like the Roman triumphs that he'd read about in the history books.

As he led his company down the streets of the capital, he wondered how many of his fallen comrades looked down at the pomp and extravagance and laughed. Still, it was better than what the Confederates were doing. They had given their all to their cause and lost. They simply didn't have the manpower or the industrial base even from the start.

Stan thought he'd be mustered out like most of the other men, but the Michigan Brigade was sent packing to Leavenworth, Kansas to serve in the District of the Plains, Department of Missouri. When they finally arrived, they had one horse for every four troopers. As a company commander, Stan had his own animal, of course, but they all knew the situation couldn't last, and it didn't.

Shortly after their arrival, the Brigade began mustering out men. First to go was the Fifth Michigan, and it was soon followed by others. Stan was debating about his future, knowing that he'd never keep his captain's rank because there were too many West Pointers that needed to stay in the army.

But he did know one thing: he'd really like to see Ellie again. Despite the absence of letters even after he was in the army, he knew it hadn't been of her own choosing. Her parents were fine with Ellie being his friend when her teeth made her appear to be headed down the road of spinsterhood, but once she changed dramatically into a pretty young woman, they didn't want her to spend any time with him.

She had defied them as much as she could, but they were insistent. Stan had always believed that the move to Wyoming was partially driven by their need to separate them, even though he had finally figured out the primary reason for their unexpected departure. But he still needed to know where Ellie was and if she had married.

No longer the chubby kid that elicited so many barbs and insults, he wanted to see if there was a place for him in her life. If not, then he would move on.

He was thinking of mustering out in Kansas and heading northwest, but then the rumor mill began to churn out all sorts of news. What was left of the Michigan Brigade would be sent to the Dakota Territory and then to Montana Territory. But he knew it was further away from Wyoming than where he was now, so he put in his papers for mustering out.

Of course, the army being the army, by the time they were finally approved, the unit was at Fort Union in Montana Territory.

FINDING BUCKY

The army's reputation for red tape had just proven itself and added hundreds of miles to his journey, but it was a journey he had to make. He knew the territory was vast, and the populated areas were few, at least those populated by white people.

But Captain Stanley Murray was determined to make that ride across the Plains and even into the Rockies if necessary, to find Ellie and settle that one, driving question in his mind. *Would she still be his Ellie if and when he found her?*

CHAPTER 1

May 21, 1867
Fort Union, Montana Territory

"Say, Captain, you finally getting mustered out?" asked Sergeant Hanratty.

"About time, don't you think? They should have let me out in Leavenworth, but those administrative bastards messed that up."

"No surprise there. Say, Captain, some of us are going to join up with General Custer's 7th. Why don't you join us?"

"He's a Lieutenant Colonel now, Hanratty. When they finally get around to me, I'll probably be working for you as a private."

Hanratty laughed at the idea, and said, "C'mon, Captain. You were a first sergeant before you put on them bars. They'd give you that at least, wouldn't they?"

"Does the army ever do anything that makes a lot of sense, Hanratty?"

He snickered and said, "Now that you mention it, it does seem a rare occurrence."

"I just need to do the final paperwork. I get to keep my saber and my Spencer. They don't want either one back for some reason, so how much ammunition can you spare?"

"Want one ton or two?" he asked as he laughed.

"Let me have six boxes. That should keep the Injuns at bay for a little while."

Sgt. Hanratty stacked the boxes on his shelf, then asked, "You want one of the infantry's Sharps?"

"Any advantage to it?"

"It's more accurate at range than that Spencer of yours. I've got a whole passel of 'em back here. Since they've been mustering out all the walkers, they've got a bunch left over. Some are almost new, too."

"Sure, why not? Got any ammo for 'em?"

"About twice as much as the Spencer rounds."

"Give me six boxes of those, too, and a bunch of percussion caps."

"Want some ammo packs for your pistol?"

"Sure."

Once all the ammunition was stacked, Sgt. Hanratty got a burlap bag and began shoveling them inside. He grabbed three other boxes he didn't mention and tossed them inside as well before returning to his stores and selecting a new Sharps rifle. He really didn't have that many new ones, but he really liked the captain. He was a real officer, not like some of the new ones that were beginning to arrive at the fort. *The man had been a blacksmith, for God's sake!*

He brought the rifle out and laid it on the counter.

"How far do you think you'd be able to hit some Rebel sniper with this thing, Hanratty?"

"Depends if I didn't like him. If I didn't, I figure I could touch him from seven hundred yards."

Stan whistled and said, "I'd sure like to see that."

"So, would I, Captain. So, would I," he said as he grinned.

"Well, I guess I'd better lug this to the Q and wake up those shavetails they've stuck me with."

"Better you than me, Captain."

Stan picked up the heavy bag and slung it over his shoulder before grabbing the rifle, then glanced back at the supply sergeant and grinned.

"You keep 'em all in line, Joe," he said as he began to leave.

"I will. You take care out there, Captain."

"You just helped me to do that."

Hanratty waved and Stan lugged the heavy bag and rifle across the parade grounds to his quarters, nudged the door open with his foot and went inside. The room was empty for the time being, Second Lieutenants John Ellsworth and Frank Bishop were somewhere in Fort Union doing something or other. He really didn't care where or what. He'd be on the road tomorrow, and it was a hundred and fifty miles to the nearest trading post.

He knew that Ellie's family would probably have had to stop at Cheyenne City if they were headed for anywhere else in the Wyoming part of Dakota Territory. Her parents had never told her exactly where they were going, probably to keep her from telling him.

He knew that Ellie was probably married by now and more than likely has two or three children, and he wouldn't blame her a bit. *Why would she wait for a chubby kid for almost ten years?* He just needed to know about her. He knew he could never get on with his life if he didn't know what had become of Ellie. After he had replaced the fat with serious amounts of hard muscle, just as Ellie had experienced with boys when she was no longer Bucky, the girls began paying attention to him. But none of them mattered, only Ellie mattered. Only after he was convinced that Ellie was out of his life would he look for the right woman.

He walked out to the stables to get his horse ready for the long ride. He'd get to keep his current mount, saddle and gear as well, in a manner of speaking. He'd have a hundred dollars deducted from his mustering out pay for the horse and was supposed to pay ten dollars for the carbine, too, but the unit was so late in being mustered out that the Spencers were just becoming a nuisance. His horse had recently been reshod, too, and was a good horse, not spectacular, but a solid, dependable horse. He had two canteens, his bedroll and tent, and his army blanket. Tomorrow, he'd pick up the mule and pack saddle he bought last week.

He already had a money belt to hold all his cash, and it was a significant amount. He didn't let anyone else know just how much he had. His current salary was $115.30 a month, and he'd rarely spent more than twenty dollars a month since he was commissioned in '63. And even without being paid in the last six months, he still had almost four thousand dollars in his money belt and kept another three hundred in his pockets. He'd had to convert the smaller bills to larger bills so they would fit, but it was still a thick wad of bills, and it was all U.S. currency, not bank notes, which meant that it was always accepted at face value. Some of the less reputable banks printed notes like autumn leaves.

He left the quarters and walked to the administrative building, met Sergeant Crenshaw and filled out the necessary mustering out forms. He was given his discharge papers and shook his hand. There was no big ceremony or parade, it was just a routine process. He then walked to the paymaster to collect his mustering out pay. Not being paid in six months wasn't an unusual situation as some units hadn't been paid in over a year, but they had to pay him now. The paymaster checked his records and counted out the $591.80 that Stan was due after the horse deduction. Zack signed the receipt and that was that. He was officially out of the United States Army.

He returned to his quarters and began packing. He'd wear his uniform out of the fort tomorrow and go to the sutler's store after he picked up the mule then get his supplies for the trip. He'd get civilian clothes as well, having not worn anything but a uniform for six years now. It would definitely feel odd wearing a color other than blue. Even though he was supposed to take the saber, Stan felt it was a useless encumbrance and left it on his bunk.

———

The next morning, after his last free breakfast, Captain Stanley R. Murray rode out of Fort Union as Mister Stanley R. Murray. He had his duffle across his lap with the Spencer and the Sharps in his two scabbards.

He left the fort entrance and turned left to the sutler's store, then stopped outside, tied off his horse, lowered his duffle and stepped down. First things first, he needed the mule that he had purchased two days earlier.

He walked to the corral and saw that the hostler had already saddled the mule, so he was ready to go. He led the mule out of the corral and walked him to his horse, trail-hitched him to the saddle and walked inside after hanging his duffle temporarily on the mule's pack saddle.

The sutler, Jake Christian smiled and said, "Morning, Captain."

"Not captain anymore, Jake. Just Stan. I need to get those supplies for my trip. It's only a hundred and fifty miles or so to Miles' trading post, but I'd rather have too much than not enough. Here's what I'll need," he said as he handed him the supply list.

"I'll start getting it together while you go and buy your clothes."

"Say, Jake. Is that what I think it is?" he asked pointing behind the counter at a brass rifle with a loading gate in the side plate.

"It is. A Winchester 1866 model, and I've got three of 'em."

"How'd you get them?"

"A gun drummer told me that they were available, so I put an order in for a dozen, but they only sent me three, and I got 'em in two days ago. Glad to have even three of those repeaters."

"You got ammunition for them?"

"Quite a few really because they use Henry .44 cartridges, which makes sense because it's a Henry with some serious improvements."

"Can I see it?"

"Sure. It's a lot better than the Henry," he said as he took the Winchester '66 from the wall behind the counter and handed it to Stan.

"I heard about these. It uses a loading gate, so you can keep going rather than going through that annoying process of opening the magazine tube and taking the time dropping those cartridges into the tube. How much is it?"

"They're kinda pricey, Captain. Twenty-six dollars, but those Henry cartridges are only eighty cents a box. If you bought them in a big town, they'd be cheaper, but freight costs run up the price a bit."

Stan didn't care about the added cost as he cycled the lever of the Winchester a few times and found it much smoother than the Spencer and it didn't have to be manually cocked either. It fired a smaller round than the Spencer, and the range was significantly lower, but having fifteen .44 caliber rounds available for rapid firing was a huge advantage and the ability to load more cartridges into the loading gate quickly added to the lure of the new repeater, which was the carbine version of the weapon.

"I'll take this one and if you'll let me buy six boxes of cartridges, that will be great."

"Seeing as how you're going cross-country, I'll let you have the cartridges. It you were just hanging around here, I'd only sell you four. I have an order in for more ammo anyway."

"Thanks, Jake."

Stan set the rifle back on the counter as Jake stacked the ammunition next to it.

While Jake was filling his order from the list, Stan went to the clothing section and bought his civilian clothes: four shirts, three pair of heavy britches, a Stetson hat, a heavy and a lighter jacket, and a scarf. It may be May, but up here, it was smart to play it safe. He'd wear his cavalry gloves rather than buying some more, though. He bought two more Union suits and four more pairs of heavy socks as well.

When he returned, Jake was already filling the first pannier with his cooking gear and other hardware. While he was doing that, Stan pulled the second pannier and began unloading the heavy bag that Sgt. Hanratty had given him. He pulled out the three boxes that the supply sergeant had slipped inside and smiled. The smaller boxes contained a new army compass, field glasses, and a heavy pocket watch. Stan didn't even know the army stocked watches, but it made sense, he guessed. He slipped the compass and the watch into his pockets but kept the field glasses out until he'd put them into his saddlebags along with one box of each of the three different size cartridges, percussion caps and the reloading supplies for his Colt Dragoon pistol. He was glad that Hanratty had included a cleaning kit for the Sharps because he had totally forgotten.

It took a while to pack all his purchases and then to hang them on the mule's pack saddle and secure them, but he finally left the sutler's store at 8:45. He had added two scabbards to the pack saddle as well, one held the Spencer and the other the Sharps. He wanted his new repeater with him and had already filled it with cartridges before putting the rest of that initial box of ammunition in his jacket pocket. He had his army long coat packed and wore his lighter jacket and the Stetson as he mounted his gelding. If it wasn't for the gold stripes running down his pant legs, he'd pass for a civilian, which he really was now. He waved to Jake and set his horse in motion to the southwest with Miles' trading post as his destination, expecting to be there in four or five days.

Ellie was having a frustrating day. Her husband, George, hadn't returned home again and the cook had quit, so she sat in the kitchen drinking coffee. She was just so tired of it all. This wasn't the life she had envisioned for herself. She didn't care about the nice house and the hired help. She just wasn't happy.

She picked up her coffee, walked out of the kitchen and down the hallway past the sitting room, the dining room, and the library until she reached the parlor. She sat down and thought how silly she was being. Every woman she knew would be insanely jealous of her situation. She had a handsome, well-to-do husband, a big house with servants to do all the work, and even her own bank account with a substantial balance. But she was lonely. and no one could understand or even seemed to want to understand. She had no one to share her deepest thoughts or feelings any longer.

Her husband, George Rafferty, was a member of the Denver Rafferty family. His father had started with a bank and had diversified into other areas of commerce in and around the city. They were at the hub of what passed for Denver society.

George worked with his father at the bank and was a vice president, was paid a handsome salary and was well-respected. She supposed she shouldn't complain. After all, he never hit her. In fact, he barely touched her. Ellie knew why, too. She wasn't really a wife; she was window dressing.

The successful businessman needed a wife to show around, and Ellie was a beautiful young woman, almost ten years younger than George. The whispers had already started about George when he was still unmarried at thirty, and Ellie had been holding out until the war ended because she knew that Stan had enlisted in '61, and she hoped that he would find her. But her parents were insistent that she forget that part of her life, including her friendship with that hideous Murray boy. They even intercepted her outgoing letters she wrote to Stan letting him know where she was living, and she hadn't realized it until almost five years ago, when it no longer mattered. Their daughter would marry well, and not some fat, directionless boy with no future. Ellie's future would be their future.

When the McCormicks first arrived in Denver, Ellie was dismayed, having expected to be going to Wyoming as she had told Stan. They had deposited the money from the sale of the family farm into the Rafferty's First Colorado Bank, and her father went to work in a clothing store as a clerk.

Years later, when George Rafferty had been told by his father in no uncertain terms that he must marry, George had seen Ellie in the lobby, waiting while her father made a withdrawal. She was a beautiful young woman and George decided that she would suffice.

Ellie was far from enamored of George, and he had acted as if the whole concept of his calling on her was tiresome. But her parents were thrilled with the prospect and told her that if she didn't accept his offer of marriage, she'd be locked out of the house. *She was almost twenty-one for goodness sake!*

So, eight months ago, she and George Rafferty had been married in a very elaborate wedding that appalled Ellie for the sheer waste. She was set up with a bank account by George and told to buy whatever she wanted, which was overkill, really. She could buy any clothing she wanted at the stores by just having the bill added to the family account. Two of the better stores were owned by the Rafferty family anyway, so her money just sat there, both useless and unnecessary, just as Ellie felt she was.

George would come home for dinner and then disappear. Sometimes he'd come back around ten o'clock, but most nights, he'd be gone all night. She didn't really mind, but it was somewhat difficult when her mother would press her about when she would give her a grandchild. Ellie at times would love to throw it back at her that she was still a virgin and that a grandchild was not in her future, but never did.

George had made more than one subtle threat that the peculiar nature of their marriage was to remain a secret, and she took him at his word.

Now the cook had quit, and she'd need to find another. Both the cook and the cleaning woman only showed up for the day. George never allowed anyone else to remain in the house after dinner. He didn't want any gossip from the servants. The laundry was taken to the Chinese laundry and returned by the maid. It meant that Ellie spent most of her days alone in the big house and the only repeat visitor was her mother.

She toyed with the idea of just cooking herself but knew George wouldn't allow it, which was one more reason for her frustration. She wanted to be a wife and mother, and this wasn't the life she had hoped to have. She wanted a life with a man who understood her and loved her as a woman and as a person. She wanted a man she could spend time just engaged in lively, meaningful conversation who understood who she was behind the pretty face and impressive figure.

She wanted her Piggy.

CHAPTER 2

Stan had estimated that six days was the longest he would need to get to Miles' trading post. The traveling would be rough, but he was used to living outdoors and being uncomfortable. His biggest shortcoming on this trip was one that could get him killed. He knew little about the Indian tribes he'd probably be meeting. The Lakota were pretty much behind him now, but he'd be traveling through Cheyenne and Crow territory soon. The Crow he knew a little about, as the army had three Crow scouts at the fort, but of the Cheyenne, he knew nothing. He knew some basic universal sign language that was understood by the majority of the tribes, but he didn't know if it would be enough. He hoped it was enough to keep him alive.

He and his horse led their new traveling companion across the Great Plains keeping a steady, but not overly aggressive pace. There was no need to rush. There was plenty of grass and water for the animals at this time of year, so all he needed to do was pay attention to his surroundings. The compass provided by Sergeant Hanratty was turning out to be his greatest gift. Between the watch and the compass, Stan was able to make sure he was heading where he wanted to go. He never did learn how to use a sextant, but he did have an instinct about distance and location, and the compass kept that instinct honest.

He crossed his first major waterway, an unnamed creek that was bordering on being a river at 11:15. It took almost half an hour to find a ford and knew there'd be more creeks and streams to cross, many of them wider, deeper and faster than the one he left behind. His only concern entering the creek was about the mule's reaction to the swiftly flowing water. He'd been relieved when the mule didn't even flinch as it crossed the creek and hoped it would be the same in the deeper crossings. The panniers were mostly waterproof and the only item that were inside the packs that could be ruined by water was his supply of coffee, and he'd wrapped that in a spare set of saddlebags which were tied off with some cord.

He stopped for lunch and a rest break for the animals just before noon. They grazed and drank while Stan had some hard tack and jerky washed down with a half canteen of water. He emptied both canteens and refilled them with fresh, cold water before stepping back up and continuing the journey. The weather was being helpful on this first day, so he was making better time than he'd hoped and overall, the ride was going well.

He had travelled about twenty-five miles from the fort when he had his first encounter with Indians. But before he actually caught sight of the Indians, he found the reason for their presence. As he was cresting a rise, he felt as much as heard a deep rumbling and even the shock absorbing legs of his horse didn't lessen the shaking. He had never felt anything like it and thought it was an earthquake until he reached the top of the rise, then stopped the horse and marveled at the sight. It was a mammoth herd of buffalo, thousands of them. They were moving fast, heading north across a wide valley. Then he spied the Indians. There were eight of them, and Stan guessed they were Cheyenne. It was a hunting party, and even though they were very good at it, hunting the big hairy beasts with their sharp weapons was still dangerous.

He set his horse to a trot down the slope of the rise but didn't pull a gun yet. He didn't want to antagonize the hunting party but suddenly thought this might be a good opportunity to try the Sharps and maybe make some important friends in the process. He knew the Winchester would probably not have the power to take down a bison. The Spencer would probably be up to it, but he really wanted to try the Sharps. He figured he could bring down a half dozen of the bigger animals for the Cheyenne with no risk to them and hoped that there wasn't some measure of pride in them that would make such an offer an insult.

They had spotted Stan after he had crossed the crest and were torn about what to do about him. They needed some meat and buffalo hide, but this white man presented a threat.

Sudden Water pointed to the oncoming rider and said that the white man didn't have his rifle in his hands, so Running Antelope told them they'd wait until the white man was close and be ready if he drew his rifle, even though they couldn't mount much of a defense until he was within fifty yards or so.

They all watched Stan trotting toward them, and each warrior had nocked an arrow and could unleash them much faster than he could pull a gun.

Stan neared the eight Cheyenne warriors and held up his palm in the gesture of peace, and Running Antelope did the same.

Stan got within fifty feet, dismounted, then walked to within ten feet of the Cheyenne warrior who had returned his gesture and made clear his intent that he would shoot six big buffalo for them to take.

Running Antelope was curious and gestured, 'Why?'.

Stan smiled, then turned and retrieved the Sharps. He indicated to Running Antelope that it was new, and he wanted to try it.

Running Antelope looked at the shining rifle and nodded. He wanted to see it as well.

C.J. PETIT

Stan ground hitched his horse and took out six cartridges for the Sharps, along with the percussion caps. They were the biggest cartridges he had ever seen. It was a .52 caliber monster that dwarfed the thicker Spencer cartridges. He and the Cheyenne trotted to the edge of the now stopped herd where he began to set up. He had never shot a buffalo before, so he signed to Running Antelope asking which the best spot was to put the round into the big animal. Running Antelope pointed to his neck.

Stan knelt and slid a round into the chamber and after closing the breech, pushed a percussion cap in place. He was only two hundred yards away and wondered if the loud report would send the herd running. There as only one way to find out, so he set the ladder sight to a hundred and eighty yards to make up for the altitude. There was little wind, and the temperature was perfect.

He cocked the hammer, aimed the rifle, held his breath and squeezed the trigger. The big cow he had selected crumpled to the ground as the boom echoed across the prairie. The rest of the herd didn't even seem to notice either the cow's sudden drop or the noise, which Stan thought was strange.

Running Antelope and the rest of his warrior hunting party were stunned. *The gun had made hunting so easy!*

Stan reloaded, selected another animal and repeated the process. Three minutes later, six large cows were down, then Stan stood, blew out his rifle's smoke-filled barrel, turned to Running Antelope, and signed that the buffalo were his and he would ride on.

Running Antelope wanted the rifle but knew that the white man had given them a gift and it would be an insult to ask. Instead, he put his hand on Stan's shoulder and said something that Stan didn't understand. But Stan nodded as if he did and

36

returned to his horse while the hunting party left to retrieve their gifts. They would take as much meat as they could in one trip and return with another sixteen warriors to take the rest. The huge amount of meat would provide the whole village for at least a week, and the hides and tallow would all be just as useful.

Stan remounted his horse and began heading southwest again, his only concern was that having seen the power of his rifle, the Cheyenne would send someone after him to get it, but it was too late to worry about that now.

After riding another fifteen miles, Stan began hunting for good campsites, and it didn't take very long. He turned his horse and mule to a bend in a strong stream and was soon dropping his supplies on the ground, then unsaddling the two animals before setting up his camp.

———

Back at the Cheyenne village, the second group of warriors returned, laden down with the last of the meat and hides from the six buffalo shot by Stan. There was rejoicing in the welcome supply of so much meat with no injuries. Running Antelope told his chief what had happened, and the chief commended Running Antelope for his decision.

But it was the war chief, Spotted Horse, who objected. He pointed out that if they had his rifle, then they could continue to supply the band with as much meat as they would ever need, along with the precious buffalo hides.

The chief, One Who Makes Fire, argued that they didn't know how to use the gun and they didn't know how much ammunition the white man had. Even if he had a lot of ammunition, it would run out soon. Spotted Horse asked Running Antelope how difficult it had seemed to shoot the gun and his honest answer was that it didn't seem that difficult. The white man had just pulled back one lever and put in a bullet. After returning the lever back against the gun, he had just pulled back a dog-eared piece of iron and pulled the trigger. He hadn't noticed Stan popping the percussion cap onto the nipple as it appeared as if he were just wiping something clean.

Spotted Horse was winning his argument. Then, he asked a critical question. How long did it take the white man to reload the gun?

Running Antelope told him the truth again, guessing the average was about fifteen seconds. He didn't mention that Stan was taking his time on purpose, because he didn't know that he was. He had noticed the Winchester and the Spencer carbine, but the white man could only fire one of his three rifles at a time. Having three was a stupid thing for the white man to have. *What was the purpose of that?* To Running Antelope as well as the other members of his hunting party, a rifle was a rifle.

Spotted Horse was given the mission of returning with the rifle and all the ammunition that he could get the white man to give him. He'd take eight warriors which was more than enough. They had two muskets in their camp, but no ammunition, and maybe the white man had ammunition for them as well. He was told to bring back the rifle and ammunition and to trade him two war hatchets and four blankets for them, but to let the white man continue because Running Antelope had promised him safe passage.

Spotted Horse acknowledged the order but knew it didn't matter. He knew that to get the rifle, they'd have to kill the white man, and it didn't bother him in the least.

They would wait until morning when they could track him, knowing that he probably was resting for the night already.

———

Stan had made himself a full dinner, cleaned up and settled down into his bedroll, but didn't bother with the tent. It was going to be chilly tonight, but he liked seeing the stars. If it was cloudy and raining or snowing, he couldn't see them anyway, so he'd use the tent. Just before going to bed, he had carefully stripped off the gold stripes from his army uniform pants. He wasn't ashamed of them; he just didn't like the way they stood out.

He laid there and wondered if this whole trip was just a futile gesture. Ellie may not even remember him at all as they had been still so young when she had gone. But he had never met another woman with her gentle nature and ability to look past his appearance and accept him anyway. Even after she had changed into the pretty young woman, she was still Ellie inside, and the only other student who would really talk to him.

He had met other women during and after the war. And now that he was physically acceptable, actually more than acceptable, he'd admit, there were more chances than one might expect during a war. But even though he had several dalliances which were necessary to keep him sane, it was always Ellie. No woman would ever be able to push her out of his heart, unless Ellie did it herself.

He hoped that Ellie wasn't just turning into a non-person after all this time, a dream woman who wasn't close to the real Ellie. The only way he would ever know would be if he found her, and if he did, it wouldn't take long to find out.

He drifted off with the almost eternal hope of finding Bucky again.

———

Spotted Horse and his eight warriors set out at dawn to return to the place where the white man had last been seen. He'd be easy to track, and they probably could move a lot faster than he could as he was trailing a heavily loaded mule. They would rely on their numbers for their advantage. They all knew that at least one, maybe as many as three, would die in the attempt, but it was an honorable way to die. If they took the white man's weapons, it would provide for the entire band for a long time and probably save at least as many lives as they would have lost on the buffalo hunts, making it a noble cause.

Running Antelope had been left in the camp and was stewing in his anger. He knew that Spotted Horse would ignore his promise of safe passage to the white man, and that would become his shame. Everyone would know that he had spoken against the mission, but it didn't matter. He could blame the chief or Spotted Horse for going against his word, but it was his shame he would have to live with and there was nothing he could do about it. He had briefly thought of riding ahead and warning the white man, but that would be an even bigger shame. The gods were cruel and seemed to hate him.

———

Stan may not have been up and moving at dawn, but it wasn't much later. He cooked himself a good breakfast and packed everything quickly because he was still anxious about the Cheyenne. The warrior that he had signed with seemed genuinely grateful for what Stan had done, but that was only one man. He knew how valuable the Sharps would be to the tribe, and he was sure that they had seen his other rifles as well. As he packed the mule, he kept one box of .44 cartridges out for the Winchester, which he still hadn't fired. He also made sure other cartridges were readily available for the Spencer and the Sharps.

FINDING BUCKY

He had just started moving when Spotted Horse's band picked up his tracks and quickly followed at a medium trot. They were fifteen miles behind but gaining rapidly.

Stan had his new field glasses around his neck and would have to write a thank you note to Sergeant Hanratty when he finally got settled. He was grateful for the ability to identify problems at a greater distance. Although he hadn't seen any trailers yet, he just felt as if he was being followed. Other than his own feeling of self-preservation, he had no reason to believe that anyone was behind him.

He had gone further than he had expected on the first day, having traveled almost forty miles, so he'd reach the trading post in three more days if he kept up the pace, the only possible delays were the rivers. He had planned his route before he left and there shouldn't be any large rivers crossing his path, but some of those unnamed creeks and streams could be close to river-sized, as he already learned. Army maps weren't always very accurate.

———

Spotted Horse and his group of warriors were able to maintain their fast pace as they could see the white man's trail a full hundred yards ahead as it traced westward. They had cut the following distance in half by ten o'clock.

———

Stan was checking for a place for lunch and to rest the horses an hour later, wanting someplace that was defensible as well. If the Cheyenne had decided to relieve him of his Sharps and probably his hair, they would have left early and easily picked up his trail. If they were there, and he wasn't convinced they were, they'd be less than ten miles behind him. In fact, they were only five.

He found an acceptable location and turned his horse to the spot, stepped down and let the animals rest and graze. There was a creek nearby that had a deep bank that he marked as his defensive location. He might get his feet wet, but he'd have someplace to hide. Besides, he had the Winchester, and doubted if they even knew about the rifle yet. He figured with the Sharps, the Spencer and the Winchester, he'd be able to handle as many as eight to ten, as long as they didn't have any long guns themselves. If they did, then there wouldn't be any reason for them to come after him in the first place. Besides, they didn't have any with them on the buffalo hunt.

He turned his eyes to his back trail, could see a good three to four miles without obstruction, and didn't see anyone.

He took out some jerky and some hard tack and began to chew his lunch, continuously watching to the east. He had just popped his last piece of jerky into his mouth and was drinking some cold water to wash it down when his eyes picked up distant movement.

He quickly set down his canteen and pulled the field glasses to his eyes, counting nine Cheyenne warriors, making this a real problem. What made it worse was that he didn't really know their intentions until they got closer. At this distance, they were still specks. He'd have to let them close to less than a mile before he could see if they were wearing war paint or not.

He did know that the Cheyenne, like most of the Plains Indians, would wear their death mask only if they were going into an engagement where there was a good chance they would die. Just like the Rebel yell, it served a dual purpose as it also scared the bejesus out of their opponents.

He quickly walked both animals to the other side of the stream and led them another hundred yards away. He hitched the horse to a nearby bush, pulled out a full box of .44

cartridges and another for the Spencer. He only took three more rounds for the Sharps and some percussion caps, put them into his pocket, then splashed back across the stream with his three long guns and then set them down on the bank facing the oncoming Cheyenne. He didn't even think about his pistol beyond taking off his hammer loop.

He watched them approach with the field glasses. They were less than two miles out now and was sure they had seen him, but surely, they weren't going to come straight at him. They'd know he had three rifles, but maybe they didn't know that the Spencer had seven rounds and the Winchester had fifteen. If he was commanding a squad and he suspected that his enemy only had three rounds available to him, he'd make a bull rush at them, but only if he was positive that's all they had. Bad intelligence leads to bad results.

He continued to watch as they rode toward him, and when they were close enough, he could see that they were wearing war paint, which meant that all bets were off. He had no way of knowing that Spotted Horse had convinced the other warriors that the white man would never give up the rifle without a fight.

Stan planned on using the Sharps at five hundred yards, then putting it down and using the Spencer until they were within a hundred yards before switching to the Winchester. He may reload the Spencer, depending on how far away they were when it was empty. If they were within three hundred yards and moving fast, there wouldn't be time. One of the drawbacks of the Spencer was the way it reloaded. After the magazine was empty, he'd have to open it, slide in seven more cartridges, close it and then cock the hammer again. Even firing the Spencer was a lot slower because he'd have to cock the hammer after each shot and sometimes that expended brass wouldn't leave the breech. The Winchester, on the other hand, when he thought he was getting low, he'd be able to quickly ram in three or four cartridges on the fly, which was a tremendous advantage, even over its predecessor, the Henry, which still had to be loaded all at once. The Winchester could also be fired very quickly, about a shot every other second. But even with the Winchester's impressive capabilities, it would still be close if those Cheyenne were determined to get his guns, and they certainly looked determined.

———

Spotted Horse and his warriors had all seen the white man prepare for their arrival and knew that this would not be a finesse attack. All he could do was to have them spread apart to reduce the number of hits and when they made their rushing attack, they'd zigzag to make harder targets. He didn't doubt for a moment that even if some of them died, they'd leave soon with all of the white man's guns. It was just a question of which of them would die.

They slowed to a walk after they got within a mile or so, then rode another hundred yards and stopped, letting their horses rest for the final dash.

———

Stan saw them stop and understood what they were doing. As an experienced cavalryman, he knew one of the cardinal rules was never to go into battle with a tired horse unless you had no choice. He guessed that they would fan out, giving him more difficult targets, and as much as he didn't want to have to do it, he knew he'd be shooting horses sooner or later. They were much bigger targets, and each downed horse would put the Cheyenne on foot and possibly injured. He also expected them to come at him in a zigzag which would make it a difficult hit with the long-range guns. He still hoped to get at least one or two with the Sharps, though.

FINDING BUCKY

He took out his Sharps cartridges and percussion caps and stood them on a nearby rock. He decided to take more than one shot with the big gun, maybe even as many as three. Five hundred yards to three hundred yards should give him the time.

His biggest worry now was smoke. The rifles put out a lot of gunsmoke, and a large cloud would obstruct his vision, but the breeze, luckily, had picked up and was blowing from the south, which was a real blessing. It would clear the smoke rapidly, leaving his field of fire open.

As the Cheyenne waited until the horses were rested, Stan used the time to improve his defenses. He built up small revetments on either side to prevent the lucky arrow from getting through. They weren't much of a defense, but he felt better.

———

Spotted Horse was ready. He'd given his instructions to his warriors and all understood what had to be done.

He suddenly whooped loudly, and his warriors repeated his cry as they charged, fanning out until each was at least ten yards from the other. After spreading, they began their attack, but in their excitement, not one warrior bothered to zigzag, but rode straight at the white man, firmly believing, as all young men did, that it wasn't going to be his day to die.

Stan had the Sharps ready, the ladder sight set for six hundred yards, then aimed at the center horse. He waited until he thought they had passed six hundred yards and squeezed the trigger. He didn't wait to see what he'd hit or missed, as he grabbed a second big cartridge, levered the breech open, tossed the empty brass to his side then slid a second round into the block and replaced the percussion cap and closed the breech.

His first round had crossed between the ears of the rider's horse and punched into Standing Buck's gut. He felt the kick of the heavy piece of lead, dropped his spear, and clutched his stomach feeling blood running through his fingers, but continued to ride for another three seconds before falling off the ride side of his horse, slamming into the ground and rolling several times.

Stan looked for a second target, and quickly made his choice, and not rushing his shot, he took a second, then squeezed the trigger again.

As he was reaching for his third round, Spotted Horse saw his second warrior's horse collapse and fall face forward into the ground, flipping Rising Star over his horse's head and saw his forehead strike the ground and his neck bend at a horrible angle as his body jackknifed over the top. He rolled twice and stopped cold. They were down to seven already and still four hundred yards away from the entrenched white man. He would tell Running Antelope how wrong he had been about the time to the white man took to reload his weapon when they returned.

He never had a chance to tell anyone anything. When the attackers were at three hundred and fifty yards, Stan's final Sharps round punched into his chest, splintering his breastbone, and pulverizing the soft tissue underneath, before he somersaulted backwards over his horse and bounced on the dirt, never knowing what caused his death.

Despite the loss of their war chief, the other six warriors pressed the attack. By the time they had crossed three hundred yards, Stan had shifted to the Spencer and began the cycle of cocking the hammer, pulling the trigger, levering in a fresh cartridge, then cocking and firing again.

The last six warriors were shaken by the rapid sequence of firing, a totally unexpected development. Two more horses hit the dirt, and one of the riders was impaled on his own spear as

FINDING BUCKY

he fell, no longer issuing his war cry, just a scream marking his pain and then his death. The second warrior who had been unhorsed, One Who Sees, even after losing his mount, was still running toward the white man.

Stan was still firing the Spencer but had lost track of how many rounds he had fired when the hammer struck on an empty chamber, and he immediately set it down and grabbed the Winchester.

There were only four mounted Cheyenne as they passed the one-hundred-yard mark. One Who Sees was running as fast as he could but was still almost fifty yards back already.

Stan wondered why they still came. This was almost shameful if he wasn't fighting for his life. He waited until they were a little closer and then the Winchester's first bullet left its muzzle and found Black Buffalo's chest on the right side, breaking two ribs, and when he fell awkwardly to the ground the broken ribs punched through the skin, leaving a huge hole into his lung, letting air in and blood out.

If the Cheyenne were surprised by the rapidity of the Spencer, they were shocked by the Winchester's even faster rate of fire. The sound was so different from the Spencer and the Sharps that they knew it was a different weapon, adding confusion to their growing fear.

As Stan continued to work the Winchester's lever, he took out two more warriors, hitting them rather than their horses now that they were closer. The first was a low chest shot, that ripped through a Cheyenne's heart before he slowly leaned over his horse's neck, then just slid off to the side and crumpled to the ground. The second one took his death shot on the left side of his neck, taking out a huge chunk and severing his left carotid. He automatically grabbed the wound with his right hand, as

47

blood pulsed out of the gaping hole but finally fell back onto his horse before dropping to the ground.

That left a single mounted warrior who had continued to attack, his spear raised above his head, preparing to let it loose at thirty yards.

As he drew the shaft to his ear, Stan fired from derringer range, and the .44 caliber missile drilled through his chest at an upward angle, and because he had twisted to throw his spear, it also entered the left side and passed diagonally through his left lung and then his right, destroying his heart as it did. His spear never left his clinched hand as he was thrown from the horse, only being dislodged when it hit the ground before he did.

The still running warrior, One Who Sees, knew that he was alone now and would soon die. He stopped, breathing hard, and dropped his war hatchet, then spread his arms wide and began to sing his death song.

Stan didn't know why he was singing, but knew he was no longer a threat, so he just lowered his hot, smoking Winchester to the rock, climbed over the creek's high bank, picked up the Spencer, then snatched a full box of ammunition and walked toward the standing Cheyenne warrior.

One Who Sees had finished his death song and lowered his arms, as he watched the white man approach, waiting to join his brothers.

Stan walked up to his fellow warrior and held the Spencer out in front of him, handing him the carbine. One Who Sees wondered what the white man wanted. *Was he arming him, so they could fight fairly?* But it wouldn't be a fair fight at all because he didn't know how to shoot the gun.

FINDING BUCKY

Stan handed him the box of cartridges and then showed One Who Sees how to load the carbine. Then he made gestures that said he should go back and shoot buffaloes with the gun, but not him.

One Who Sees finally understood. The white man was telling him that they should never have attacked, but simply asked. The chief had been right, and Spotted Horse had been wrong. He nodded, took the gun and the ammunition, then he walked to the nearest horse, took the bow and quiver of arrows from the horse, and returned to the white man, picked up his war hatchet, and handed the weapons to Stan.

Stan nodded, understanding that the warrior couldn't accept the rifle as a gift without giving something in trade. The two men looked at each other and then Stan turned and walked back across the stream, leaving the Cheyenne the job of loading his fallen warrior brothers onto the surviving horses for the long return to their camp.

Both he and One Who Sees knew that the rifle and ammunition were worth much more than the bow, arrows and war hatchet, but honor had been satisfied and right now that was all that mattered.

Stan admired the war axe, bow and quiver of arrows as he walked to his horses. He knew that his Spencer was getting tired, noticing the difference when he fired. It still had the power for taking out big animals like the buffalo, but if he hadn't been firing at the horses, he would have been lucky to hit a man over two hundred yards. The Winchester, on the other hand, had proven its effectiveness. If only he had one of them in the war, he wouldn't have suffered the two wounds he had received. One was from a Rebel captain's pistol shot from ten feet and the other was a stab wound from a Confederate trooper. Arm a cavalry troop with Winchesters and it would be a formidable weapon of war. But the army, in its usual wisdom, had rejected

49

the Henry repeater because they thought soldiers would waste ammunition. They probably wouldn't buy the Winchester, either.

The delay had cost Stan more than time. It had notified every Indian within ten miles around that there was an armed white man in the area. He hoped that there weren't any, but there was always that possibility.

After storing his new weapons on the mule, he mounted and resumed his journey. As he rode, he realized how lucky he had been. The Cheyenne hadn't known about the Winchester, but now they knew, and word would go out among the tribes of a fast-firing gun. The Henry had been around a while, but it had a different sound than the Winchester, even though they fired the same round. He wondered why that was.

––––––––

Hundreds of miles away, George was not happy with Ellie. When he had come down for his normal breakfast of a soft-boiled egg, biscuits with marmalade and coffee, he discovered that Ellie had cooked it. It was cooked perfectly, but that wasn't the point.

"Why did she quit?" he demanded.

"She said she didn't like having to walk two miles each way before and after work. Besides, she was offered more money at a closer residence and could sleep there."

"Well, when you hire a new cook, give her another ten dollars a month."

"I'll go and see the agency this morning."

"You do that. I won't eat here tonight anyway, as I'll be taking my supper at the club. I may be back by in the morning, but under no circumstances are you to cook me a meal. Is that understood?"

"Yes, George," Ellie replied, wanting to hurl something at him.

George wiped his upper lip, tossed down the napkin on the table, then ran his finger over each side of his beloved mustache, rose and walked out of the room and the house.

Ellie sat down and took a biscuit, split in apart, then spread some marmalade across the soft surface and had her coffee. At least she'd get a George-less day again.

"How sad is that?" she thought, "I'm happy to be alone."

She finished her breakfast and cleaned up. The maid wasn't due to arrive for another twenty minutes, but if George knew that his wife was cleaning up the kitchen every day after he left, he'd explode. Ellie smiled at the thought, then remembered that her mother was stopping by that day after lunch, and her smile dissolved.

There would be the usual winks and suggestions that she must be so lucky to find a catch like George and that she wouldn't mind having George in her bed. Ellie always wanted to tell her that it was more likely her father would wind up in George's bed than she would, but she had promised George that she'd never say anything. Besides, the less she had to talk to her parents, the better.

She still resented having been used as a pawn in her parents' desire to move up in the world. Before the wedding, her father had been given a position as a vice president at one of the stores, and she made a point never to shop there. But he seemed to fit in and was hobnobbing with the snobbish elites that she hated so badly.

She knew that this was her fate now. Piggy wouldn't find her here. He'd be up in Dakota Territory if he was looking for her at all. *Then, what would happen even if he did find her?* It could make everything worse for her. She'd have her heart broken all over again. He could arrive, say hello, then spend an hour telling her about his wonderful wife and their three children.

She often wondered if he ever lost the weight. It didn't matter if he had, he'd always be Piggy to her, even he had shed the weight and become an Adonis. But the idea of a slim, handsome Stan Murray did thrill her. His face had always been handsome, even with the roundness. Lose that roundness and he would be something special. *But would that change him from the thoughtful, caring boy she loved so much?* She'd rather have the heavy Stan with his warm heart than a handsome Stan without it.

———

The erstwhile Piggy was taking a bath in a deep stream. The water was frigid, but he needed to get rid of the day's trail dust. If Ellie had seen this Piggy, she would never have recognized him. The only thing he had in common with the Piggy that she remembered was that he still harbored a deep affection for Ellie, and yes, he still had the warm heart and gentle ways that she loved.

His new campsite was well situated with water and grass for his horse and mule. He had only traveled thirty miles that day because of the altercation with the Cheyenne.

After drying himself and dressing, Stan wandered over to his campsite, figuring that he may as well take time to consolidate his cash now that he had a chance. He had never moved his mustering out pay into his money belt.

FINDING BUCKY

After counting out his scattered cash, he managed to squeeze another four hundred and fifty dollars into the bulging money belt. That left him just under three hundred dollars in his pockets and over four thousand in his money belt. He could buy a nice ranch with that much money, but he knew it wouldn't be anywhere near here.

After he found Ellie, if she was still available and wanted to go with him, he'd take her to Colorado. He wanted a ranch near Boulder but had no idea why he chose that as his final destination, he just did. He knew that Yankee cash was hard to come by these days, and he should be able to buy a ranch with less than half of his stash. Even if Ellie wasn't there, or didn't want to come with him, that was the plan.

He spent the remaining part of his daylight cleaning the Winchester and the Sharps, grateful he hadn't had to fire his Colt.

―――――

By nine o'clock the next morning, Stan knew he had passed the halfway mark to Miles' trading post, and for some reason that cheered him up. He still scanned the horizons for visitors, but only saw four legged ones. He saw one in the distance he swore was an elephant, but knew his eyes were playing tricks on him. By the time he got his field glasses to his eyes, it had moved behind some trees. With that wooly coat, it was probably some big buffalo bull looking for his herd.

The rest of the day was going very smoothly. There were no crossings that caused any problems and he wound up stretching the miles until he pulled up to set up camp less than thirty miles outside of the trading post.

After his campsite was set up and his dinner was cooking, Stan did one other thing with his money. He broke up the cash he had in his pocket into smaller stashes. He put forty dollars in each boot and then split up the rest into his other pockets. He knew that bad things happened when you flashed money around. It was best to give the appearance of being low on money, and he didn't even shave that morning. He'd go into Miles' trading post looking a bit tired and scruffy. He guessed he'd be in around noon or thereabouts. He needed some more eggs anyway, but other than that, he was in good shape for supplies.

———

Ellie had hired a new cook before noon, and the young woman seemed competent and was very pleased to be able to make the money offered. She was mildly surprised that she wasn't being offered a room in the house, but with that amount of pay, she could afford to take a room at Iverson's Rooming House two blocks west of the big, empty house.

Betsy Brumfield was very pleased with her new job and had even told Mrs. Rafferty that the reason she had to leave her last place of employment was that the man of the house would catch her in private locations and let his hands run all over her. Ellie assured her that it wouldn't be a problem at their home, which she took to understand to mean that Mrs. Rafferty was in charge of the home and besides, what man would even look at her if he was married to a woman like Ellie Rafferty?

George didn't come home at all that night, nor did he come by for breakfast. Ellie wound up sampling Betsy's soft-boiled egg and biscuits, not that it was a particularly difficult culinary challenge, but it was good.

———

Stan made himself a much more filling breakfast than a soft-boiled egg, but he didn't have any biscuits or marmalade, either.

FINDING BUCKY

He was on the road by eight and four hours later crossed a rise and saw the trading post in the distance, about three miles away. He was surprised how much larger it was than he had expected. It had several buildings and looked more like a small town than a simple trading post.

He picked up the pace and reached the post before noon, and decided to get himself some lunch first, so he trotted the horse down what passed for a street to an eatery and stopped outside. He tied off the reins, entered the place and found a table, then took a seat where he had a view of his horse and mule. He really wasn't expecting anyone to take the horse or mule, but he didn't want his new Winchester to go wandering.

The owner/cook/waiter walked up and asked, "What can I getcha?"

"What's the special?"

"Buffalo stew. Same every day," he replied as he grinned.

"I guess I'll have the special," Stan said as he grinned back.

"Wise choice," he said before he walked back to his kitchen.

Thirty seconds later, he brought a pot of coffee, a cup, and a bowl of stew with a spoon sticking out of it. There were two biscuits on top of the stew.

Stan poured the coffee, removed the biscuits off the stew and put them on the table, hoping that no additional flavors were being transferred from the wood to the biscuits because the Lord only knows what was on that table before.

The stew wasn't bad at all, and he finished the stew and tossed the two biscuits back into the bowl. They were as rocky as the hard tack he chewed in the army for all those years, and he had never grown to appreciate them either.

He left a quarter on the table for the twenty-cent meal before returning to his horse and mule, mounted, then rode down the street looking for someplace to stay for the night and was surprised to see a sheriff's office, assuming that he had either been self-appointed or selected because he was the biggest bully.

He saw what passed for a hotel of sorts, as all it had to identify it as a place where he could rest his head was a sign out front that read, ROOMS. He rode past the hotel until he found the livery and stepped down.

He walked inside leading his animals and found the liveryman leaning against the door.

"Afternoon. What can I do for ya?" he asked cheerfully.

"I need to leave my horse and mule overnight, get some oats and get them reshod. I've got to get to Cheyenne, so I'll have to get them in good shape."

"That'll run you four dollars and I'll have 'em ready by morning. You in the army?"

"Up until four days ago, then they figured they'd had enough of my ugly mug and sent me packing."

The liveryman smiled and said, "Thought that might be the case. That army saddle is lookin' kinda sad. You know, if I was going that far, I'd take an extra horse and probably buy me a better saddle, too."

Stan smiled at the sales pitch, but it did make sense. This was going to be a long trip and if the horse went lame, he'd be in bad shape.

"Okay. You've sold me. Let's see what you've got."

The liveryman said, "I think you'll be impressed. Just got me a few new ones in last week. There's a feller that breaks mustangs and has a ranch nearby. He runs some of 'em here so I can sell 'em for him. Two of them look mighty good."

Stan wasn't so sure, as these local guys tended to exaggerate their horseflesh to unsuspecting newcomers, but as an ex-cavalry officer, he knew he wasn't one of them.

As it turned out, he wasn't exaggerating at all. When he reached the corral, he saw the two he was talking about. One was a buckskin mare and the other was a slightly taller deep red mare with no markings at all.

"I see which two you're talking about. The two tall mares. The buckskin and the red. How much are you asking?"

"Those two are kind of special and I couldn't let either one go for less than forty dollars."

"Oh, please. Now that the war's over, there are a lot more horses available, and out here you have mustangs all over the place, but I'll tell you what. I'll take both of them and you can keep my horse in trade. He's not spectacular like these two, but he's solid. I'll give you fifty-five dollars for the pair and my horse."

The liveryman feigned thinking about it. He would have sold them for thirty dollars apiece without the trade.

"All right, you've got a deal. They're both newly shod, too. So, I'll only have to put new shoes on the mule."

"Let's see what you have for saddles."

"I've got three. One is in great condition and the other two are okay."

Stan walked into his dry room and spotted the saddles, and found he was right again. One was in very good shape and was made by a much more talented leather smith than the one who'd made his cavalry saddle.

"How much for the good one?"

"I'll let you have that one for twenty-five."

"I'll tell you what I'll do. I'll give you seventy-five dollars cash for the two horses and the saddle and you throw in the shoeing and the overnight and oats for all three."

"Now, you're making me sweat. Let me think about it."

He really didn't have to. It was the biggest sale he'd made all month and it was near the end of May.

"You got me again. Seventy-five dollars and you've got a deal."

Stan smiled, shook his hand and paid him the money.

"Do you know why I had to buy the buckskin?"

"Aside from she's a beautiful horse?"

"Besides that. For the past six years, I've had to ride army horses. They all had to be dark and had to be geldings. That buckskin is my way of saying that I'm really a civilian."

The liveryman hooted and said, "That's the truth, ain't it?"

Stan pulled his Winchester out of its scabbard and pulled off his saddlebags.

"Say, you don't have another set of saddlebags, to you?"

"They're part of the rig you just bought."

"Great. See you in the morning."

Stan left the livery in a good mood. The buckskin was impressive as was the red. He'd ride the buckskin and use the red as a sort of pack horse, carrying the Sharps and all the ammunition and cooking supplies. Then, he'd switch off riding the horses every day, and use the mule for all the food and other camping necessities.

He stopped at the almost-hotel and got a room for the night, picked up his saddlebags and went to his room, stepped inside and put his saddlebags on the bed and his Winchester in the corner. He wondered if the post store had a map of the area. He doubted it, but he'd check.

He left the hotel and stepped over to the store, glancing at the large sign over the front: Garnett's Dry Goods.

He went inside and strode to the counter.

"Yes, sir. What can I do for you?" the proprietor asked as Stan approached.

"I'll be needing to stock up for my ride to Cheyenne. You don't happen to have a map of the area, do you?"

"It so happens that we do. Right over by the books. They're army maps."

"If I leave you my order, can I pick it up in the morning? My horse and mule are in the livery right now."

"Not a problem. We open at seven o'clock."

"Perfect. I'll head over there and pick up that map."

Stan stepped over to the last aisle and found the books and right below them were tubes of maps. One said Montana Territory, and another said Dakota Territory, which included Cheyenne. He never understood why the government always seemed to be behind the times. Everyone he knew referred to the area as Wyoming Territory, but they still had it as part of Dakota Territory. He heard that Congress was going to change that soon and it would be a state soon after that. The State of Wyoming of the United States of America, he said in his mind, and thought it sounded odd. But then, he thought it sounded a lot better than Massachusetts or Connecticut, which were much more difficult to spell. He never could figure out why that second 'c' was there, either. He'd never heard anyone say "Connect-i-cut', but then again, he never heard anyone say, 'Arkans-as', either.

He took both maps, and as he was walking out, stopped and picked up a nice pocketknife. It was just too handy to pass up and had a tin opener as well which would save the sharp edge on his big knife.

He dropped his purchases on the counter and pulled out a pencil and paper then wrote out his order for pickup in the morning, and when he'd finished, he handed it to Mister Garnett who totaled his order and included the two maps.

"$33.30," he said when he was done, "them maps cost more'n anything else."

"And worth every penny," Stan replied as he paid the bill.

FINDING BUCKY

Stan left the store, crossed the street to his room, and once inside, opened the two maps, spreading them out on the bed. It didn't look that bad of a trip on the maps, but he knew better. On any map, the distance between stops didn't look very far apart at all. There were only a few inches between Miles Trading Post and Cheyenne City, but he knew the real distance from the scale on the bottom of each map. It was going to be a long grueling journey from now on with few places to restock. He spent a long time examining his route to Cheyenne City, memorizing the terrain and landmarks, but acknowledging that he was lucky he wasn't going further west where the real difficult terrain began.

He slid the two maps back into their leather tubes and resealed them to keep them dry.

At quarter past five, he left the room, closing the door behind him, but there was no lock, so he had his Winchester with him as he crossed the lobby and walked down the street to the diner. He stepped inside and took a seat at a table, then when he asked the owner what was available, Stan was gratified to be able to order steak and a baked potato for dinner. It was a buffalo steak, but it didn't matter, the thought of a thick cut of meat made his mouth water.

As he waited for his food, he became very aware of two rough-looking men sitting at another table glancing his way time to time and talking. In a compound of rough-looking men, they stuck out, which was saying a lot. But it was their surreptitious glances that had him wondering if they had plans involving him. Traveling strangers made good targets for those who preyed on other men. They'd let them leave the post and then drygulch them away from town, or in this case, the trading post, and nobody ever knew what happened to the stranger. He was leaving anyway and would never be missed. They get your supplies, guns and money and you get your life snuffed out and left to rot in the vast wilderness. These two had all the earmarks of drygulchers as they continued to talk and give him quick onceovers.

When the do-it-all owner came to deliver his steak, he looked over at the two who had been nursing the coffee for a while and was obviously displeased that they were still there.

"Zeke, you and Frank get your asses outta here. You been here for over an hour and ain't ordered a thing."

"We got this coffee, Al," shouted Zeke from across the room.

"Get your lazy asses outta my place until you can afford to buy some food."

They both rose slowly, shot the owner a nasty look, and were grumbling as they left the establishment.

The owner glared at the pair, and was mumbling something about 'no good lazy bastards' as he returned to the kitchen.

Stan smiled as he cut into the big steak and forked a large piece into his eager mouth. Again, he was pleasantly surprised by how good it tasted. He'd had buffalo steak before, but the army cooks never took time to add anything to the meat as they needed to cook for hundreds of men. This was cooked exactly the way he liked it and had some salt and pepper sprinkled on top while it was being fried. There was a crock of butter for the baked potato and some fresh biscuits rather than those rocks that had graced the stew earlier.

When he finished eating, he left fifty cents on the table, picked up his Winchester, left the diner, then crossed to the hotel and walked to his room.

After entering, he closed the door, set his Winchester down in the corner and kicked off his boots. He flopped on the small bed, his feet hanging off the end, and wondered what those two were planning.

Even though trying to guess what their plans were for his demise should have been the only thing on his mind, his thoughts drifted back to Ellie, as they always did. He kept trying to focus his mind on possible defenses against what he assumed was going to be a shootout tomorrow, but his mind kept returning to Ellie.

He eventually did fall asleep after setting the alarm on his watch for six o'clock. He had a really long ride starting tomorrow, and now he'd probably have someone lying in wait to try to keep him from reaching his destination.

CHAPTER 3

Stan rolled out of bed, literally, a half an hour before his alarm was set to go off. He had simply rolled once in his sleep, and with the blanket wrapped around him, thumped to the floor probably waking the other guests, if there were any. It was a rude way to start his day, but he shrugged it off and walked down to the washroom where he washed, shaved and even combed his hair. He didn't have time for a bath, which wouldn't have worked anyway as there was no bathtub.

Ten minutes after returning to his room, he had his saddlebags packed, his hat on his head, and his revolver at his waist as he picked up his Winchester and left the room. He had originally planned on skipping the buffalo breakfast but wanted to see if Zeke and Frank were at the eatery or already gone. He walked out to the lobby, gave a short wave to the man at the desk, left the hotel and crossed the compound to what he now called the Buffalo Bistro.

As he approached the diner, he noticed that there were two horses parked out front, each with a Springfield Model 1861 musket in a scabbard. He acted as if he didn't notice and entered the building.

He was very familiar with the Springfield. It was a muzzle loader, but the ammunition was in a single paper tube containing both powder and bullet. It still had to be rammed in, but the shooter didn't need to measure and pour in the powder which improved accuracy. A good rifleman could get off four shots in a minute with the gun and put that massive .58 caliber bullet three hundred yards downrange. Some might laugh at the muzzle-loaders nowadays, but he didn't. For a back-shooter, it was a good weapon. But if he knew where they were, he could take advantage of their slow reload times.

As he entered, he noticed that Frank and Zeke were at the same table they were yesterday when they had been evicted. Stan took a seat and when asked by the owner what he wanted, he was grateful that the owner took his order for bacon and eggs without batting an eye and wondered if there was such a thing as buffalo bacon.

While waiting for his order, he was thinking about possible routes to take out of the post. He had checked the map, and the best path toward Cheyenne City was south-southwest for a while. The only landmark listed on the map was a point called Parker's Butte about six miles along that route, and if they were going to try to ambush him, they'd probably use that as cover.

He'd need to see if there were any possible locations on the way, but with no other landmarks on the map, he would have to wait until he was riding south. If they intended to get on the other side of the butte though, it would mean they'd have to leave before him, and that had to be very soon. They'd have to go around the other side or risk being seen as he rode behind them.

He had barely finished with that assumption when they stood, went outside, mounted their horses, and rode off quickly to the west. Stan figured that they'd have about a four or five-mile head start on him at least because he had to go and get his horses and then his supplies. It would be more than enough time to go around the western slope of the butte to get on the southern edge and set up their ambush.

After his four eggs and four strips of bacon arrived, Stan ate quickly. He didn't want to give those boys too much time to set up, so he finished in three minutes before leaving two bits on the table as he departed.

He jogged down the main street until he reached the livery, and true to his word, the liveryman had the three animals ready to go. The new saddle and scabbard were on the buckskin, and old army saddle and the new saddlebags along with its Sharps-filled scabbard were on the red. The mule was loaded with his supplies and two empty scabbards.

The liveryman helped to move the animals out of the barn and after checking to make sure the supplies were lashed down properly, Stan turned and shook the liveryman's hand.

"I appreciate the service, sir," Stan said.

"Thanks for the business. You have a safe trip now."

"Speaking of that, if someone were planning on making my trip unsafe, you know, maybe a bit of a drygulch. Where would be the best place if I'm heading south?"

"That's easy. Parker's Butte. It falls off real sudden on the south end. That's where I'd look. There ain't anythin' else that close to the post."

"That's what I was thinking, too. But I've never seen it."

"Well, good luck. Hope you're wrong."

"Me, too, but I'm pretty sure there are a couple of gents waiting with their rifles on the south end of Parker's Butte."

"If they are, you be sure and leave 'em for the critters, cause there ain't nobody here who cares. That so-called sheriff ain't really a sheriff. He just put up the sign and wears a badge he made. He's just a no-account thug."

"I thought as much. Thanks for the information," Stan said as he shook the man's hand.

Stan climbed aboard the buckskin, slid his Winchester into the scabbard appreciating the extra height over his army horse, and noted that the red mare was even taller. He felt a lot better having the spare horse as he set them moving away from the livery.

He fast walked them down the main street to the dry goods store, stepped down, tied off the buckskin and walked inside, noticing that his order was ready to go. Suddenly, he wished he hadn't given away his Spencer to the Cheyenne warrior. He could have used the extra lead-spitter.

"Excuse me, what do you have in the way of firepower?"

"Not much. Seems like you've got enough, but I do have a few surplus Spencers in back. I got 'em in trade a few months ago. Don't have any ammo for 'em, though."

"Let's go and have a look."

"Sure, come on back."

Stan walked back and saw six Spencers leaning against the wall. He'd look at the serial numbers and pick out the newest one and then check its condition.

He looked at what looked to be the oldest and flipped it over to look at the serial number, and then rubbed his thumb across the dirty stamping believing that what he saw was impossible. Yet after the grime was removed, he found that the impossible was very possible and was in his hands. The serial number read 6100992. *It was his first Spencer!* The one he was issued when he enlisted, and after a year's heavy use had turned it in for a replacement. There was no doubt he'd have to buy this one.

Then he found one that was made in '64 and was in excellent shape, then turned to the proprietor and asked, "How much do you want for them?"

"Give me two dollars and you can have your pick."

"I'll give you three dollars for this one and that old one right here."

"You can take that old one. Why would you even want to carry that thing with you? It's darn near useless."

Stan smiled and replied, "Would you believe that this was issued to me in Detroit, Michigan in August of '61? It was my first carbine of the war."

"Well, I'll be danged. It sure took a roundabout way coming back here. Didn't it?"

"That's the truth."

Stan still paid him three dollars for the two carbines, just because he felt that the old carbine was still worth a lot more to him. Then they began loading up the mule with the large order. Stan would get it all sorted out later tonight, provided those two assassins waiting for him south if the butte didn't get lucky.

He slipped both Spencers into the mule's scabbards and stepped up into the saddle of the buckskin. He thought about going west and sneaking up behind the pair of would-be murderers, but thought he'd have to be sure that was their plan, otherwise he'd be wasting time. He decided to stick to his original path, but he'd make sure to keep a sharp eye out as he rode.

He turned his animals east and left the trading post, then turned south after clearing the almost-town, took out his compass and headed south-southwest. That would keep him on the right path.

He could see the butte ahead, and probably saw it when he rode in, but hadn't paid attention as he was studying the trading post. He definitely paid attention now. He noticed that the ground to the east of the butte rose suddenly to a low ridge, leaving a pass between the two geological features. He estimated the pass to be about three hundred yards wide or so and decided that he would ride as close to the eastern side of the pass as possible putting him at the edge of the Springfield's effective range. As he rode, he wondered how good they were with those muskets.

———

Frank Porter and Zeke Liston had their horses moving as quickly as they dared without getting them too tired.

"That feller had a ton of supplies, Zeke, and must have a lot of money on him, too," Frank said loudly.

"It sure looks that way!" agreed Zeke who was already wearing a grin in anticipation of the job.

If either one had known just how much money Stan was carrying, they would have peed their pants in excitement.

They were still excited, though. This was going to be a great payday, and it was far enough away from the trading post, so no one would know. The army man just disappears as he said he was going to do, and nobody would investigate the huge flock of vultures that would be seen south of the post because they had protection. They'd have to share their take with Benny Laskins, the sheriff, but that was okay, they'd cheat him anyway.

They reached the butte as Stan was leaving the town, and it took them another forty minutes of hard riding to circle around to the south side, and another twenty to reach the eastern edge of the butte. They both stepped down about fifty yards away from the south end, tied off their horses on a nearby pine, then took out their muskets. Both were very comfortable with their Springfields, having used them during the War Between the States. Zeke, in particular, thought of himself as a marksman, and knew this would be a simple shot. That ex-soldier would probably be within a hundred yards as he came through the pass. Everybody rode in the middle to avoid any boulders that might decide to leave the highlands on either side of the broad pass.

They reached the edge of the butte, and looked across the flat ground, expecting to see their victim riding through the pass soon.

As they peered north, Zeke said, "Now, I'll take the first shot and you wait ten seconds until the smoke clears a bit and then you fire if he ain't on the ground. That'll give me time to reload. We should have him down by then, anyway."

"Sounds like you got it all planned out good, Zeke."

Zeke grinned and replied, "This will be a piece of cake, Frank. The easiest job yet."

_____

Stan had just entered the pass and guessed it would be about another twenty minutes before he reached the southern edge of the butte at the walking speed of the horses and mule, and that's where he expected them to be, on the southern edge of the butte, and suspected that they were already there.

FINDING BUCKY

Earlier, he had taken the time to move the Sharps back to his second scabbard on the buckskin and had already loaded the rifle. Now, his only real concern, other than being shot, was whether the buckskin would be skittish around gunfire, or the red for that matter, because if she reared, the trail rope would jerk his mare enough to ruin his return shot. It would be a hell of a time to find out, but Stan had no choice.

———

Frank pointed and said loudly, "There he is! I think that's him, anyway. He's riding a buckskin instead of the brown horse and he's trailing another tall horse and the mule. That boy must have lotsa money, Zeke. But he's on the other side of the pass. That's gonna make the shot a lot harder."

"That ain't gonna be a problem. I'll still get him all right, Frank. You get right behind me. Remember, ten seconds."

"I'll be ready, Zeke," Frank said as he moved back from the edge slightly to give Zeke more room to take the shot.

They had set all their reloading supplies and tools on a nearby rock, not believing that they would be necessary.

———

Stan had his animals moving at a slow walk so his vision wouldn't be jarred. He was riding on the far edge of the pass away from the shooters and was just about four hundred yards from the end of the butte when he thought he spotted them. It looked like a stick jutting out from the rock, but it was a very deadly stick. It was the barrel of an 1861 Springfield musket, and depending on the condition of the gun and the skill of the shooter, they could be effective to five hundred yards. He always assumed the worst situation, and if that were true, the assassin was a sharpshooter and the rifle was almost new,

71

which would have him already in range. But that distance did give him a slight advantage. There would be a gap between the instant that he'd see the muzzle spit out the cloud of smoke and the arrival of the bullet. It wouldn't be much, less than a second, but it could be enough to save his life.

He kept the muzzle in sight without appearing to be staring at it. He didn't want them to realize that he was aware of their presence, but he desperately wanted that fraction of a second to react when he saw the bloom of smoke. Depending how soon the shooter let it go, it could be as long as a second, but with each step that his horses took, the time and distance dropped. A second could feel like an eon if you knew it was coming. The only possible problem was if they targeted the horse, just like he had when he had engaged the Cheyenne, then all bets were off.

If he saw the muzzle flare, he was planning on kicking the horse to a faster pace and dropping to the mare's neck, but a shot at the horse would definitely still hit. If the shooter was impressed with his own skills, then he'd go for him and he'd miss. It might be their greed to keep the horses for themselves that would make him the target and not the buckskin.

He kept the horses walking and he had almost reached the southern edge, two hundred and fifty yards out when he saw the cloud of smoke burst from the Springfield's muzzle. Stan dropped to the buckskin's neck and gave her a hard kick to the sides, as the big round hissed past him followed immediately by the loud report of the Springfield.

He quickly pulled the mare to a stop, knowing that the shooter couldn't reload quickly, but there was the second one, and Stan hoped he had time. He yanked the Sharps from its scabbard, sighted on the smoke, but shifted his aim slightly to the right, centering on the edge of the butte itself, and squeezed the trigger. The gun jolted and boomed, his own large cloud of gunsmoke boiling into the air. The buckskin just jerked a little, and he immediately began to reload.

As soon as he fired, Zeke had stepped back to reload without seeing the impact of his shot. He'd let Frank do that when he aimed his musket. Frank quickly stepped to the edge, and was bringing his Springfield to bear, when the rock three feet to his left exploded into hundreds of shards and a cloud of dust.

"Jesus Christ, Frank! What the hell happened? Did your gun explode?" Zeke screamed from behind as the Sharps' report echoed off the rocks.

Frank was too stunned to answer for a couple of seconds, but then replied loudly, "I don't know. The gun looks all right, but the rock blew up."

Zeke trotted next to Frank, looked across the pass and saw Stan reloading his rifle before shouting, "Damn! That bastard shot at us!"

"I'll get him now, Zeke!" Frank shouted back as he tried to reacquire the target.

He swung the long barrel of the Springfield back toward the pass, and as he took aim, he saw another cloud of smoke blow out of the muzzle of Stan's rifle. Frank never got a chance to warn Zeke of the incoming round, as the heavy mass of lead passed through Frank's upper chest, ripping out a good section of the soft tissue, snapping three ribs and after exiting his back, smashed into Zeke's left upper arm, shattering the humerus and severing his brachial artery. Zeke screamed, but Frank was well beyond making noise as he crumpled to the ground, with blood still bubbling from his massive chest wound. It continued to bubble for another eight seconds before he stopped breathing and the blood stopped gurgling.

73

Stan heard the scream and dropped the Sharps into the scabbard and grabbed the Winchester before he set the buckskin to a trot toward the eastern edge of the butte, still trailing the horse and mule, arriving less than a minute later.

He had his Winchester's sights still centered on the edge of the rock as he approached but heard the continued screaming. *He knew he'd hit one of the two, but why wasn't the second one firing?* He suspected that the other man was waiting for him to get closer, but with the Springfield's size, it would be easily spotted. He'd be able to send two or three .44s their way before that long muzzle-loader even was pointed his way.

He reached the edge of the butte, still wondering where the second shooter was, but slowly stepped down, keeping his Winchester at the ready, then slowly walked to the corner of the butte. The screaming had stopped, but he could hear a blubbering whimper coming from the other side of the rock outcrop.

He stepped forward carefully, his Winchester ready to fire as he reached the corner of the rock, then quickly swiveled it around the edge and knew that he had nothing to worry about any longer. He lowered the Winchester's muzzle and walked slowly toward Frank's body as Zeke was on the ground nearby, sobbing as the blood leaked from his arm into the growing syrup-like red pool beneath him.

He gave Frank a hard kick to make sure he was really dead and not playing possum then looked at Zeke.

"You gotta save me, mister. I'm gonna die," he pleaded.

"We are all going to die, Zeke. You're just going to die today."

"How'd you know my name? You ain't gonna help me?"

FINDING BUCKY

"No, I'm not going to help you. I'm going to let you die. I couldn't get you back to the post fast enough anyway. But it doesn't matter. You're dying and I'm not, so you won't get anything from me other than the few ounces of lead you already got. Enjoy your trip to Hell."

"You bast..." was all that leaked out of his mouth as his blood finally stopped leaking out of his arm when his heart stopped pumping.

Now it was salvage time, one didn't leave anything of value just lying around. Stan looked at the horses and knew they were worth keeping, as he'd seen them before. Both were dark geldings, one a brownish-red and the other black. About six or seven years old by the looks of them. They could have been army horses for all he knew, so he checked, but neither had USA burned on their butts, so at least they weren't army issue, which could have presented a problem in the future.

The saddle on one of them was a lot nicer than the army saddle he had, so he'd swap them when he saddled the horses tomorrow morning after he camped. He'd alleviate some of the weight from the mule, too. He didn't need the Springfields, but he'd take the powder. He didn't bother going through their pockets, though, because if they had a hard time paying for a meal, they wouldn't have anything worth finding. Stan made another trail rope and hooked up the other two horses and attached them to the back of the mule. One man, four horses and a mule made an odd-looking train.

Stan wasn't about to waste the time or energy to bury them. Let the wolves, coyotes, buzzards and crawly things eat. They were God's creations too.

He climbed back on the buckskin, and after the thirty-minute delay, set them all off at a slow trot to the southwest.

He made another twenty miles before Stan found a good spot and pulled over for a break. He had a quick lunch of jerky and hard tack and let his long trail of animals graze and drink before he returned to the saddle and resumed his long journey.

He kept going until after sunset, having gone another thirty miles before Stan decided to call it quits for the night. It was the longest he'd been able to travel, despite the interruption.

After unloading the mules and unsaddling the horses, Stan led them to a nearby stream and let them drink, then hitched them in an area where they could graze while he prepared to graze himself but decided to go through Zeke and Frank's saddlebags before he did, just out of curiosity. They weren't in bad shape and could be used to carry the ammunition.

He dumped out their contents, finding nothing of value whatsoever, which hadn't surprised him in the least. He took the saddlebags down to the nearby stream, rinsed them out and shook them dry, then hung them from a branch and left the flaps open to dry. It wasn't the best way to treat leather, but they were at least clean. He'd oil the leather later. The clothing that was in the saddlebags hadn't smelled very good, and he'd rather not be reminded of the two lowlifes every time he opened the bags.

After leaving the saddlebags, he dug a fire pit and soon had a small fire going. The sun was long gone, and he could already feel the chill in the air, which he'd grown to expect in the high plains, even at the end of May. He cooked himself a decent dinner and then cleaned up before going to the supplies and rebalancing the load.

———

Ellie was lying alone in her bed as usual.

FINDING BUCKY

George had expressed his bland approval of Betsy, but she had made one major faux pas. After she had served dinner to him and Ellie, she had asked, "Would you like anything else, Ellie?"

George had chastised her severely, reminding her that she was help and was never to use either of their Christian names again. She is to refer to his wife as Mrs. Rafferty.

Betsy had been terrified at his vehemence, and thought she was going to be fired on the spot. Ellie had never objected to Betsy calling her Ellie, but she had apologized and agreed demurely to Mister Rafferty's order, and he seemed to accept her apology.

After Mister Rafferty left, Ellie had to explain that he set great store in position, and to accommodate him when he was there, but it wouldn't be that often.

She also was still irritated with her mother from the day before. She had spent almost two hours badgering her about her failure to become pregnant and had asked very private questions about whether she was doing everything possible to satisfy her husband. Ellie really wanted to scream but kept assuring her mother that she was everything her husband would ever want in a woman, an honest answer that seemed to satisfy her mother.

But secretly, her mother doubted that she was and placed the blame for the delay squarely on her daughter and began to suspect that Ellie might be barren.

Ellie was getting tired of the charade. She'd only been married for eight months and she was already being pushed on two sides. George was demanding that she play the dutiful wife at the many parties and soirees that they attended, but always leaving her in her bedroom alone afterwards. Yet her parents both continuously demanded that she have a child to cement their marriage and their positions in society. Everything about her life was so phony.

All she had was her memory of the overweight boy who had loved his buck-toothed girlfriend; the two misfits that no one liked, just liked to torment. But they had liked each other, and Ellie knew that even from the very start, she had loved Stan. He was her Piggy and she was his Bucky.

She sighed, remembering those simple days. It was her and Stan against everyone else. Now, she was against everyone else and she was alone with no Piggy to talk to and comfort her.

———

The next four days on Stan's journey went well. The weather cooperated, and the Indians stayed away. He was riding the red mare today, as he had decided to alternate to get used to each horse's quirks and give the others a day with a lighter load. He had even taken some shots from the back of the red to see if she was skittish and found that she wasn't. He was able to take down a nice doe for a few days' worth of fresh meat yesterday and had even ridden the other two horses occasionally, but of the group, he was much fonder of the two mares he had purchased at the trading post.

But this was the fifth day, and it would bring its own problems. He was almost two hundred miles south of Miles' trading post and was getting close to Fort Fetterman. The day had started normally, but the clouds were building quickly by mid-morning, and he knew it was going to get wet, so he pulled out his slicker and pulled it over his head before replacing his Stetson.

The rains began an hour before noon and started out innocently enough as an almost pleasant spring shower. Then the nice shower suddenly became a nightmarish deluge, when the clouds opened up like Stan had never seen before. There was no thunder or lightning, just buckets of water pouring from the sky.

Stan began looking for shelter for him and his animals. He had the horses in a line and the mule at the end of the long tether, but there wasn't much available in the way of protection until he spotted a ridge nearby that had an overhang. It wasn't much, but he angled toward it.

He was almost there when he heard a roaring sound from the ridge behind him. He quickly swiveled in his saddle and to his horror, saw a massive mudslide rolling down the ridge and flattening when it hit the ground and spreading quickly, churning and swallowing anything it its path. He pulled the red mare south and snapped his legs together hard to give her the message. The horse didn't need any hints from its rider as she and the other animals heard the threat behind them and began to run. The roaring was getting louder as the faster moving mudslide gained on them, even at their fast pace.

Even the mule was moving as fast as it could, it wasn't fast enough. Just as Stan thought they were going to make it to safety as the mudslide began subsiding, the mule was caught in the thick flow, picked up from its hooves, and spun to the left of the still moving horses. He was flailing wildly as the mud carried him alongside the buckskin, whose eyes were white with terror. The mule fell and was sucked under the mud as the buckskin's rear hooves fought to gain footing. Then, the mud slide suddenly stopped, its deadly momentum gone.

Stan slowed the red down quickly and stepped down to see if the horses were all right. He knew the red mare was okay, as were the two geldings, but he was worried about the buckskin. It was still panicked, its hind legs thrashing about wildly in the mud, even though it was only four inches deep. The rain was still coming down, just not as hard as before as Stan walked to the buckskin and began talking to her. Then he sang to her to calm her as he rested his hand on her neck.

The buckskin finally felt some purchase on its right foot and stepped away from the mud to join her companions. There was no point in hitching the horses as there was nothing to hitch them to, but the mule's trail rope was still holding them. Luckily, it had been a longer rope than normal. Stan had done it intentionally because of the mule's tendency to slow down suddenly.

He used the rope to lead him to the mule and the supplies, knowing he'd have a job turning one of the two extra horses into a pack horse.

As he followed the rope to the muddy bulge that covered the mule, the heavy rain continued to wash the mud from the body. Stan began wiping the mud from the mule and supplies thinking that at least they were close to Fort Fetterman.

He was startled when the mule suddenly jerked its head out of the mud and snorted the mud out of its nostrils. It scared the daylights out of Stan, as he had been standing just a foot in front of the mule's nose.

The animal then rolled around for a few seconds, scrambled out of the muck, then stepped away from the mud toward the horses like nothing had happened, the pack saddle and panniers still attached. The rain began to clean the mule of the clinging mud and Stan was surprised that in addition to the panniers all being secure and still covered, the two Spencers were still in their scabbards, although Stan surely didn't want to fire one now. They'd have to be severely cleaned before he even thought about it. He finally managed to get them away from the ridge and moving south again. He'd settle for putting up with the rain until the heavens finally turned off the spigot.

FINDING BUCKY

The rain subsided by early afternoon and around three o'clock, the sun came out as if it had all been a big joke.

Stan kept them all moving while the sun dried the ground, and by five o'clock, even though there would still be another three hours of daylight, he pulled them over to a swollen stream for camp, estimating that Fort Fetterman had to be less than twenty miles away.

He set up camp and unpacked the mule. The panniers were still dirty, but the supplies had miraculously stayed dry. He then unsaddled the horses and let them graze and drink before hitching them, dug a fire pit and soon had his dinner cooking. It was more of a breakfast, with scrambled eggs, bacon and coffee. The few remaining eggs had already been scrambled in their bag when the mule went down, which was why they made it to the menu.

After eating, he cleaned and oiled all his weapons. Tomorrow he should find Fort Fetterman and add to his supplies, but right now, he needed to sleep. The horses and the mule were already passed out and Stan joined them shortly.

———

The next morning was like the nightmare from the day before hadn't happened. Stan packed the revitalized mule, who had been given a name overnight. Lazarus. What else?

He saddled the horses and was on the move by 7:45. He had looked at the map earlier and had turned southeast, looking for a small river. He wouldn't have to cross the river, just follow it to Fetterman. He recalled meeting Captain Fetterman briefly at Leavenworth when they were both in transition and the man didn't make an impression, one way or the other. He just had a bad taste about any officer that would lead his men into an ambush of any sort. A good commander always expects an

81

ambush. Maybe Fetterman just thought the Sioux were stupid and couldn't figure out how to lure him into a trap. Stan had his own opinion about who the ignorant leader was in the action.

He plodded his horses along the small river until the buildings of Fort Fetterman came into sight, and a welcome sight it was. Even from a distance, the size of the fort looked like a good-sized settlement that easily surpassed the trading post at Miles. Construction was still ongoing, and there was a lot of activity.

He wound his way across the flat plains in front of the fort and rode toward the sutler's store on the outskirts of the main buildings. There were already quite a few barracks, and he wondered how many troops the army was planning on sending here. It was surely a remote posting, but then again, in the West almost all of them were remote, but this one was more remote than most.

He stepped down in front of the store and tied off the buckskin. Stan was confident that the buckskin was the only one of its type on the fort and bound to catch some attention. He walked inside leaving his Winchester in its scabbard this time.

"Good morning, what can I do for you, young feller?" asked the proprietor.

The man couldn't have been five feet tall and surprisingly heavy set, but he seemed pleasant.

"I need to pick up some supplies. I just rode in from Miles' trading post and need to head down to Cheyenne City."

"You'd better be careful. The Sioux are getting all the Nations riled up."

"So, I hear. I had a run-in with some Cheyenne about sixty miles northeast of the post myself."

"Get many of 'em?"

"Eight. One got away."

"Still pretty good shootin'."

"I'll need to get my horses and mule reshod before I shove off, and I'll need a bath and haircut, too."

"No problem. Got a tub in the back room, and I'll trim your hair. Do it for lots of the boys. The livery is just to your right as you leave the store. Give me a list and I'll get your stuff together."

Stan wrote out what he needed and handed it to the sutler.

"I'll be back for the haircut and bath in a bit. I'm going to head over and drop off the horses."

The sutler was already filling the order and waved him off.

Stan went outside, then led his animals to the livery where he stepped into the large barn and found the liveryman mucking out the back stall.

"Howdy. What can I do for ya?" he asked as he looked Stan's way.

"Can I get the animals reshod? I've got to make it down to Cheyenne."

"All five of 'em?"

"All five."

"I can do 'er, but it'll take a couple of hours, and cost you five dollars."

"That's fine," Stan replied as he paid for the work and left the livery.

An hour later he was clean and felt better, then stayed in the sutler's store and had a filling beef stew but declined the offer for some whiskey. He told the sutler that he had a bad experience with the stuff and swore off.

The sutler just snickered and Stan let his imagination decide what the experience was. There never had been a bad experience, other than that first taste when he was seventeen, and the blacksmith had offered it to him. He just had never developed a taste for it but found that his fake explanation for not drinking was always accepted more readily.

"Whatcha heading down to Cheyenne for?" the sutler asked.

"I'm looking for a woman."

The sutler slapped his thigh and laughed, saying, "Ain't we all?"

"You hear about Cheyenne's big doings?" the proprietor asked when he finished laughing.

"Nope. Haven't heard a thing," Stan replied.

"General Dodge is heading out there to set up for his Union Pacific Railroad to come through there pretty soon. The town that was there is gonna get bigger awful fast."

"I sure could have used a railroad on this trip. I'm going to go down there and see if her family went through there."

"Well, good luck, young feller."

FINDING BUCKY

Stan lugged his two heavy bags out the door and across to the livery. He had to spend some time balancing the supplies again, but the only things he added to his saddlebags were the four boxes of cartridges for his shooting Spencer and more ammunition for his Sharps. He wasn't about to use his worn-out issue carbine, and not because of its sentimental value. The thing would probably blow up when he pulled the trigger.

His horses and mule were newly shod, watered and fed, and it was time to head south to Cheyenne City.

He left Fort Fetterman just two and a half hours after arriving, so he didn't lose much time, and he was more than halfway to Cheyenne City. The question already haunting him was: *what if she's not there?* She had said Wyoming, and that meant a lot of territory. *If she wasn't in Cheyenne City, where would she be?*

After that, he'd be close to Colorado, and began thinking of just settling down in Colorado and trying to forget Ellie. Then he thought about maybe finding another woman and settling down, but he knew that would be unfair to the other woman. Ellie owned him, heart and soul. They spent more time together when they were young than most married adults did. She was more than sweet. She was thoughtful and sincere but had a wonderful sense of humor that meshed with his and that was their greatest defense against the continuing onslaught of insults and abuse. They'd laugh together about how they were treated, because it was all that they had in those days before she changed.

She had changed physically, and what made Stan love her even more was that she hadn't suddenly become a stranger to him. As pretty as she had become along with its potential for popularity, she had stayed beside him and talked to him exactly as she had before. Not too many young people could resist the allure of being popular just for friendship. *How could anyone not love someone like that?*

He may go to Colorado and build his ranch, but he would never let Ellie go. Without her, he felt like he was nothing. But he still had to know. *Where was Ellie? Was she happy? Did she still even think of him anymore?*

He stopped for the night about twenty miles south of Fort Fetterman, knowing that now he could push it a bit. He had another hundred and fifty miles to go, all of it in Sioux and Cheyenne territory. He'd make sure all his weapons stayed loaded, maybe even his old Spencer. Lord knows where the bullets would go if he had to fire the thing.

He cooked his dinner and when he was finished, loaded all the guns. Thirty rounds plus the five in his Colt New army. That's acceptable, he thought.

———

The next morning, he began early. After a hasty breakfast and cleanup, he was traveling by seven. He wanted to get at least fifty miles done today, and felt as if it was urgent, but knew it was just his imagination driving him. He and Ellie had separated almost ten years ago, and one or two days wasn't going to make any difference, or even a month probably wouldn't make any difference, but he still kept up the rapid pace.

———

Ellie had enough. She was so tired of all the phoniness and lies. She had six thousand dollars in her personal account, but how could she get it? *Did she need it?* It would take time to get the money out. *But then, where would she go? Should she return to Michigan to see if Stan was still there?* But then there were the legal problems. She was still married to George and he had every legal right to take her back against her will. She felt trapped by the extraordinary set of circumstances not of her making.

86

She just felt like she had to do something, and thought maybe she should have an affair, let George find out about it and divorce her. But she knew that it wasn't even remotely possible, even though she was often the recipient of some of Rafferty male acquaintances to do just that. It simply wasn't her. She wanted a man to love her first, and not just someone who would just say the words, either. Before a man would make love to her, it had to be one who knew her and loved her completely. And the only one who would love her that way was her beloved Piggy.

But how could she find him?

She didn't know that her Piggy was moving south, heading in her direction, and he had no idea where she lived either.

For Stan, it was almost a hopeless mission, one he must undertake. But at least he knew he was on his way to find Bucky while Ellie had no idea where he was or what he was doing, nor did she have any plan to try and find him. He could be back in Michigan sitting at the kitchen table with his wife and four children for all she knew.

But Ellie refused to believe that. She just couldn't. She needed to believe he would come for her. The war had been over for almost two years now, so he could be out there somewhere, hunting for her. That hope; that belief, was all she had now.

Suddenly a new thought popped into her head. One that had never once entered her mind in the ten years they had been separated. *What if he'd been killed in the war?* So many had died. *Why shouldn't Stan have been one of them?* One of the masses of blue uniforms marching across an open field to artillery fire and fusillades of bullets. Or even more likely, he could have been one of the tens of thousands to die from the diseases that ran rampant through the armies. He could be dead, but again, she refused to believe it. She firmly believed that she would have felt it in her heart and soul if he had died and had to convince herself that Piggy was coming. Coming to take her away from all this luxury, her gilded cage.

––––––

Stan had made almost sixty miles that first full day from Fetterman, stretching the ride until the sun had gone down. He was almost halfway to Cheyenne now, and if he could duplicate today's distance on tomorrow's ride, he'd be less than eighty miles from Cheyenne. He didn't realize that he had just committed the cardinal sin of being optimistic.

He set up camp for the night in the lee of a ridge near a large creek. There were plenty of trees around and lots of deadwood. He let the horses eat and drink and set up his cooking grate over his fire pit. It had been dark for over three hours, so it was a very late dinner, probably close to midnight. Everything was quiet, and for some reason, the silence was eerie. The normal noises of the night, the bugs and other night creatures had stopped making noise.

Stan felt spooked by the absence of sound, so he stood, removed his pistol's hammer loop, then slowly walked to the saddles and pulled the Winchester from its scabbard. He cocked the hammer, then walked to the ridge, put his back against a big boulder, and waited.

He didn't see anything as he avoided looking at his cooking fire. Maybe the pistol would be better, but the Winchester could be reloaded faster and had ten more shots to begin with. He just didn't know who was out there, or what, if anything. He stood with his back against the ridge for ten minutes and still nothing stirred. The long wait in the silence was adding to his nervousness.

FINDING BUCKY

Then his eyes picked up something to the right. Something had moved, but it wasn't much. He tightened his grip on the rifle and stared at where he had seen the movement. *There!* The shadow moved again, then he heard something moving slowly as well. *What kind of an Indian makes that much sound?* He was beginning to sweat, and decided then to fire at the next movement, but the sound bothered him. If it was a hostile Indian, he wouldn't have heard that much rustling, so he held his trigger finger.

He heard another rustle off to the right and finally spotted the source. It was an Indian, but he was crawling. He kept his Winchester pointed at the Indian as he crawled toward the fire and then collapsed. Stan waited for two minutes to make sure it wasn't some trick before finally walking slowly forward, keeping his Winchester pointed at the prostrate Indian. He didn't look like a Cheyenne or Arapaho, nor Sioux either and it was too far south to be a Crow. *Could he be a Ute?*

He finally got near enough to realize it wasn't a warrior at all. It was a Ute woman, and she was injured, or she could just be exhausted.

Stan released the hammer on his Winchester and set it down. He knelt next to her and rolled her gently onto her back, his right hand supporting her head.

"Ma'am? Can you hear me?" he asked softly.

Either she didn't hear him or didn't want to, because her eyes stayed closed. It was difficult to see in the firelight what her injuries were, if any. He couldn't see any blood, so maybe she was just hungry and thirsty. She looked pretty worn out, like she'd been on the run for a few days.

He didn't have to stand, but just pulled his bedroll over and slid it under her head before standing and jogging to his supplies and finding a tin of peaches, then grabbed his canteen as well. He didn't see how she could be thirsty with a stream nearby, but the cold water might wake her up.

He crouched down on his haunches, put the can of peaches nearby and opened the canteen. Stan then slowly poured a trickle of water onto her mouth and tongue slid across her lips, so Stan poured more. After the third time, her eyes flickered, then opened.

"Do you want more water?" he asked, showing her the canteen.

"Yes. Water. Food," she uttered hoarsely.

Stan was surprised somewhat, but many Utes spoke English, so he wasn't that startled.

He gave her more water, but she was weak.

He laid her head back down, took out his pocketknife and opened the can of peaches, taking the top of the tin completely off. His coffee cup was nearby, so he poured half the can inside and used the blade part of the pocketknife to chop the half peaches into smaller pieces. When it was done, he lifted her head again, put the cup to her lips and let the sugary syrup pour into her mouth. Her eyes widened as she tasted the sweet fruity liquid, then she reached for the cup with both hands and lifted it higher, letting the chunks of peaches enter her mouth. She closed her eyes as she emptied the cup, chewed the peaches and swallowed. Then she opened her eyes again and looked at Stan.

"More?" she asked.

Stan repeated the pouring and chopping with the other half of the can, poured it into the cup and handed it to her. She reverently took the cup and put it to her mouth, emptying it in seconds.

"You are Ute?" he asked.

"Yes. Yamparika Ute."

"What happened?"

"Three days ago, I was scraping hides with three other women. Arapaho came and took us. I fought but the others submitted. They were going to kill me, but I hurt one and ran. They hunt me still and will come for me now. Soon."

"How many?"

"Six in the beginning. Four now. Two stayed with the other women."

"How soon before you can ride?"

"One hour, maybe."

"Alright. I'll cook some food. I was ready to start cooking anyway, so it won't take long. We'll eat, and I'll saddle and pack the animals. Would you like to wear some pants, so you can ride? They will be too big, but it will be better, I think."

"I will. My village is more than a half of a day ride to the west if we ride quickly."

"We should be halfway there by daybreak. I'd better get started."

Stan was out of eggs, so he fried up some bacon and then, after pulling the bacon out of the pan, dumped in some beans, tomato, canned beef and sprinkled some salt. Not the tastiest concoction, but it would fill their bellies, and she needed it. Stan handed her the bacon and began to pack the mule, returning to the pan to stir the mix every minute or so. She greedily ate the bacon and watched Stan as he worked.

Stan finally pulled the pan from the grate to let it cool before returning to getting the mule loaded. After he had the mule packed, he pulled out one of his spare pairs of pants and brought it to her. Stan quickly turned away to give her some privacy and began saddling the horses. He'd ride the red mare today, so it got the two scabbards.

He returned to the skillet, pulled out one of his two plates and spooned the food onto the plate, leaving the spoon with it. He handed it to her and left her the canteen.

She began to eat quickly as Stan took out another spoon and ate directly from the pan. When he finished, he then cleaned the pan and collected her empty plate and spoon. He washed them quickly, returned to the camp site and packed them in the cookware pannier.

Stan then dumped a canteen on the fire, extinguishing it in a cloud of steam, then kicked dirt onto the smoldering coals, filling the fire pit before turning to the Ute woman.

"How are you feeling?" he asked.

"Much better. Thank you. What is your name?"

"Stan Murray. Yours?"

"It translates to Giver of Light, but my English name is Mary."

"I'll call you Mary, if that's alright. It's just shorter."

"It is. Why are you here? This is Arapaho land."

"I'm on my way to Cheyenne City. You know of it?"

"Yes. It is two days ride southeast. But will you take me west to my village?"

"Of course. Can you shoot a gun?"

"No. But you have a bow. A Cheyenne bow. They are enemies to the Utes as are the Arapaho."

"I was attacked by nine Cheyenne a few days ago. I killed eight."

She spit, then said, "I am sad that one escaped. We must go quickly. The Arapaho will come at night and will be here soon."

Stan needed no further urging. He helped her into the saddle, deciding to give her the buckskin mare instead of one of the geldings. She might need the speed if he failed to stop the Arapaho. She looked a bit ludicrous with her deerskin dress pulled up around her waist and the baggy britches underneath, but it worked. Once she was aboard the buckskin, Stan handed her the reins and stepped up onto the red. They left the camp, heading west by the light of a quarter moon.

They moved at a walk as the forested area near the stream had given way to plains, so their visibility was better. Their night vision allowed the limited light from the moon to give them a clear view of the surrounding area out to a mile.

They had ridden for over an hour already in silence when Stan asked, "Were the other three women killed?"

"Not when I escaped. Because they had given themselves to the Arapaho, they will probably live. I would rather have died. My husband would wish it."

"You have children?"

"Three. Two boys and one girl. My daughter is special. Why do you journey to Cheyenne?"

"For a very silly reason. When I was young, I was fat. Other children made jokes and called me names. I knew a girl who had very large teeth, and they also made fun of her. We became best of friends. When she was older, her teeth became normal and she was very pretty. I thought she would no longer be my friend because I was still fat, but she did stay my friend. Even when her parents took her away, she was as saddened by our separation as I was.

"Her parents told her they were going to Wyoming. But they could have lied to her. They joined a wagon train, but I don't know where it went. I left my home and fought in the great war and just left the army twelve days ago. I am looking for her now. It is silly because she has probably married and has children. But I must find her to make sure she is happy."

"You love this woman very much."

"I do. Until I know how she is, I can never marry another."

"That is wise. Too many settle for another because it is easy, or they do not wish to wait. Then they are unhappy for the rest of their lives thinking of the one who was not there."

"I'm not sure how wise it is, but it is something I must do. Your husband will be proud of you for fighting off the Arapaho."

"He will be, but he will seek revenge against them. I fear his anger may make him foolish."

"I think you will be able to talk sense into him."

"Perhaps," she said as she smiled.

Stan had been scanning their backtrail as they rode. He thought he saw shadows in the distance, but it was too dark to use the field glasses.

"I think your Arapaho friends are behind us. Do they have rifles?"

"Two have them."

Stan noticed that they were gaining and guessed there was another hour before sunrise, but the predawn would arrive soon. That would give them enough light. But would it be enough light for him to pick out targets? He tried to wish the sun to rise sooner.

"I have four rifles. I can shoot a long way and much faster than they probably can. Mary, I want you to ride ahead. I'll slow down a bit and draw them in closer. I'll stay between you and them. If it looks like they have won, go. The horse you are riding will outrun their horses. You can return to your family with honor."

She looked at him and asked, "You do not fear death?"

"Of course, I fear death. Only a fool does not. But you are needed by your children and husband. You are more valued."

She had no reply. She knew that none was possible because she knew that what he had said was true. She nodded and pressed the buckskin to a faster pace while Stan slowed the red. There were no defensible positions anywhere he could see, so this would be a standing fight.

She kept pulling away until she was a reasonably safe half mile to the west, then slowed to match Stan's pace.

C.J. PETIT

Stan kept an eye on the four approaching Arapaho warriors. Unlike the Cheyenne, he had no intention of allowing any of them to leave alive. If he walked away, none of them would. Taking women from their homes wasn't honorable. They had earned their deaths.

As the predawn arrived, meaning there would be another thirty minutes before dawn, Stan continued his slow pace while he observed the Arapaho. He could pick out the individual warriors now and saw the two that were armed with rifles, but only one had his in his hands. He knew from experience that Indians were very miserly when shooting. Ammunition was worth more than gold, so they would want to get closer than needed to be to make sure their shots counted.

He'd go with the Sharps/Winchester combination, but no Spencer interim shots this time. With only four potential targets, he'd take two shots with the Sharps which may either turn them back or invite them to fire at long range, then he'd be able to hear their shots and figure out which weapons they carried.

The sky continued to get lighter as the gap closed. He noticed that Mary was staying about a half mile ahead, and he thought she was a smart woman. She knew she had more speed and endurance with the buckskin but didn't want to run the risk of running into more Arapaho on the other side. If she saw more, she'd be able to race back to Stan.

But the concern now was for the four followers. They probably knew when they found the abandoned campsite that they were dealing with a white man. Maybe they thought they could knock off two birds with one stone. Maybe they were angry because he had stolen their prize. *Who cares?* They were there, they looked like they wanted a fight, and Stan was going to give them more than they bargained for.

96

FINDING BUCKY

The sun cracked the horizon and Stan stopped. They had been coming from the east, but the sun was rising more to the north, so it wasn't the problem it would have been a couple of months earlier. He stepped down, pulling his Winchester from his scabbard, then pulled the Sharps from the mule. He still had three rounds for the big gun in his right jacket pocket with six percussion caps. He opened his saddlebag and took out ten rounds for the Winchester and put them in his left pocket, then ground hitched the red and began walking toward the oncoming Arapaho.

———

Hiding Deer asked his cousin, White Bull, if his rifle was ready. He said it was, so he told the two bow-armed warriors to spread out to the sides. After White Bull had fired his first shot, they were to shout their war cries and attack. He and White Bull would join them, firing their guns.

———

Stan stood and just let them come. He had both rifles ready. He had laid his slicker on the ground to protect the rifles from the morning dew on the beautiful late spring morning. It was already around fifty degrees, with no wind and not a cloud in sight. It was the kind of morning that makes one happy to be alive, and he hoped it wouldn't be his last.

He was getting impatient with the Arapaho. They were still moving, but slowly. They were about a half mile away, so he reached down and picked up the Sharps. He set the ladder sight for five hundred yards, compensating for the altitude and cooler temperature. At six thousand feet, he basically let them both work against each other, the higher altitude adding range and the denser air reducing it. He'd go with the range on the ladder sight as it was.

97

C.J. PETIT

————

When they had walked their horses within four hundred yards, Hiding Deer whooped once, and the attack was on. The two bow shooters peeled off to the left and right and then straightened out as Hiding Deer pulled his rifle into position as White Bull fired his gun, the large report breaking the silence of the morning and the large discharge of gunsmoke fouling the cloudless sky as the four Arapaho warriors accelerated their horses to attack the white man who challenged them so blatantly.

————

Stan saw the bloom of the rifle and ignored where the shot was going. If it was aimed correctly, there was nothing he could do about it. Just seconds later, the second rifle-armed Indian fired, stunning Stan. It was the lighter crack of a repeater. He shifted his aim away from the first shooter with the big rifle and focused on the one whose rifle was still out of range but posed a bigger threat. He cocked the hammer, blew out his breath, held it and squeezed the Sharps' trigger ever so gently. The big gun slammed back into his shoulder as the massive round left the muzzle and crossed the three hundred and fifty yards towards Hiding Deer.

White Bull was still riding, reloading his rifle and firing, as Stan's bullet creased Hiding Deer's horse's ear before plowing into the left side of the warrior's chest. With a .44 caliber round from the Winchester, it might not have been fatal, but the Sharps' more massive, faster moving projectile took out two ribs then eviscerated his left lung. He dropped his rifle, rolled to his left, fell to the ground and rolled, creating a cloud of dust in the bright morning sunlight.

White Bull was incensed and fired again, opened the breech, then inserted another cartridge before pushing a percussion cap

98

on the gun's nipple, aiming his rifle at Stan and fired hastily, breaking the rule about conserving the precious ammunition. His horse was still running, causing his sight to bounce wildly, but he thought he had the white man, now only two hundred yards away, but when he fired, the shot flew across the ground, finally striking the earth eighty yards behind Stan.

Stan had him already in his sights, took two extra seconds to aim and gently pulled the trigger. The hammer struck home, and the Sharps' second round ripped through the air and struck White Bull almost in the center of his chest, pulverizing bone and soft tissue to an enormous degree, sending White Bull tumbling over his horse's rump.

Stan quickly dropped the Sharps and grabbed the Winchester, as the two bow wielding Arapaho closed to less than a hundred yards still moving quickly. Stan took aim at the one on the left who was marginally closer and fired but missed. He levered in a second round and fired more carefully and struck the Arapaho in the left upper chest, just below the clavicle. He didn't wait to see the whether he was dead, the other warrior was getting much too close.

As he was turning to fire, the last Arapaho warrior let loose with his arrow and was reaching for a second when the first struck Stan in the right thigh. Stan grunted and jerked as his finger snapped back, throwing his shot off wildly. He levered a new shot as the warrior fired another arrow from less than fifty yards. His second missile glanced off the Winchester's stock as Stan had been ready to fire. It rocked the rifle for a second, but Stan waited until he could reestablish control before taking aim and firing his second shot. This one didn't miss and caught the last Arapaho in the neck, spinning him from his horse, and after he hit the dirt, he continued his rolling motion for another fifteen feet before coming to a stop in a cloud of dust.

Stan looked at the arrow sticking out of his leg. This was going to hurt, but better now than later. He grimaced as he yanked the arrow free, then quickly examining the arrowhead for any signs of something on there that wasn't him.

Many Plains Indians had been known to add fecal matter or decayed meat to their arrowheads to ensure death to their enemies even if the initial wound was insufficient to kill. It looked clean, so he tossed it aside. It hadn't penetrated too deeply from the range it was taken, but it had only stopped because the tip of the arrowhead had found the shaft of his femur. That warrior had hit him from seventy yards from the back of a moving horse. It was an incredible shot, or a lucky one, but not for Stan.

He limped to the fallen rifle shooters, having to pass some of the others, wanting to see what his first victim was using, expecting to find a Henry, but instead found a Winchester lying on the dirt. *How did he get one already?* That did not bode well for the army if the Indians had a source for repeaters, especially when the troopers were still using the Sharps carbines or Spencers. He picked up the carbine and levered it until three cartridges had been ejected, but no more. He had started the fight with four rounds.

He then picked up warrior's war tomahawk, slid the war tomahawk into his belt and returned to pick up the other shooter's rifle, not surprised to find was the familiar Sharps carbine, similar to the longer-barreled musket version he had with him. There were just so many of the carbines around after the war, just like the Spencers, especially with cavalry units in the West. He found the warrior who had been using it and picked up his ammunition pouch, and when he looked inside, he found nine more cartridges and a dozen percussion caps. He hung the pouch over his shoulder after picking up his war tomahawk.

FINDING BUCKY

As he was walking toward the third warrior, he heard hooves approaching from the west, and slowly turned knowing what he would see. Mary was almost there as Stan reached the third man and pulled his war tomahawk. He then stepped over and relieved the last fallen warrior of his, then walked over to the mule and slid the new Winchester into its empty scabbard, the Sharps carbine went into the scabbard of one of the geldings, then placed the four war tomahawks in one of the panniers, before sliding the Sharps and his Winchester back in the red mare's scabbards. Stan turned to Mary as she was stepping down.

She led the horse as she walked toward him, holding up the pants with her other hand as she said, "You are wounded."

"Not badly. The arrowhead looked clean. I'll patch it up in a second. Mary, did you want to collect their four horses?"

"I will," she replied.

Stan took the reins of the buckskin as Mary dropped the pants from her legs and let her dress slide down. They were so oversized for her that she just walked out of them.

Stan trail-hitched the buckskin to the second gelding, then rummaged through his saddlebags and took out his sewing kit and a small flask of whiskey.

He took off his gunbelt and unbuckled his belt, lowered his britches and sat down, straightening his damaged leg. He tightened his jaws, poured some whiskey on the wound, feeling the stab of pain when the alcohol came into contact with the wound. He opened the sewing kit and began to close the wound. It wasn't too bad, and had the job done in eight minutes, although the suturing job would probably make an army doctor wince. He poured more whiskey on the newly closed wound and then cleaned it off with some water from his canteen. He stood,

101

pulled up his trousers and buckled his belt, then snugged his gunbelt over his hips and picked up the flask and the sewing kit.

He spotted Mary returning, leading the four horses. She looked tired. In the morning light, Stan could see her more clearly. She was a slim, but handsome woman, and he guessed her age to be around thirty years or so.

"You sewed your wound?" she asked as she approached.

"Yes. It'll be fine. Mary, did you want to go and get your friends? There are only two warriors left to guard them."

"No. They gave themselves to the Arapaho. They are no longer Ute. We must be going."

"Mary, you look tired. Would you like to at least have some jerky?"

"That would be good."

"I'll tie off the horses, so they can be trailed. Are you riding one of their horses or the buckskin?"

"I'll ride one of the Arapaho horses and trail the rest. I'll need to wear your pants again."

"I know. Let me get the jerky and the rope."

Stan grabbed a fistful of jerky and his rope, then handed the jerky to Mary as he began fashioning an extended trail rope for the three saddle-less horses. He ran it around the lead horse's neck and waited while Mary pulled on his trousers.

He stepped up on the red mare and Mary rode to his left as they began the return to her village.

———

FINDING BUCKY

In Denver, Ellie had come up with a plan of sorts. At least she'd be able to find out what happened to Stan and chastised herself for not thinking of this before. She left the house at nine o'clock and walked into the center of Denver.

Across the street from her husband's bank were the offices of the Pinkerton Detective Agency. She went inside and approached the man at the desk.

"May I help you, ma'am?" he asked.

"Yes, I'd like to engage your agency to find the whereabouts of an old friend."

"Have a seat, ma'am, and I'll see what we can do for you."

Ellie sat in the chair next to the desk.

"I'm Agent John Bickerstaff. Now, when was the last time you heard from your friend?"

"When my family left Michigan in 1857."

Agent Bickerstaff wanted to say that he was from Michigan, but that would be unprofessional, and an inappropriate thing to say to a woman. He would have mentioned it to a man, though.

"This might be difficult. What can you tell me about him or her?"

"His name is Stanley Murray. We lived near the town of Southfield, near Detroit. He was a year older than I am, but after that I have idea."

The detective's eyebrows arched before he put down his pencil after writing the information down.

He looked at Ellie and said, "I recall a Captain Stan Murray in the Michigan Brigade. I was with the 5th Michigan Cavalry, but I only met him once or twice."

Ellie felt her heart skip a beat and asked, "Can you describe him? He would be fairly tall but was he tending to fat?"

"Tall, yes, but not fat at all. In fact, if I were to pick out an image of the ideal cavalryman, it would have been Captain Murray. From what I heard, he was very highly respected among the troops and his superiors, but I don't know what happened to him after our units were separated."

"He's probably not the same man. Stan tended to fat and was the son of a mill worker."

"You're probably right, although he probably did go into the army during the war. We'll just ask the army what his last status was, and we'll get a reply quickly. They're usually very good at responding to our requests. If he hadn't been in the army, they'll let us know and we'll start over."

"How soon do you think you'll find out?"

"I'll get this out on the wire today and I should have the results by tomorrow at noon. It's just a simple records check."

"Could I stop by around two o'clock tomorrow?"

"That would be fine. And your name?"

"Mrs. Ellie Rafferty."

Agent Bickerstaff wrote down the information and Ellie left the office.

———

FINDING BUCKY

Mary and Stan came in sight of the Ute village just after one o'clock. The perimeter guards had alerted the village of her approach with a white man, and the whole village turned out to watch them ride in.

Her husband, Red Hawk, trotted to meet her, followed by their three children. When she saw him, she smiled and waved. He broke into a grin and ran up to the horse just as she dropped down and fell into his waiting arms. Stan watched with a smile as his britches dropped to the ground and Mary's feet automatically kicked them away.

There was a lot of chatter that Stan couldn't understand as he sat on the red gelding. Mary was talking at a furious rate, periodically pointing at Stan as Stan just watched. From a woman who appeared near dead just a few hours ago, she seemed energized, probably by the return to her village and her family. At last, she finished her diatribe, then turned and walked close to Stan.

She looked up and said, "My husband wishes to thank you for rescuing me and killing those who offended me. He is proud of me for fighting for my honor. Will you stay with us for a few days?"

"I'd like to do that, Mary, but I need to get to Cheyenne City."

She turned to her husband and began rapidly speaking again. The village elders had been listening to the conversation and one of them interrupted her with a comment.

Mary turned back to Stan and asked, "When did you say your woman came from the east?"

"That would be 1857, ten years ago."

She began talking to the elder who had interrupted her. He shook his head and pointed to the south. She asked him some questions and he shook his head and pointed again. Then he spoke for almost two minutes. Mary listened intently, asking one question at the end.

He replied to her query, and she nodded, then turned to Stan and said, "He tells me that no wagon train made it successfully to Wyoming that year. The only one that tried had many problems with the snow, and turned south, but the survivors were killed by the Sioux when they tried to build homes in their land. There were two others that did reach our southern areas, but he's not sure where they went or if they continued on."

Stan felt his stomach contract into a twisted knot. *Had Ellie been massacred by the Indians? Was this whole journey useless?* He had known going in that she might be married, but he hadn't given any thought that she might be dead. There may not be any point in going to Cheyenne after all.

"He's sure that no wagon trains made it into Wyoming that year?"

"All of the elders confirm what he said."

"I guess there's no point in going to Cheyenne now," he said quietly.

"Maybe your woman traveled the southern route."

"Maybe. Maybe this was all a futile gesture."

"Stay with us and meet my children."

Stan smiled, dismounted and picked up his discarded britches, then was greeted by Red Hawk with a strong handshake and a left hand gripping his shoulder.

Mary then led her three children out of the crowd and told them that this was the man that saved her from the hated Arapaho and had killed four of them.

Stan smiled at them, then turned to the mule and opened the weapons pannier. He pulled out the two of the war tomahawks and handed them to Red Hawk and gestured toward his boys. Red Hawk grinned and summoned his two sons. He handed each one a war tomahawk and said something to them. They both smiled young boy smiles and took the weapons. Then Stan went back to the second gelding and pulled out the Sharps carbine. He grabbed the ammunition pouch that he had hung over the horse's saddle horn and walked back to Red Hawk.

He handed the carbine to Red Hawk along with the ammunition pouch.

"Mary, tell your husband that he will be able to feed his family better and protect you and your children with the gun."

Mary smiled at Stan and repeated his words to her husband, who had already understood most of what Stan had said.

He looked at Stan, nodded, then said, "Come," and walked toward the center of the village.

Stan led his horses and mule, following Red Hawk into the village and was impressed with its size and organization. It reminded him of an army camp, with everything in its place and similar operations placed closely together.

Stan was led to what he assumed was the family tipi. It was large and well made. One of Mary's sons, who looked around nine, took the red's reins and smiled at him. Stan relinquished his horses and followed Mary and Red Hawk inside. He was taller than any of the Utes he had seen and had to bend over to go into the dwelling.

Mary bade him to sit, so he did and then Red Hawk noticed his leg wound.

"You are wounded?" he asked.

"Arrow. Not bad. I fixed it."

"Good. Better soon. Not good to wait."

Mary sat and said, "I've told Red Hawk about your shooting of the Arapaho and he is very pleased that you avenged the wrong they committed. He asked about the Cheyenne bow and I told him you had killed eight Cheyenne who attacked you. He asked why you did not kill the last one."

"I could have, but I was struck by his bravery. His fellow warriors were all dead, and I had a rifle. I could have killed him easily, but he stood there looking at me. How could I kill a man with such courage?"

Red Hawk nodded. He could understand English much better than he could speak it.

Mary said, "Stan, I think when you leave, it would be wiser to follow through Ute lands into Colorado. I will give you a sign to wear that will mark you as a great friend to the Utes. It will ensure your safety and provide you with aid if you need it. But it also means something else."

Stan wanted to ask what other meaning it had, but she rose and walked to the other side of the tipi.

Despite her weariness, Mary prepared food for Stan and her family. She said that there would be a feast in his honor in the evening.

FINDING BUCKY

"Would you like me to get some fresh meat while I am here? I can hunt buffalo and antelope from a long distance."

Red Hawk smiled and nodded, saying "I would like to see you shoot."

They finished lunch and a smiling Mary watched as her husband and new friend left the tipi and walked outside. Stan found the red already unsaddled so he stepped up on the buckskin and moved his Winchester and Sharps to the horse. He walked to the mule and took out eight more cartridges for the Sharps along with another dozen percussion caps. He sometimes fumbled the small things and had a hard time finding them if they reached the ground.

They mounted their horses and Red Hawk led the way. They rode silently for over two miles and then Red Hawk slowed as they came to a small hill. He stepped down and Stan did the same, taking the Sharps with him. Red Hawk crouched down and climbed the hill with Stan trailing. When he neared the crest, he stopped and waited for Stan to catch up.

He turned to Stan and said, "Buffalo."

Stan nodded and replied, "Your gun and this one load the same."

Red Hawk nodded, and watched as Stan opened the breech, slid a round into the Sharps, and closed it again. After putting a percussion cap carefully onto the nipple so Red Hawk could see it, he snuck up to the top of the hill and looked beyond. It was a good-sized herd, probably around five thousand animals and all of them were just standing or on their haunches about three hundred yards out.

Stan lay prone on the hilltop, set his ladder sight, cocked the hammer, and took aim at a cow at the edge and fired. He quickly reloaded and fired again, and soon had fired all eight cartridges. The other buffalo hadn't moved.

Red Hawk had watched as the six large cows and two bulls had fallen, then they both stood, and he slapped Stan on the back with a grin on his face.

"We will send men," he said as they turned to go down the hill.

They returned to the village and Red Hawk told the chief that there were eight buffalo down and they needed to send some men and litters to retrieve the animals. The chief looked at Red Hawk incredulously. He and the white man had been gone less than an hour and there were eight buffalo down?

Red Hawk grinned and said something as he pointed at Stan.

He called Stan over and said, "Chief Walking Eagle wants to know if anyone can shoot like that."

"Some, but not all."

Stan's horses and mule were unloaded for him, fed and watered as he and Mary spoke to the tribal leaders who wanted to know all he had discovered about the Cheyenne. When they found out he had been serving at Fort Union just two weeks earlier, they asked more questions.

They also told him of the massing of Sioux, Cheyenne, Crow and Arapaho against the bluecoats. He told them that the army had been aware of the call to arms, but the tribal leaders assured him that this was far larger than the army probably expected. Stan didn't doubt it. The army's intelligence on the warring tribes was usually inadequate. He told the leaders that and they all nodded.

The feast was held six hours later. It was a lot of food and Mary introduced Stan to her younger sister, who was soon to wed. She was such a tiny maiden who couldn't have been over four feet and eight inches. He'd seen taller women when they were ten. He smiled at her and wished her every happiness.

They finally adjourned to the family tipi and Stan talked with Mary and Red Hawk for two more hours before turning in.

CHAPTER 4

Stan woke when Mary's young daughter tickled his nose. His eyes popped open and he immediately smiled at the cute, curious face just inches from his.

"Good morning," he said to her.

She grinned and just danced away.

Stan sat up and pulled on his boots, then went outside and was wondering where he should relieve himself when Red Hawk appeared from the tipi, smiled at him and pointed to some trees. Stan waved, then trotted over and barely made it.

When he returned, he found his horses all saddled, and the mule packed. All his weapons were in their proper locations.

He entered the tipi, Mary smiled at him, then said, "After breakfast, I will give you your sign of passage."

"Thank you, Mary."

"Red Hawk wonders why you have two guns that are the same."

"I was going to buy one and found that the oldest gun the storekeeper had was the same gun that was issued to me when I first went to war. I used it for over a year and was issued a new one. I don't know how it made it all the way out here. It shouldn't be used anymore. It's too old and worn out."

"Maybe it is the gods telling you that you should come here."

FINDING BUCKY

"Or an army ordnance department trying to squeeze every last penny out of an old gun."

She laughed and said, "What you said is probably the right one."

After breakfast, Mary presented Stan with an elaborate shawl, and told him that he just needed to show the shawl to any member of the Utes, or its associated tribes and he would be welcomed as a friend.

Then she looked into his eyes and said softly, "But it also is a sign of perfect love. Give this to the woman you will love to give her safe passage to your heart."

He thanked Mary and Red Hawk for their hospitality and stepped up on the buckskin. He rode out of the village to waves and smiles and hoped that the army never had to turn its anger on the Utes.

He was heading due southwest toward Boulder, Colorado when he left the village and estimated it was a hundred miles or so away and found it ironic that he'd soon be where he had decided to settle, but without finding Ellie.

He felt somewhat empty with the knowledge that his Ellie may no longer be alive. Then he realized that when he thought of her, he always used the possessive, and realized that she was no longer his Ellie or his Bucky. If she was alive, she probably belonged to another, and the idea saddened him.

He made good time in the balmy weather, and by noon, he was entering Colorado, not that Stan knew it precisely. He knew he was either in extreme southern Wyoming or northern Colorado, but his exact location didn't matter as he pulled aside for lunch and a rest for the animals around one o'clock.

———

An hour later, Ellie was sitting next to Agent Bickerstaff's desk. He had pulled out the telegram he had received from the War Department.

"Mrs. Rafferty, I have to admit that I'm as surprised as you are. The Stan Murray you asked about was the same Captain Murray that I told you about. He mustered out at Fort Union in Montana Territory a couple of weeks ago. If you had asked before then, we could have sent him a telegram. But he left the area and his whereabouts are unknown. It would cost you a lot of money to try and find him now, and it is unlikely that we could. The area is very extensive and added to that are the growing hostility of the Plains Indians. If he crossed into Montana, he'd more than likely run into trouble. If he went east across the Dakota Territory, he'd run into the Sioux. Either way, trying to find a single man in that much territory occupied by hostiles would be remote at best. Impossible is a better probability."

Ellie was stunned by the news, but nodded and replied, "No. I understand. This information is quite enough. Thank you. What is your fee?"

"Ten dollars. All we did is send a telegram."

Ellie paid the fee and took the telegram with her. *Stan did not only survive the war but had left the army in Montana!* She hadn't a doubt that her not-so-piggy Piggy was coming to find her. She was ecstatic, but the fact that Stan expected her to be in Wyoming and not Colorado dampened her joy, and the detective's comments about his difficulties in crossing the territory tempered it even more, but she would continue to hope. It was all she had.

FINDING BUCKY

As she reached the house, she was smiling about the detective's comment yesterday when he had said that Stan had become the very picture of what a cavalryman should look like. She tried to imagine a tall, svelte, and handsome Stan Murray and found it difficult. She laughed at the thought of the overweight, shy boy she knew and loved becoming a fearsome and respected leader of men, a man they all admired, and an unmarried man at that. She prayed that he would return safely to her. What she would do if he did find her was the new question. *Or was it a question at all?*

She no longer cared about the consequences. If he still loved her, she'd leave with him. *Repercussions be damned!* She entered the house and found Maria Elena waiting for her.

"Maria, what do you need?"

"Mrs. Rafferty, Mister Rafferty said to tell you that you both are going in Mister Johnson's surrey tonight."

"I understand. I'll be upstairs getting my clothes selected."

"Clothes?"

"Yes. He meant Mister Johnson's soiree. It's like a party."

"Oh. I make a mistake," she said as smiled, then returned to her duties.

Marie Elena Menendez had worked for the Rafferty family for twenty years, and George's father had sent her along with the house when they had married. She was a friendly and competent housekeeper, but still had issues with some English words and phrases, especially the odd ones like soiree, which wasn't even English. She still lived at the older Rafferty's house two houses down the street. George's father had never questioned why he didn't have her living with him, but assumed it was because he wanted some private time with his gorgeous young wife, and he didn't blame him.

Ellie walked upstairs to her room and selected an appropriate gown and the petticoats and corset to go with them. She set them down on her bed, then sat down and reread the telegram. She yearned for the simple days, when she could dress in a minute or two. She hated wearing all the lace and that damned strangling corset! She wanted to feel a horse beneath her legs as it raced across a field, the wind blowing her hair back and the sun on her face. Now, she was expected to be pale, the whiter the better. She was expected to carry a parasol to keep the sun off her skin, too. It hadn't sunk that low yet, but knew it was just a matter of time before they insisted that she did.

She absent-mindedly ran her fingers over the satin cloth wishing it were rough homespun, or at least a comfortable cotton. She sighed, folded the telegram and slid it into the drawer on her nightstand. She knew one thing without a shred of doubt in her mind; she would wait. She didn't care how long it took; she would wait for her Piggy. She would go along with her situation as long as necessary. If he had died in his last journey to find her, she'd know. She'd know because he wouldn't come to her.

———

Stan had resumed his ride at one-thirty and continued to make good time. While he had stopped for the noon break, he'd consulted his map, and needed to change to a south-southwest heading. He had discovered that he was in Colorado while he ate, too, so tomorrow he should be able to reach Boulder. *Then what?*

He still had all his money and needed to get into a bank as soon as he arrived. One doesn't walk around with over four

FINDING BUCKY

thousand dollars in cash. He also figured he'd stay in Boulder for a few days and come up with some semblance of a plan.

He finally pulled over to camp for the night at just after sunset. There was still light in the sky, but he found such a nice spot and the animals must be tired. An hour later he was well situated, and the animals were all happily munching grass. He prepared and ate his dinner and when he was finished, he examined the shawl that Mary had given to him. It was quite intricate, and he thought that the shade of blue they used in some of the designs was the same color as Ellie's eyes. He found himself thinking more of Ellie now that he was nearing the end of his journey. *If she had died, how would he know?*

He'd search for McCormicks in every town and village he'd go to. Here in Colorado there were many more than in the territories up north. He just couldn't give up. He needed to find his Bucky.

―――――

He reached Boulder the next morning just before noon and was exhausted. He needed a bath and a lot of other things, but first, he needed a real lunch. He rode the red to the first diner he spotted, stepped down and after tying off his string of animals, walked inside and found a table. The waitress stepped over quickly and took his order, leaving a pot of coffee and a cup on the table before she left.

As he sat drinking his coffee, he scanned the tables and watched as the diners ate their food. He contrasted the view with what he had seen on the long journey, and even the five years he had spent in the army. Everything seemed so clean and quiet in comparison.

She brought him his steak and potato lunch a few minutes later, and he ate every morsel, even the fat on the edge of the steak, then paid for his meal before returning to his horse. He stepped up and rode down the street looking for the biggest building, which was invariably a bank. He spotted it three blocks down the main street, stepped down in front of the impressive brick building and tied off his horse. He walked inside the bank and crossed the large lobby to the desk of a clerk.

"Could I help you, sir?" he asked.

"Yes, I'd like to open an account."

"Very well. Let me get the paperwork started."

While the clerk started writing, Stan opened his shirt and removed his money belt, glad to get rid of it. His stomach had already begun to turn red from the leather, and he wondered if it would wash off. The clerk looked at the bulging money belt and was debating how to ask the man how he had come into such a large amount of currency, wondering if it was stolen.

Stan saw his difficulty and said, "I spent five years in the army, most of it as an officer. I never spent any money, so I just accumulated it."

"Ah. Thank you, sir. It's just that we don't see that much cash these days."

"I understand. It was a worrisome trip from Fort Union in Montana carrying that amount of currency."

"*You rode all the way from there?*" he asked in astonishment.

"Yup. Over six hundred miles."

"Meet any Indians?"

"A few Cheyenne and Arapaho that didn't seem to like me and some Utes that did."

"Have to shoot any?"

"Eight Cheyenne and four Arapaho."

"Sounds like you had your hands full. Get hit?"

"I took an arrow in the thigh, but it wasn't too bad."

"Sounds like it would make an interesting story."

"It sure was exciting at the time, but it sounds kind of boring now."

"Maybe to you. I'll just need you to sign here and here," he indicated as he handed Stan the pen.

Stan signed the paper and the clerk began counting the money. He wrote some numbers down and handed a receipt to Stan. He gave him a bank book and five drafts. Stan's balance was $4274, and he still had over $300 in various locations on him as well.

"So, you're staying in Boulder, then?" the clerk asked.

"Looks like it. I've got to find a place to hang my hat, though."

"Would you like to see Mister Harkins? He handles real estate, and there are a lot of properties available right now because of the war. Some have been on the market for over two years."

"Sure. Let's go see him."

Stan stood and followed the clerk to Mister Harkins office. Mister Thaddeus Harkins was thrilled at having a potential buyer enter his office, and the clerk left Stan in his care.

"So, Mister Murray, what are you looking for?"

"I'm not sure. I'd like some property and might get into ranching."

"We have several properties available. We have four ranches already established but without any cattle, I'm afraid. They all sold off their herds to pay off debts."

"How large are they?"

"The largest is eight sections. It might be too large for what you need. We have a nice four section ranch that might be exactly what you'd like. It has a healthy spring, two wells and a creek. It has a nice ranch house, barn and corral. Its only flaw is that the northeast section is almost half into the foothills of the Rockies."

"How much is the asking price?"

"Well, I'll be honest with you, Mister Murray. It's been on the market for over a year now. The price we're asking is twenty-six hundred dollars."

"That does seem a bit steep for only four sections, or, three and a half, really," Stan said without any idea of what he was talking about.

How much did a section of land cost these days? He knew how much a section of Michigan farmland cost before the war and it was a lot more than what they were asking for a whole ranch.

"We might go lower if it's a cash sale, Mister Murray. Or would you be needing a mortgage?"

"No, I'd deal in cash. I'd like to examine the property, if I could."

Mister Hawkins' smile broadened as he replied, "Absolutely. Let me get the keys."

He opened his file cabinet, took out a folder and slid a key ring with two keys onto his desk, then turned back to Stan and handed him the keys.

"Now, the land is all fenced except for the section that's in the foothills. The furniture is all there as well. It may be quite dusty, though."

"I'll go and take a look. How far out is it?"

"It's not too far. Just head west out of town and you'll find a wagon trail heading southwest after about two miles. The ranch is located three miles down the road. It has a sign over the access road. It used to be the Bar M, although that brand has since been lost to another ranch."

"I understand. Would it be alright if I left my spare horses and mule there? I'll probably be back tomorrow."

"Not a problem at all. Take as long as you need."

Stan took the keys and shook his hand, then left the bank feeling relieved and excited. He had thought a ranch with buildings would be much more, but by the sound of it, the ranch was still overpriced. He wondered how much less he would be able to drive the price down.

He stepped outside and onto the buckskin, turned him west and left Boulder a few minutes later. It wasn't difficult finding the turnoff and as he rode, he was impressed with the beauty of the landscape. The rolling hills and the mountains appealed to him, and if the banker was right and it had two wells, a creek and a spring, it would be hard to say no.

He found the access road to the ranch thirty minutes later. The sign was in bad shape, but it didn't matter as it was wrong now anyway. He turned his animals down the access road and saw the ranch house and barn in the distance. They needed paint but seemed all right.

He reached the house and stepped down, tied off the buckskin and walked up the steps to the porch, bouncing as he did to test the board strength and found them to be sound. Then he took a minute to walk around the porch. The boards all seemed solid, so he returned to the front door, opened the screen door with a squeal and put the key in the lock. He opened the inner door without a squeal and half expected to find the property vandalized after two years without habitation, but when he entered the main room, he was pleasantly surprised.

There was a large fireplace with a mantle, and even the fireplace tools were still sitting on the hearth. The furniture, as expected, was dusty, but not damaged in any way. So far, so good. He checked the bedrooms and found them in similar condition. If it had been on the market for that long, then it hadn't had time to deteriorate too much in the dry air. He found the bathroom with a large clawed tub and sink. Then he walked into the all-important kitchen. Again, he was pleased to find all the cookware still present along with very dusty dishes and glassware. The cook stove was in excellent condition with a minimum of rust. Everything looked well organized and his decision was already made when he found the empty cold room. It was fairly large, and he was already smiling before he walked outside. The privy was sixty feet from the back door, but he'd check it later, maybe after he bought the place. He could always dig a new one.

He walked across to the barn and pulled one of the large doors open. It moved smoothly, which did surprise him until he looked at the hinges and found that they still had some grease on them. He went inside, and the first thing he noticed was a wagon. It looked in remarkably good condition, which was another surprise. He rolled it forward and it moved easily. Amazing. Then he looked at the rest of the barn.

There were six stalls with wooden flooring. That was a big plus. There were even six pegs with rows of horseshoes. *Why so many?* There was even a small smithy, so he could work iron here. He climbed up into the loft and found some bundles of hay still there. He pulled one out and dropped it onto the floor of the barn, climbed back down, pulled his knife and cut the steel wire, letting it split open, then spread it over the floor and into the stalls. Each stall had a feed bin and a small trough for the horses. There were lots of tools in the smithy area as well, and four large buckets. It was a well-equipped barn, and he knew he had finally found his home, but he wanted to see the land.

He walked back to the front of the house and untied the buckskin. He led all three animals into the barn and stripped down the mule and three horses, leaving the buckskin saddled. He led them to their stalls and made sure there was enough hay for them to eat, grabbed two buckets and went outside. He had to prime the outside pump but soon had the trough full, then filled the two buckets and brought them inside. It took two more trips to fill each small trough, but the horses and mule seemed to appreciate it.

He led the buckskin outside and let him drink from the big trough, then he mounted and began his check of the property. The pastures were undulating hills, and if he wanted to raise anything, he'd raise horses. He knew how to ride and care for them, but he knew he'd have to learn a lot more to be able to raise them.

As he rode, he found the ride very pleasant. There was plenty of grass and he ran across a flock of turkeys while he was riding. Then he turned toward the northeast corner, found the creek and followed it to the spring. It took almost three minutes of riding to get there, as the ranch was two miles by two miles, which Stan thought was a nice, manageable size. The spring was a sight to behold. It was an oval shape, with the spring itself at the western edge. The water flowed out of the southern tip into the creek. The water was clear and inviting, so he stepped down and stuck his hand in the water. It was frigid, but it was getting warmer outside now, so he hitched the buckskin to what looked like a blueberry bush, looked around and stripped off his Stetson, gunbelt, and continued to disrobe. Soon, he was stark naked and leapt into the pool. It shocked his body when he hit the icy water, but his system adjusted, and he reveled in the release of the built-up tension. He had to have this place. After six hundred miles of stress and worry, he had found his home.

He exited the pool and quickly dressed, stepped back on the buckskin and returned to the barn. He stripped the buckskin and began hauling the panniers into the house. It took a while to bring them all inside with the rifles, but he finally closed the door and began to clean enough so he could stay the night. The blankets and quilts weren't bad at all. He guessed it was because of the dry climate. He simply took the quilts from each of the three bedrooms and shook them out on the front porch.

He hung them over the rails to air out for a while then returned to the house and pulled the blankets off next. He buried his face in one and found no bad odors. In fact, it had almost a pleasant, airy scent. There were even sheets on the beds. He took the blankets and added them to the porch railing, and soon the house was blanketed in bedding.

He checked the two heat stoves, found them both in operational condition, but he would need to chop some more wood. There was a large stand of pines on the western edge of the property that he could use for firewood but he'd clear it of the dry deadwood first. He found a broom in the pantry and began sweeping the dust from the furniture and then the floor. It took over an hour to get it mostly clear of thick dust, but he'd still have to invest a lot of time to finish the job. His army training when he was a private gave him those skills.

He began putting away his food into the pantry and cold room. He'd need to get a pair of draft horses for the wagon, so he'd be able to get large supply orders. He'd be able to have milk and butter, too. He felt like he was gaining paradise, a paradise he wanted badly to share with Ellie.

After the food was put away, he made the third bedroom his weapons room and put all the guns and ammunition inside. Finally, he decided to cook himself a real dinner in his new home. He fired up the cook stove and listened to it crack and pop as the iron felt the flames for the first time in a while. But after it settled down, he was able to prepare his supper. He'd get fresh meat at the butcher, too. The town was only an hour's ride with the wagon, but much less with just a horse, even if he led a pack horse.

After he had eaten, and washed his dishes and pans, a contented Stan Murray sat at the kitchen table drinking a cup of coffee. He had found his home, and now, he needed to find his Ellie.

He brought all the bedding back into the house and made the beds, then checked the lamps and found them all dry, so he'd need to pick up some kerosene when he made his next trip into town.

He crawled into his bed early, just because it was his bed, well almost, he still had to buy the place.

The next morning, he made it official, and was able to get the property for $2140. Mister Harkins had a painful expression as the price kept getting lower, but when they reached an agreement and Stan handed him the bank draught, he was all smiles, and so was Stan.

He stopped at the butcher's shop and Brewster's General Store for some kerosene on his way back. He had also bought some lye soap for cleaning and some white soap for himself. He stopped at the livery and asked about draft horses and the liveryman told him he could get two for him in two days. The pair cost him eighty dollars, down from the original asking price of a hundred. When Stan had registered the new ranch with the land office, he applied for a new brand, the B-P connected, which would only mean something to him and one other person, whose whereabouts were unknown.

He returned home and filled each of the lamps while there was still light, then began to seriously clean his house. He had thought of painting the house and barn himself but decided against it. He was never a fan of painting.

He picked up the draft horses two days later, and while he was there, he mentioned that he might like to have a few horses of his own and inquired about a stallion and six mares. The liveryman said he'd check.

He made a large supply run and contracted for the painting. It was only ninety dollars, including the paint. He ignored the traditional colors and went with a medium gray paint and white trim. Even the painters admitted it looked much better than a white house and red barn.

While Stan was getting settled thirty miles northwest, Ellie was getting more unsettled in Denver. With the warmer weather, it was cotillion and party season among the social elite and climbers. It seemed like it was one right after another. Each involved her smiling and pretending to be the adoring wife of a handsome banker. She literally couldn't eat at any of the affairs over concerns that she would vomit all over the pretentious crowd.

They'd return in the carriage to the house and George would let her off to enter the dark residence before driving off.

She'd walk into the house, close and lock the door behind her and not bother lighting lamps until she reached her bedroom, then go up to her room and close the door behind her. There was no reason for her to close the door, really. The house was always empty, just as her life was, she admitted.

She'd take off the beautiful gown and toss her hated petticoats and corset into a pile, then don a shirt and a pair of pants that she had bought right after she had been married. She'd take a book and curl up on her bed and read, letting her imagination take her away from this vapid life she lived.

Tonight, though, after reading a few pages, she set the book down and stared at the far wall. It had been almost a month since the detective had told her that Stan had left the army and had set off across the wild Plains. *How long would it take to ride six hundred miles? Three weeks?* Then he'd have to find her, but her name wasn't McCormick any longer, so he knew that it would be difficult. But her parents were still here, so maybe that would help Stan find her. She sighed and returned to her book.

———

Stan was getting well known in the Boulder community over the next few weeks. He had bought a fine stallion and six handsome mares for a very steep $345, then had let them roam the property, which seemed to suit their needs, or at least those of the stallion. There was no reason for them to leave. He also let the red and buckskin mare join the harem, while he would ride the two geldings.

It was on his way to the feed and grain store just before noon on a Thursday to buy some more oats that his life took a drastic change.

Sheriff Harry Hastings was on his morning rounds as three men walked their horses into town. They came from the east, and the sheriff didn't like the looks of them, so he kept an eye on them as two of them stepped down and entered the bank. They may as well have worn signs that said BANK ROBBERS when they rode into town. Harry turned and ran to his office to get his Winchester.

Stan was less than a mile out of town when the sheriff returned to the street with his Winchester cocked.

The lookout, a nasty piece of work named Horace Belknap, saw the sheriff as he ran back to his office and pulled his Henry out of its scabbard when he did. He cocked the hammer and watched for the sheriff to come back into the street.

Inside the bank, Whitey Spradlin and Charlie Roberts had their pistols drawn and were demanding cash from the cashier, and just as the cashier was preparing to comply, Horace saw the sheriff come back out with his Winchester and didn't wait for the sheriff to draw a bead on him but fired as soon as he exited the jail.

FINDING BUCKY

From fifty feet, the .44 caliber round smashed into the sheriff's chest, dead center, knocking him stumbling backward against his office wall, then he fell forward face first into the boardwalk, leaving a surprisingly small patch of blood on the wood as his heart had ceased pumping blood when the bullet passed through the right atrium.

Whitey and Charlie heard the gunfire outside and accelerated their actions, not knowing who had been shot or how many lawmen would be involved.

Charlie ran to the window and grabbed the money that the cashier had been putting on the counter, then fired his pistol point blank at the cashier for no apparent reason other than his proximity.

Whitey figured it was a free-for-all now and began firing his revolver at other bank employees, as they both backed out of the bank, Charlie taking one more shot at a customer who was already on his knees praying. *Damned Bible-thumper!* Charlie hated all those religious types.

Horace had their horses waiting and White jumped on board his horse without even touching the stirrups, while Charlie took a second to take his handful of bills, ram them into his saddlebag, then quickly mounted using his stirrup. Once he was in the saddle, the three thieves and killers kicked their horses into a full gallop and raced out of town heading west leaving a huge cloud of dust.

Deputy Sheriff Gus Jorgenson, who was in the diner having his lunch, had run out of the eatery when he heard gunfire, pulled his Colt as he saw them racing his way, and as they thundered past, took three hasty pistol shots at them as they left the town without hitting any of them.

Stan heard the erratic fire and knew it wasn't anyone practicing. He was on the road into Boulder and was still a mile out when he saw the clouds of dust being churned up by three men racing in his direction. They were all facing backwards, firing at someone.

Stan trotted the gelding to the right, off the road. He lost the men for a while, which also meant that they couldn't see him. He stepped the gelding into the trees and turned him around to face the road, then cocked the hammer of the ever-loaded Sharps. He'd take one shot and then chase after them with the Winchester. He was only twenty yards off the road, so the Sharps might be overkill, but he might be able to get two with one shot if they were overlapped, but that was a remote possibility. He brought the Sharps level and waited.

A minute and a half later he heard the pounding hooves approaching rapidly from his left. They'd ridden more than a mile at full gallop, and their horses were already winded and slowing down.

Stan spotted them through the trees, they were riding abreast, and they had already put away their weapons.

Stan followed them with his sights, leading them as they continued their gallop. When they were almost in line with him, he fired and quickly rammed the Sharps into its scabbard and grabbed the Winchester.

At twenty yards, the large chunk of lead reached his target in the blink of an eye at the same time as the thunderous report. The round shot hit Charlie in the right side of his chest and exited the left, leaving nothing but mangled body tissue behind before it struck Whitey in the right side of his gut. Charlie was knocked to the left and as he died, dropped from his horse, then crumpled to the dirt landing awkwardly. Whitey felt the thump of the bullet as it lost its energy and buried itself into his liver. He automatically clutched at the wound as blood poured from the hole and the ruptured hepatic artery. He continued to ride beside Horace for another ten seconds as the blood flowed down his right side and then down his leg. He finally blacked out and dropped to his horse's neck as his blood pressure kept falling.

Horace was stunned by the unexpected shot and the loss of Charlie but thought that Whitey was just hunkering down over his horse. He turned to see what had happened when Stan came charging out of the trees, the gelding looking like a demon. Horace reacted the only way he could when he spurred his already exhausted horse forward and began groping for his Colt. He had just pulled the pistol from his holster when he was distracted as Whitey fell from his horse's neck, bounced when he hit the dirt and then rolled twice and stopped.

He then fired once at the chasing rider, but when he pulled the trigger the second time, the hammer fell on empty brass. He rammed the Colt back in his holster and laid low across his horse's sweaty neck and could hear the tortured breathing of his animal. He knew he had to make a stand soon.

Stan began gaining on him as his fresh gelding reached his stride. Horace was only a hundred yards ahead when Stan had reached the road and had cut the gap down to sixty yards already.

Horace turned again and watched as the shooter gained on him. He pulled his pistol again, and began to reload, stopping after only four cartridges before he cocked the hammer, sat up and began throwing fast shots back at him. One was so wild, it struck Stan's gelding's left front hoof. The large caliber round was centered so accurately that it didn't deflect to either side but penetrated the hoof. The gelding, more from shock than injury, lost its balance, stumbled, then fell, tossing Stan fifteen feet into the air.

131

Stan was airborne and braced for a hard landing, but when he hit, he was lucky and landed on the outside of the berm on side of the road, crashed into angled dirt, lessening the impact, before rolling into the level ground off the road. The landing and sliding created another big dust cloud to add to his horse's enormous cloud from his fall.

Horace couldn't believe his luck. He laughed and continued down the road at a reduced speed to save the horse, believing he had hit the man, probably killing him.

Stan was stunned by the sudden reversal. He was almost there, and suddenly he found himself flying through the air. He had been lucky to land on the soft sand of the berm, though. He'd be black and blue later, but right now, he was just mad. He stood and clambered back onto the roadway and quickly checked his horse. He'd be all right, but he thought he couldn't be ridden with that bullet in his hoof.

He spotted his Winchester on the road, trotted over, snatched it from the ground and inspected it for dirt, but didn't see anything that might cause it to explode in his hands, walked over to the still shaken gelding, and slipped it back into the empty scabbard. He pulled the Sharps out of its scabbard and pulled a cartridge out of his pocket, opened the breech, pulled and tossed the expended brass, inserted the new cartridge, closed the breech and popped on a percussion cap. He pulled the hammer and walked to the center of the road. The last outlaw was already three hundred yards away, so Stan set the ladder for four hundred yards. He'd fire when the man reached that distance at the time the bullet arrived. He'd be a little further to make up for the altitude difference.

He knelt and angled the rifle and the sights. He let the rider get out four hundred yards and squeezed the trigger. The heavy slug blasted out of the muzzle and began its long arc toward the last outlaw.

FINDING BUCKY

Horace thought he was at least out of a terrible situation when the large slug hit his horse in the right hind quarter. The horse screamed and they both went into the dirt.

Horace executed a flying maneuver very close to what Stan had done, but landed in the roadway itself, which was much harder than Stan's berm, smashing into the ground on his right hip. It was a jarring landing, but the hip didn't break. He rolled several times and then came to a confused and painful stop.

Stan slid the Sharps back into the scabbard, grabbed the Winchester, and began to run toward the last bank robber.

Horace finally looked back down the road in a daze and saw the man running toward him. He looked around for his Henry and finally found it lying on the road. He quickly checked the barrel, and more importantly on the Henry, the open-slotted magazine tube under the barrel. It was clean enough for Horace, and he was already in the prone shooting position, so he levered in a new round, took aim and fired.

Stan saw the smoke bloom, but was two hundred yards away, so he kept running but began an erratic zigzag to make himself a harder target.

Horace fired a second shot, but Stan continued to get closer and Horace was getting frustrated. He began rapid firing his rifle, trying to get a bead on the closing shooter.

Stan felt one shot burn the side of his boot, increasing his anger and his need to put an end to this nonsense. He suddenly halted, aimed at the base of the smoke and began his return fire. He kept cycling rounds and firing, peppering the area at the base of the smoke with .44 caliber bullets. After seven shots, he stopped. His barrel was getting hot and he knew it would affect accuracy. Besides, there was so much smoke in the area now that he could barely see the injured horse.

He began walking forward, his Winchester's barrel cooling and making cracking noises as it did.

Horace, after his sixth shot had left his Henry, suddenly had the ground in front of him explode. As Stan had walked closer, so did the rounds. The third hit Horace's left shoulder, shattering the head of the humerus. Horace dropped his rifle and was reaching for the wound when Stan's fourth round hit him in the right side of his neck angle to the shoulder, taking out a large chunk of flesh. He wasn't dead yet, but he knew he would be. Stan's next two rounds were both high, but his last round hit the top of Horace's head and deflected into the air. It wasn't a killing shot, but it knocked him unconscious and let him die in peace.

Stan hobbled over to Horace and found him already dead. He turned his rifle to Horace's suffering horse and put his eighth round through the horse's head.

He lowered his rifle and began gimping back toward his injured horse. He had lost his Stetson in the fall and had to leave the road to find it, spotting it right on the berm. After retrieving his hat and putting it where it belonged, he continued hobbling along, until he reached his horse and bent down to check the gelding's injury. He'd never seen a bullet lodged in a horse's hoof before. The horse didn't seem to mind that much after the initial shock had gone, but he'd get the horse back to the liveryman and see what he thought about it.

He slipped his Winchester back into its scabbard and began leading the brown gelding back toward town. He saw riders approaching as he passed the other two horses and bodies but didn't even look down. He was just too tired.

"Stan! Did you get them all?" shouted Deputy Jorgenson.

"Yeah. The first two with the Sharps and the last one with the Winchester," he replied as he continued to walk.

"You hurt?"

"A round grazed my right foot, but I think it'll be okay after I buy some new boots."

"We'll go and clean up the mess. Can you stop by the office and write a statement?"

"Sure. Where's Harry?" Stan asked loudly.

"They killed him with the first shot. I was having my lunch when I heard the shooting start. I ran out into the street and they blasted right past me. I got three shots off, though. They killed three others besides Harry, too."

"Bastards should have died sooner. I've got to take my horse to the livery. He took a bullet into his hoof. I'll stop by right after."

"Okay, Stan. See you later," the deputy said as he and the hastily-formed posse trotted away.

Stan walked the mile back to the town, then had to walk the length of the main street, another half mile to get to the livery, where he showed Arnie Whitaker the bullet.

Arnie was sitting on his heels, looking at the back of the bullet, and said, "I ain't never seen the likes of that before. I reckon I can just pull it outta there and let it fill in by itself. Hell, it probably don't even hurt him except for the shock of him gettin' hit. Let me try and get it out."

The liveryman began trimming around the entrance wound until he could get his pliers onto the bullet. It took him some amount of tugging before the bullet slid out of the hoof, but the gelding never complained.

"Can you give him some water and oats, Arnie? I've got to get down to see Gus and write this up."

"You get 'em all, Stan?"

"Every blasted one of those sons-of-bitches."

"Good. You can take him, Stan. He'll be all right. Just walk him and you can see if his gait is okay."

"Thanks, Arnie. How much do I owe you?"

"You think I'd charge you for that, Stan? I will keep the bullet, though. That'll be the best story I'll ever tell."

"Well, I appreciate it."

Stan shook his hand and led the gelding out of the livery. He did watch his gait and saw nothing wrong, so he stepped into the saddle, and the horse acted as if nothing had happened as he rode toward the sheriff's office. He arrived before Deputy Jorgenson, so he went inside and found a small room with some paper and pencils. He took a sheet and began to write but hadn't finished before he heard Gus enter.

"I'm back here writing, Gus," he shouted.

Gus walked back into the office and asked, "Stan, how many shots did you take with your Sharps?"

"Two altogether. One for the first two. I waited until they were lined up and squeezed it off. I was only intending to take one shot, so I thought I'd make it a good one. I was ready to pull my Winchester anyway. The last guy was getting away after I took a tumble, so I fired it again and took out his horse at about four hundred yards."

"Well, I'll be damned! I thought it looked like only one shot. We found the slug in the middle guy. We identified all of them. Horace Belknap, Whitey Spradlin and Charlie Roberts. I think there are wanted posters on 'em, too. They're bringing the bodies back here for confirmation of death. I'll check on those posters."

"How much did they steal, anyway?"

"They had $221 dollars of the bank's money. It was found in Charlie's saddlebag."

"*Those stupid bastards killed four people for $200?* Damn!" Stan exclaimed.

"I know. Everybody liked Harry, too."

"How'd they get Harry?"

"It looks like they shot him when he was coming out of his office. His Winchester was cocked, so he must have spotted them."

Stan just shook his head and continued writing.

"You want to have the doc look at that foot?" Gus asked.

"What? Oh. Let me check."

Stan put down the pencil and looked at his right boot. It had been ripped to pieces on the outside, so he pulled the boot off and found the sock discolored from the disintegrating leather, but that was it.

"Looks like I'll just be buying some new boots, Gus. It's about time, anyway. These were army boots."

"I didn't know you were in the army. Of course, most guys over twenty were. How long were you in for?"

"I enlisted in August of '61 and got mustered out in May of this year."

"That's almost six years, Stan!"

"Seemed longer sometimes."

"You get wounded?"

"Shot once and stabbed once. Not too bad."

Stan finished his statement and handed it to Gus as he said, "Gus, I'm going to head over to Blanton's and see if I can buy some more boots."

"I'll let you know about the rewards, if there are any."

"Not a problem, Gus."

Stan walked outside and headed down to Blanton's Dry Goods, stepped inside and turned to the clothing section and found a pair of boots that fit reasonably well and walked up front where Ernie Blanton was waiting.

"Morning, Ernie. How are you?"

"I'm good, Stan. That all you need?"

"That's it."

"That'll be $8.15."

Stan gave him a ten dollar note and accepted the change.

He took his boots, left the store, walked back to the sheriff's office, and climbed back on the gelding glad it was over. He headed home for some peace and quiet, and maybe a dip in the spring.

————

Pinkerton Chief Agent Gerald Hornsby called Agent Bickerstaff into his office.

"Have a seat, John. I need you to take a quick run up to Boulder. I just got a telegram claiming some local rancher gunned down Horace Belknap, Whitey Spradlin and Charlie Roberts in an attempted bank robbery. Sounds kinda far-fetched to me. It sounds like they might be pulling a fast one to claim the reward money."

"Alright. I'll leave in the morning. It's only a four-hour trip. I might even make it back tomorrow night."

"Don't stretch it, John."

"Just kidding, Boss. You're right, though. It's hard to believe that some rancher could handle one of those bastards, much less all three. Hell, I wouldn't want to run into them myself. Not alone, anyway."

"Same here, John."

John stood up and waved as he returned to his desk. The robbers were probably just three amateurs, not those wanted men, but it'd be good to get out of the office.

————

Stan returned to his ranch and went straight out to the spring. He had pulled several flat stones from the nearby foothills and made a fairly large stone patio. He stripped quickly and plunged into the invigorating water. It had its normal shock effect followed by the serenity of flowing water past his skin. He stayed in the pool for ten minutes, a little longer than usual, and after he exited, he laid on the heated stones and felt the warmth on his back from the stones and the sun on his front.

He closed his eyes and wondered if the possible by-product of the failed bank robbery would put his name in the newspapers for Ellie to find. It was possible. He was always reading in newspapers about a much less gory outcome than this. A sheriff murdered in the streets, three people shot in the bank and then the three robbers meeting their end on the road outside of town. Maybe his Bucky would read the story and send him a letter.

———

Stan didn't know that even if it was a frontpage story in Denver's Rocky Mountain News, the Rafferty clan wouldn't pay any attention. They never read sensational stories that didn't affect them. They read the financial news.

Ellie never got to see the newspaper at all.

———

CHAPTER 5

The day after the robbery attempt, events began to converge for Stan and Ellie.

Pinkerton Agent John Bickerstaff left Denver at seven-thirty and had his horse at a medium trot, expecting to be in Boulder by noon.

The *Rocky Mountain News* had a frontpage story with the banner headline, 'Massacre in Boulder', and had to print extra editions.

Stan remained on his ranch and was still doing repairs to the place, mainly in the barn, not so much repairs, but more as upgrades. Even though he hoped that his name would make it to the papers, so Ellie would find out that he was there, he would have been shocked to find just how much traction the story had. Newspapers across the west and then across the nation picked up the story. The full impact of the event wouldn't be felt for another week as more papers added it to their pages.

In Boulder, the town council had asked Gus Jorgensen to take over as sheriff, but instead of accepting, he had resigned, leaving the town temporarily without a lawman. Gus had told the county commissioners that when he had seen Sheriff Hastings lying there on the boardwalk staring blankly into the boards, he knew he couldn't do the job anymore. His departure left the council with a big problem.

Agent Bickerstaff arrived in Boulder at 11:50 and rode directly to the sheriff's office. He walked to the door and yanked on the handle only to find it locked. He peered inside and couldn't see anyone in there, either in the office or in the jail cells, which was odd in a growing community like Boulder.

He walked over to the county courthouse and found the office of the county prosecutor, Paul Belmont, entered the outer office and met the prosecutor's clerk.

"May I help you, sir?"

"I'm Agent John Bickerstaff of the Pinkerton Detective Agency. I was sent here to confirm the claims made by Deputy Gus Jorgenson about the three men who attempted a bank robbery two days ago."

"Well, that presents a problem. You see, Sheriff Hastings was murdered by the robbers and I was just informed that Deputy Jorgenson has resigned."

"You don't have a second deputy?"

"No. One had been authorized but none hired yet. Would you like to speak to Mister Belmont?"

"Please."

"Just a moment."

The clerk tapped on the door and told Mister Belmont that a Pinkerton agent would like to speak to him about the failed bank robbery.

After getting an affirmative reply, the clerk waved John Bickerstaff into the prosecutor's office.

"Have a seat. Why is Pinkerton's involved in this?" asked the prosecutor.

"Those that offered the rewards have an issue with the claim. I'm here to clarify the problem."

"I can understand their concerns. It was an incredible story. I've talked to Deputy Jorgenson before he resigned and examined the bodies of the three men."

"Can you give me a synopsis?" he asked as he took out his notepad and pencil.

"Surely. The three men rode into town, and Sheriff Hastings must have noticed their intent to rob the bank, then returned to his office and retrieved his Winchester. Their lookout had spotted him and shot him before the sheriff could even get a shot off. When the lookout shot the sheriff, the two inside the bank began shooting people, two employees and one customer. They grabbed the money and rode west out of town. Here's where it gets interesting."

Bickerstaff thought, "…and *now* it gets interesting?"

"As the three men are racing out of town, one of our local ranchers just happened to be coming into town. He'd only been here a few months, mind you, but he was well-liked. Lives by himself about five miles out of town. Good man.

"Anyway, he hears all the gunfire, sees these three racing out of town and knows they had hit the bank. So, he pulls off to the side of the road behind some trees and waits for them with his Sharps rifle."

"He had a Sharps? Just riding around?"

"From what folks tell me he had just ridden down from Montana a few months ago and had gotten so used to shooting hostile Indians, he kept it with him."

"Go on," Bickerstaff said, still writing his notes.

"Now, he figures he's got one shot with that single-shot Sharps and waits until they're lined up and fires one shot and takes out two riders. The third one panics and takes off. He goes riding out after him with his Winchester. The last one, that's Horace Belknap, starts throwing pistol shots back at him and one shot hits his horse right in the hoof, and he goes flying head over heels into the road.

"Now, Horace thinks he's home free, but no, sir, he wasn't. Our man reloads his Sharps and fires at over four hundred yards and hits the horse in the flank. The horse goes down and so does Horace. The rancher starts running at Horace, who opens up with his Henry. The man keeps going at Horace, who starts rapid firing. The rancher finally stops and starts shooting at the source of the smoke and put three shots into Horace. Jorgenson had all the bodies brought back. That's when we found papers on them identifying them and matched them to the wanted posters."

"I'll need to see the bodies and identify them myself. What was the name of the rancher?"

"Stan Murray."

John Bickerstaff felt a jolt as he asked, "Did you say Stan Murray?"

"I did. He used to be an army captain, from what they tell me. One of the Michigan Brigade."

John Bickerstaff was still stunned, then slowly closed his notebook and slid it and the pencil into his pocket.

"I'll need to go and see the bodies and talk to Mister Murray. How do I find his place?"

"It's easy. Just head west about two miles and you'll see a wagon path swing to the southwest. Just take that and you'll find it three miles down on the right. He's got a new name on the ranch, but I can't remember what it was."

John stood and shook the prosecutor's hand as he said, "Thank you for your help, Mister Belmont."

"Glad to help. I hope Mister Murray gets that reward. He certainly earned it."

"It sure sounds like it."

John walked out of the county courthouse with his mind still racing. *How could Stan Murray be so close to Mrs. Rafferty and not know where she was, and vice versa?*

He stepped up on his horse and turned it east to the mortician's and then ten minutes later, he exited the undertaker's and headed west.

———

Stan was in his house enjoying a good lunch, having been improving his cooking skills almost daily since moving into the ranch. Having a town so close was handy. Even when he was in the army, towns always seemed to be too far away. Except during the war, but then, the towns had usually been occupied by Confederates.

He finished his lunch, cleaned up and was thinking of going into town and buying a copy of *The Rocky Mountain News* to see if his name was in there but decided to wait until tomorrow, so he could pick up some more fresh food.

He left the house and was walking to the barn when he saw a rider approach his access road, then stopped and watched as

145

the rider turned toward the ranch. He continued to watch when the rider suddenly waved, and Stan waved back. He kept trying to figure out who he was. He surely wasn't dressed like someone around Boulder. He had a jacket on and matching trousers, almost like a uniform.

Stan stood still as he got within thirty feet. He looked vaguely familiar, very vaguely.

"Can I help you?" he asked.

Bickerstaff knew who he was long before he spoke, then after he pulled his horse to a stop, smiled as he looked down and asked, "Can I step down, Captain?"

"Go ahead. I think I've met you someplace before but can't quite place you."

John dismounted and replied, "I met you twice before. You were commanding B company in the Michigan First. I was with the Michigan Fifth."

Stan smiled and said, "Now I remember. We were at a staff meeting."

John smiled back and said, "That's it."

"Want to come inside? Did you have any lunch?"

"No, I missed it. Thank you for the offer."

"Well, come on in and I'll fix you something. I've already eaten, but I'll have some coffee."

"I appreciate it. Do you mind if I call you Stan?"

"Not at all."

"Do you want to try to remember my name?" he asked as he laughed.

"Bickerstaff, isn't it? John Bickerstaff?"

John was surprised and asked, "How do you remember that? It was years ago, and we only met for a few minutes."

"I remembered watching your face as some of those higher ups spouted their nonsense, and I could see you were a straight-shooter. I always remembered them because they were hard to find."

John laughed again as they entered the house and Stan led him straight into the kitchen and immediately began cooking the same meal he had just had. He tossed a small steak on the hot pan and added some of the cold hash browns.

"So, John, you just came out to rehash some memories?" Stan asked as he flipped the sizzling steak.

"No, Stan, I have a couple of reasons. I work for Pinkerton's now and I was sent here to verify the claim on the rewards for those three outlaws you took down. The story sent by Deputy Jorgenson seemed too outrageous to be true."

"I wish it wasn't, John. Those bastards killed four good people, including Harry Hastings."

"You know that Deputy Jorgenson quit? They don't have any law in Boulder right now."

Stan turned in surprise and said, "You're kidding. Gus quit?"

"That's what the prosecutor told me."

"That's bad news."

"The other news is a lot different. Have a seat, Stan."

"Just a second. I'm almost finished with your lunch."

Stan slid the small steak and hash brown potatoes out of the frypan and onto a plate. He slid the plate in front of John and gave him a knife and fork, then he grabbed two cups and filled them both with coffee, put one down in front of John and the other on the table and he sat down.

Before he cut his steak, John said, "Stan, a few days ago, I had a visit from a Mrs. Rafferty. She asked me to hunt down a friend of hers, and I did. John, she was looking for you. Her first name is Ellie."

Stan had his cup almost to his lips when John spoke that name. He stopped and slowly lowered it to the table.

"My Ellie? I rode over six hundred miles looking for her. She's married?"

"To a very wealthy banker named George Rafferty. His father owns the bank and a few other stores."

Stan let that news sink in for a full minute before he quietly asked, "Does she have any children, John?"

"I don't think so, but I'm not sure."

"Did she say why she was looking for me?"

"No. We don't ask the whys."

"Did you get the impression that she wanted to see me?"

"That was my impression. Honestly, Stan, I believe she desperately wants to see you."

"When are you going back to Denver?"

"Tomorrow morning."

"Did you want to just stay here tonight? I'll make breakfast and then I'll come with you back to Denver."

"Throw in dinner and I'm your man. You can tell me about that trip you made."

"I will, but I've got to show you something really bizarre."

"I can't wait."

Stan stood and walked to his weapons room and picked up his old Spencer, then returned to the kitchen, sat down and showed the carbine to John.

"Lord, Stan! That thing is falling apart. What's so bizarre about it?"

"I picked that up at a dry goods store in Miles' trading post in Montana. I bought a different one for a backup that was in good shape for two dollars and he offered to throw this one in for free, but I still gave him a dollar for it. I would have paid more than two dollars for it."

"Why?"

"That's the bizarre part. It's the first carbine that I was issued in Detroit when I enlisted in August of '61."

That did surprise John as he exclaimed, *"You're kidding? Are you sure?"*

"My memory isn't lying, John. This is my carbine. When I was issued my first gun, I memorized that serial number, and I'd love to find out how it traveled all the way to the wilds of Montana."

149

After that, the afternoon slipped into conversation about his travels.

When he finished, John asked, "You gonna show me this place?"

"Sure. Let's go."

Stan went out and saddled the lighter gelding and then he and John rode out to the pastures. Stan was proud of his ranch, and showed him the pool, the stallion and his mares and everything else he loved about his home.

"This is a great place, Stan."

"I can't believe how cheap it was, John."

"How much did it cost you, if you don't mind my asking"

"I paid $2140, and all I had to do was clean it up."

"You're right. That is a good deal. I wish I had something like this."

"The bank said that they had quite a few properties available, but this was just the first one I looked at."

"I'll have to think about it. This is just great."

They returned to the barn and led their horses inside, where he and John unsaddled them then brushed them down.

"Even your barn looks great," John said as he looked around.

"I did have the house and barn painted by a contractor, though. I hate painting."

"I'll agree to that."

FINDING BUCKY

They returned to the house and continued to talk through dinner and into the night and turned in by eleven o'clock.

Stan, once he was alone in his room, was almost too excited to sleep. Tomorrow he would see Ellie, although she was a married Ellie. *Why would she want to see him if she was married to a wealthy banker who could provide her so much more?* Maybe she was just getting nostalgic.

He finally drifted off, trying to imagine what his Bucky looked like now.

———

As soon as his eyes twitched the next morning, the excitement immediately returned. He almost jumped out of his bed and began dressing, pulled on his new boots and ran out to the privy. He returned and began washing for the day. After shaving, he put on a new shirt and trousers and was ready to go when John finally made his appearance. He smiled when he saw the anxious Stan before he left to use the privy and returned as Stan was cooking breakfast.

"You seem a bit antsy this morning, Stan."

"It's been a long time, John. I don't know what to expect."

"You never even asked what she looks like."

"It doesn't matter, John."

"Then I won't tell you how beautiful she is."

"I really don't care, John. You have to understand that we were both outcasts when we were in school. I was a fat kid they made fun all the time and she had really big front teeth. We were so close because of what we went through."

151

"She said you were fat, but I found it hard to believe and still can't see it. I can't see her with big teeth either. You've both changed quite a bit."

"I know, but it doesn't change what she was inside. I don't think she's any different."

"She's very big in society, Stan. I don't know if she'd give that up."

"Then I'll smile at her and wish her well. All I need to know is that she's happy, then I'll get on with my life. I've had a lot of opportunities with women over the years, but I wasn't about to settle. If she's married, then I'll have to move on."

"I wish you luck, Stan. Let me finish this and we'll get the horses ready to go."

"Let me clean up first."

After cleaning the dishes and frypan the two men went out to the barn, and Stan saddled the dark gelding.

They were on the road out of Boulder a little after eight o'clock. Stan, without even being aware of it, set a fast pace as John just grinned inside. He was curious about what would happen when they met again and suspected that it wouldn't be good for his new friend.

They reached the outskirts of Denver shortly before noon and Stan suddenly realized he still didn't know where she lived.

He looked across at John and loudly asked, "John, what's her address?"

"14 Third Street. I'm going to get to the office and file my report. I'd appreciate it if you'd stop by afterwards and tell me how it went."

"Where's your office?"

"Ironically, right across the street from her father-in-law's bank, The First Colorado Bank."

"If I haven't stolen her away, I'll stop by," he said as he grinned.

John grinned back, but still wished he could follow Stan to see what happened.

Stan, despite his grin, could feel his future with Ellie suddenly coming to an end. If she was happily married to an important, wealthy man, then that was the end of his search. For almost ten years, finding his Bucky had been his one goal, now that he knew that she was married, finding her was almost like a curse.

What made it so unusual was that he'd always expected her to be married. *Why should she waste almost an entire decade waiting for a fat boy who would never amount to anything?* Soon, he'd find Ellie, smile at her and probably deliver that disgusting, 'as long as you're happy' lie.

After they had entered the city, John pointed out the bank and the end of Third Street and shouted, "Good luck, Stan."

Stan nodded and waved to John as he turned onto Third Street. His heart threatened to pound itself right out of his rib cage as he walked his horse down the street until he reached number 14 and was awed by its size. *How could he ever compete with this?* He was so proud of his ranch, but his ranch house would be swallowed by the elaborate Rafferty home. He blew out his breath and stepped down.

He tied off his horse and strode down the fancy brick walkway, feeling more insignificant with each step. If it wasn't for the knowledge that Ellie was inside, he would have turned around and headed back to Boulder.

He stopped at the door, pulled the doorbell cord, and began fidgeting impatiently, expecting Ellie to answer the door.

Inside the house, Ellie heard the doorbell, and assumed it was someone else dropping off another invitation.

Maria Elena walked to the door and opened it, saw Stan and asked, "Yes?"

Stan had forgotten that rich people don't answer their own doors, and replied, "Yes, Ma'am. I'd like to speak to Ellie. Is she in?"

"Mrs. Rafferty?"

"Yes. Please."

"What is about?"

Stan smiled awkwardly as he replied, "Tell her that Piggy wants to see Bucky."

Maria Elena looked at him as if he was ready for the loony bin and closed the door, then walked upstairs to Ellie's room.

She saw Ellie and said, "Mrs. Rafferty? A man wants to talk to you. He says pig wants to see our buggy."

Ellie looked at her, curiously and asked, "What did he say?"

"He says pig wants to see our buggy."

"Tell him to go away," she said, frustrated at the confusion.

"I will."

Maria Elena walked back down the stairs and opened the door.

Stan, expecting to see Ellie was taken aback to see Maria Elena again.

"Mrs. Rafferty says you should go away," she said before she closed the door.

Stan was absolutely crushed as he stared at the closed door. *After all this, after all the waiting and hope, she pulls him here just to humble him? Was that the purpose of her trying to find him to prove how much better she was now?*

He was frozen in place as his mind raced. He finally concluded that he had been wrong, and people do change. He sighed and turned around, utterly deflated. This was much worse than even having to see her smiling as he told her that he was happy for her.

He stepped down the walk, then untied the gelding, stepped up and returned to the main road, still numb by what had happened. He promised John he'd see him, so he turned left and headed for the Pinkerton's office.

He reached the office, dismounted and tied off the horse, walked into the office and saw John sitting behind his desk.

John was smiling as Stan walked over to his desk.

"Well, Stan. What did she say?" John asked expectantly.

"I never saw her, John. Her maid said that she just told me to just go away."

John was shaken by what Stan said. He hadn't read that in her demeanor at all when she had come in, and even his own concerns about what impact the meeting would have on Stan all paled when compared to this.

"Are you sure, Stan? I mean, I just didn't see that attitude when she was here."

"I guess she just wanted to show me that she was so much better than I was."

"I don't think so, Stan. I think you should go back and see her."

"There's no point, John. I can't shove the maid aside and have the city police arrest me. No, I've learned my lesson. I'm heading back to my ranch."

"Did you want to get some lunch?"

"No, I think I'll just head back."

He shook John's hand, and said, "Thanks for telling me, John, at least now I know."

He left the office, mounted the gelding and headed north.

After he had gone, John wanted to grab his Stetson and march over to #14 3rd Street, but he couldn't. She was a client and it was policy not to contact a client with something that wasn't business related, so he just sat behind his desk and stewed.

———

Stan left Denver and kept the same fast pace on the way back to Boulder, but for a different reason. He was utterly crushed by Ellie's rejection. He had left the army, crossed six hundred miles of hostile territory and killed more than a dozen men to get here. *For what?* To literally have the door slammed in his face. The further he rode the more he slipped into depression. His dream of a joyful reunion with Ellie turned into a nightmare.

———

Ellie was still curious about the man who wanted to see the buggy. What was odd was they didn't have a buggy, they had a large, fancy black carriage. *Why would Maria Elena even think the man wanted to see their non-existent buggy?* Maria Elena could speak three languages, but the only time she had a problem with English was when she was presented with a word she didn't know or sounded out of context. Soiree became surrey, even though they had no surrey. *What sounds like 'buggy'?* She had totally forgotten about the 'pig' wanting to see the buggy.

———

Stan passed through Boulder at seven-thirty and reached his ranch twenty-five minutes later. He rode straight into the barn, unsaddled the gelding and brushed him down without even realizing he was doing it. He put him into his stall and walked to the house. It's all he had now. His ranch, his horses, and the mule. As he'd told John Bickerstaff, he'd start looking for a wife if he found Ellie was already married, but it would be a while. He'd simply invested too much time and love on Ellie. It would take a while to try to force her out of his heart, despite the knowledge that she must have already emptied him from her heart.

He fixed himself a flavorless dinner and cleaned up before going to sleep, but really just to lie in bed and wonder what had happened to turn his Bucky into Mrs. High Society Rafferty.

―――

When Stan finally forced himself to get out of bed the next morning, it was almost nine o'clock and considered it to be the first new day of the rest of his life, a life without Ellie or the dream of finding Ellie. He had to start thinking about what to do now because it was such a huge change in his life. Ellie had been his focus since he was ten. When she had been taken away, she became his goal. Now that goal was gone, and he had nothing to focus on. He needed to find something beyond just finding a wife.

He'd think about it today while he handled his daily chores, beginning with a much-needed run to the privy.

After breakfast, he moved the horses from the barn to the corral to let them get some measure of exercise and sun. He had just finished moving them when he saw a dust cloud from riders approaching the access road. Stan walked toward the front of the house to welcome them. He had his pistol, but it wouldn't do much good if they were hostile. He'd been a bit touchy about visitors since the bank shooting.

He was ready to get his Winchester when he noticed they were far from tough-looking hombres. They were a bit too old for anything like that. He smiled at his own nervousness and walked toward the group as they approached the house. He finally recognized them and guessed their intention at the same time.

"Good morning, gentlemen. What can I do for you today?" he asked when they were close.

"Howdy, Stan. Mind if we set?"

"Come on in. Would you like some coffee?"

FINDING BUCKY

The three men all stepped down and tied off their horses.

"Wouldn't mind, Stan," said Bill Wasserman.

Stan led them all inside and they walked back to his kitchen.

"You've really turned this place around, Stan," said Joe Baker.

"It wasn't really that bad, Joe," replied Stan as he took out four cups and filled them with coffee, emptying the pot.

Each man took a cup and sat at the table, as Stan grabbed his and joined them.

He smiled as he sat and said, "Having trouble finding a sheriff, Bill?"

"Kinda obvious, isn't it, Stan? The county is growing, and we don't have any law enforcement. We have two men who applied for the job, but one can't read and the other is a troublemaker. Seems like the violence inflicted on Harry Hastings has made it a less than desirable position."

"My problem is that I have a ranch that's an hour out of town. You'll need someone there all the time."

"It's not as big a problem as you might think, Stan. Now, we know you only have a few horses on your ranch. It's not like it's that far. Heck, I'll bet that you could make it in thirty minutes."

Stan nodded. He'd made it in less than that, far less. He'd made the trip in twenty-two minutes. It was the time he'd have to spend away from his ranch that bothered him.

"It's really not the travel time, Bill. It's the time I'd lose at my ranch. I love it out here."

"Stan, we need someone to protect the town and the rest of the county. Now, there are two authorized deputy positions. You could fill them if you find a couple of good men. That would help."

"Does the jail have a bed I could use if I get stuck in town?"

"It does, but we'll build a whole apartment in back for you with everything you need if you're stuck. We'd pay you fifty dollars a month and you could eat at the café while you're in town and the county would pick up the tab."

It wasn't the money or the food that was their compelling argument. It was that they needed someone to protect the town. They didn't know it, though.

"Alright, Bill. I'll take the job, but we'll see how it works out."

He could see the relief on all their faces as Bill Wasserman said, "Thanks, Stan. We really appreciate it. Let's get you sworn in."

They all stood, and Stan took the oath of office. For some reason, they had brought the badge of office with them, so Bill Wasserman handed it to him, and he pinned it on.

"Give me a few minutes and I'll saddle a horse and join you on the way back."

"We'll follow you outside, Stan."

All four men left the kitchen, Stan locked the back door and they walked out to the barn. Stan saddled the buckskin mare and was soon leading her out of the barn. He stopped at the front door, locked it before leaving the porch and stepping up on the buckskin.

They left the ranch a little after ten o'clock and arrived in Boulder forty minutes later. Stan had kept the buckskin at a medium trot just to verify the travel time without pushing it. They stopped at the sheriff's office, his office, stepped down and tied off their horses.

"Here are the keys to the office, Stan," said Bill, handing him a small ring of keys.

"Thanks, Bill."

Stan unlocked the door and they all filed in. Stan had been in the office a few times but hadn't really looked around. There was a rifle rack with three Winchesters and two shotguns, one with shortened barrels, an ideal weapon for law enforcement.

"Can I modify that other shotgun? I'd like to have the barrels shortened somewhat. Not as radically as the other one, but another three inches."

"Go ahead. Just drop it off at the Hank's blacksmith shop."

"I'd rather do it myself. I have a smithy in the barn, and I'll be able to test it as well."

"Have at it, Stan," said Joe Baker.

"I'm going to have to do some reading and get familiar with the ordinances."

"Well, we'll let you start, then," said Bill.

All three shook his hand again before leaving.

After they'd gone, Stan pulled the book on state, county and town ordinances. He sat in the chair behind the desk and began reading. Some of them surprised him and actually caused him to laugh at the silliness of the law. He doubted if he'd arrest anyone for spitting tobacco outside of a cuspidor.

He was so involved in reading that he missed lunch. He also realized with a start that he'd left the buckskin out front without water for four hours.

He marked his spot in the book with a folded up wanted poster and set it aside, then left the office and walked the horse down to the livery.

"Morning, Arnie. Am I supposed to leave my horse with you while I'm working?"

"Yup. I just heard you took the job. Makes me and a lot of other folks feel better."

"Good. What did Harry do about it if he needed to chase down bad boys fast?"

"If I hear gunfire, I start saddling your horse."

"That'll work."

"You know, the county is supposed to provide you with a horse, don't you?"

"Nope. They didn't mention it."

"Well, they are. As soon as I heard that they were going to try to get you to take the job, I went out to Lampman's and found you one I think you'll like better."

"I don't know, Arnie. The red and the buckskin are fine animals."

"I've had my eye on this boy for a while, I just didn't want to sell him to anyone. Come on."

FINDING BUCKY

Stan followed Arnie out to his corral in back and immediately liked what he saw. He was a tall gelding that at first glance was all black, but it wasn't just black. In the bright early afternoon sun, it shone with a blue hue.

"Look at the chest on that boy!" exclaimed Stan.

"Isn't he special?" asked a beaming Arnie.

"Arnie, he's incredible. I can't let the county buy him, though. I'll buy him myself, so they can't take him away."

"I was going to charge them fifty dollars for him, Stan."

"He's worth every penny, Arnie," replied Stan as he ran his palm over the horse's side, watching the horse's coat shift from black to blue-black and back.

Stan reached into his pocket and pulled out the cash and handed it to Arnie.

"I'm guessing he's been shod recently?"

"This morning, after I saw the commissioners riding your way," he replied as he grinned.

"Well, I'll spend my days riding him more often. I'll still ride the others, though. They need the exercise."

"You gonna name him? I noticed you never name your horses."

"It was a habit from the war. I'd lose them so often that I didn't want to get attached. I should've named the buckskin and especially the red, though."

"Well, you'd better come up with names for 'em."

"I'll do that as soon as I finish reading those state, county and town laws. Some of them are a hoot."

Stan left the corral and the livery to get started on the job.

He spent another three hours reading before deciding to call it a day. He left the office, and after locking the door, walked down to the diner to get his first free meal. He wondered if the county included a tip, but figured they didn't, so he'd stock up on change.

He greeted a lot of folks on his way to the café. They seemed genuinely pleased to have him there, and he could understand why. It must have been an uneasy situation to have no one to turn to for protection. The men who carried pistols had their own, but the innocents had no one. He would protect the innocents.

He reached the diner and found a table. Laura Price saw him enter and walked his way.

"Hello, Stan. I'm glad to see you wearing that badge. I was getting worried they'd let Jimmy Ryder have the job. He's kind of mad he didn't get it, too."

Stan looked at Laura and cocked his head as he asked, "He wanted to be sheriff?"

"He'd been telling his little group of skunks that he was a shoo-in for the job because you'd never take it."

"Then I'm glad I did. Give him a badge and there'd be no holding those boys back."

"I know. Stan, they scare me sometimes. Like when I'm getting ready to leave, Jimmy and his pal Ed Crenshaw will hang outside the diner waiting for me. They follow me saying all sorts of things about what they want to do to me."

"What time do you get off, Laura?"

"Seven-thirty or so."

"Well, you come out the front door tonight and don't you worry. I'll escort you home."

She smiled, and Stan could see the relief in her eyes as she said, "I would really appreciate it, Stan."

"Anytime, Laura. What's the special tonight?"

"Roast beef and roasted potatoes."

"I'll have the special, then," he said as smiled at her.

"I'll be right back," she replied as she smiled back.

Laura was a nice girl, but Stan didn't know her particulars, like her family life or even where she lived. She was unmarried, he knew that. Married women didn't waitress. Whatever else, she was an innocent.

Jimmy Ryder and Ed Crenshaw were nothing more than local bullies, much like those older boys who used to call him Piggy. They talked a lot and got into a lot of minor scrapes and had a small following of younger kids, no more than boys, really. Take those two down a notch or two and they'd lose their little entourage. He just wondered how to do it.

Laura brought him his dinner and a pot of coffee.

"Laura, I'm new to this whole sheriff game. How does the county know how much to pay?"

165

"I'll give you a bill and you just sign it."

"Okay. Thanks."

She smiled again and left.

Stan ate his dinner pondering what to do about Jimmy and Ed. He didn't think it would escalate to gunfire, so he was thinking of leaving his pistol in the office when he escorted Laura home. But that would leave him vulnerable if there was any other trouble. He'd have to just see how it played out.

He signed the bill that Laura left him, and he left her a quarter tip that was almost the cost of the meal.

He left the diner and returned to his new office, his home away from home. It was six o'clock, and there was plenty of daylight. He wondered if the county would remember their promise to build an extension apartment onto the jail. He looked at the bed in the back office and figured it would do in a pinch. It was just a cot, really, but it was still a lot better than lying in an 'A' tent with the rain pounding on the canvas and turning your bed into a swamp.

He leaned back, and his mind wandered back to a familiar subject…Ellie. He was still in disbelief that the girl he thought he knew so well, the girl with the big heart and soft eyes could have turned into such a heartless woman. *Why would she try to find him just to turn him away? Was it so important to her that he see how far she'd moved up in the world?* That was just the opposite of the Ellie he knew, his Ellie.

His Bucky would never do anything to hurt him. Ellie was the first and most innocent of the innocent. Until she rolled away on the tailgate of that wagon, she was still the only true innocent he had known. He didn't think anyone was capable of such a massive change, but Stan finally concluded that money could change anyone.

He blew out his breath. He had to stop thinking about Ellie. He had a job to do now. She was only thirty miles away, but she may as well be standing on the moon. She was lost to him.

Despite everything that had gone his way recently, he felt empty and vowed to get over it. He had to. He was only twenty-three but would be twenty-four next month. Of course, then he had to remember that Ellie would turn twenty-three just four days after his birthday. So much for not thinking about her.

He stood and pulled the short shotgun off the rack and checked the shells. It was loaded with birdshot, which made sense. With such short barrels, the spread would be very wide. It would hurt a lot of folks but shouldn't kill anyone unless they were really close.

He pulled the long shotgun and checked its load and found #4 buckshot shells. This was the serious shotgun. If this was used, there would be dead men at the other end. He decided to only shorten it by a couple of inches. He wanted a moderate spread, but still keep the effectiveness. He'd want it to take out bad men from across a street without having to aim too carefully.

He'd take the short one with him to escort Laura home.

At seven-fifteen, he left his office, turned left and walked along the boardwalk. There was still daylight, and as he looked down the street, he could see two men waiting by the diner's front door. No doubt Jimmy Ryder and Ed Crenshaw had arrived for their nightly fun, if that was all it was. He noticed only Jimmy was armed with a holstered pistol. Ed may have a blade somewhere, but no gun.

He arrived before Laura had emerged from the diner and asked, "What are you boys hanging around the diner for? Need some late chow?"

"None of your business," Jimmy snarled.

"That's not true, Jimmy. It is my business. Now, you two are loitering. Why don't you both move along?"

"We're not goin' anywhere," Ed replied.

"Now, boys, I'm new to this job, but I'll be taking it seriously. I don't want to have to toss you two in jail on my first day, but you're pressing your luck."

Jimmy challenged him with a witty retort, saying, "You ain't throwin' nobody in jail."

"Do you want me to give you the town ordinance number you're violating by standing there without purpose?"

Before they could answer, Laura exited the door, saw Stan, and despite the presence of her two regular problems, she smiled.

"Good evening, Laura. You ready to go?" Stan asked.

"Thank you, Sheriff," she replied, taking his arm.

"She's my girl, you bastard. You take your hands off her," shouted Jimmy.

Stan stopped, turned and said, "I beg your pardon? You have to be joking. You couldn't come close to being good enough to be Laura's boyfriend. You and your pal Eddy, are nothing more than crude bullies. You've been harassing her nightly as she tries to walk from her work to her home. Now, I'm here to make sure she can peacefully walk the streets of our fair city and I'm going to give you both a warning. If I find you outside the diner, or bothering Laura in any way, you'll both be arrested for making threats."

"You can't do that!" protested Ed.

"Now, you're surely smart enough to know that I can, and I will. Now, why don't you both just go enjoy the beautiful evening, say goodnight to Laura and while you're at it, you can apologize for being so rude to her in the past."

"You're feeling mighty big with that badge and that shotgun. How about you and me just have a go? Afraid?" Jimmy said while taking a challenging posture.

"Of you? You're just full of jokes tonight. How about this? You leave your pal Ed out of this and I'll let you have a shot. How's that?"

Jimmy was suddenly unsure of what he was getting into. He'd beaten up a lot of guys, but none had ever challenged him before, and none were as big as the sheriff. But he regained his confidence, as no one had ever beaten him, either.

"Alright, Sheriff. If that's what you think you are, they shoulda give me that badge."

Stan cocked the right hammer on the shotgun, which made both Jimmy and Ed twitch, then he handed it to Laura.

"Laura, if anyone, meaning Ed, tries to interfere, aim in his direction and pull the trigger. It won't kill him, but they'll be unhappy for a long time,"

Then he looked at the four-foot distance to Ed and said, "On second thought, I think it will kill Ed at that range."

Laura smiled as she took the shotgun, saying, "I'll be happy to help, Sheriff."

Then Stan turned back to Jimmy and said, "Okay, Jimmy. I'm going to give you one more chance to apologize to Laura and walk away. If you don't want to do that, drop your gunbelt and I'll take mine off."

Jimmy didn't hesitate. He'd rarely even fired the pistol, so he unbuckled the gunbelt and let it fall. Stan unbuckled his and set it carefully on the ground, giving Jimmy a free shot, or so he thought.

Jimmy saw Stan's face turn as he lowered his gun to the dirt, but Stan was watching Jimmy's feet. When he saw Jimmy suddenly shift his weight by pulling his right foot back an inch, he dropped his head and shoulders, following the gunbelt. Jimmy's sucker punch swung by and Stan smashed a vicious uppercut into his gut with his right. Jimmy folded over and hit the dirt, curling up in the fetal position, and that was all there was to the big fight.

Stan picked up his gunbelt that had been on the ground for all of fifteen seconds and strapped it back on, took the shotgun from a beaming Laura and released the right hammer.

"Ed, help Jimmy up, will you?" he said.

Ed was stunned by how quickly Stan had turned Jimmy into a blubbering mess. He reached down and took Jimmy's left elbow and pulled him to his feet. He was still sobbing.

"Ed, I believe you and Jimmy owe Laura an apology."

"Laura, I'm sorry for all the things I said. I think Jimmy would say the same thing if he could."

Stan turned to Laura. "Is that an acceptable apology, Laura?"

"Yes, thank you, Sheriff."

"Ed, you'd better help Jimmy home. Remind him it's better not to start trouble in the first place than to try to get out of it."

Ed turned Jimmy away from Stan and led him down the street.

"Laura, do you still need an escort, or are you okay now?"

"Would you mind?" she asked with a smile.

"Not at all. My pleasure," he replied, offering her his arm.

He led her all of a hundred and twenty yards to Mason's Rooming House where she stopped, turned to him and said, "I have a room here. Thank you so much, Stan. That was wonderful."

"You're welcome. I don't think they'll bother you anymore, but if they do, you'll know where I'll be."

"I know. I'll see you tomorrow, Stan."

For a few seconds, he thought Laura was going to kiss him, but he tipped his hat and turned to go back to his office. He was right, as it turned out. She was giving it serious consideration.

Stan walked into his office, replaced the short shotgun and took the long shotgun, before leaving the office, closing and locking the door then heading back to the livery.

Arnie had been watching the Jimmy Ryder confrontation and after Jimmy had plowed face first into the street, had turned and begun saddling the black gelding.

Stan stepped up onto the big horse and rode west out of Boulder. He was home in less than thirty minutes, but he felt like he was leaving a gap in town. Bad things didn't stop at night.

He rode the black into the barn and unsaddled him. He'd have to trail the buckskin back tomorrow, maybe at lunchtime. He took out the shotgun and locked it in a vise, using a leather strap to keep the metal from getting gouged, then took out a hacksaw and had the shotgun shortened by two and a half inches in twenty minutes. He filed the burrs off his cut and sanded the edge smooth, before he released it from the vice and carried it into his house.

He cleaned himself up, undressed and crawled into bed. It had been a long day.

———

Ellie couldn't sleep at all. For some reason, the buggy man, as she came to call him, kept haunting her. What had he said to Maria Elena? She had fixated on the 'uggy' part of the word and couldn't come up with anything that made sense.

She was beginning to let her mind wander, though. That can be a good thing at times when concentration is making it focus on all the wrong things. As she let her mind drift, it moved into the one realm that was always present, Stan and Piggy. She thought of how they would sit together in class and on the steps during recess and lunch talking. How painful it was when the other children made fun of her but how when Piggy had called her Bucky, it gave her a warm feeling. It was funny how the same derisive name could have two…

She almost hit her head. *How could she have not made that connection quickly? Almost instantly?* The man at the door had wanted to see Bucky! She sat up with a start. *Had she turned away Stan?* She felt her heart and stomach plummet at the same time. She refused to believe it was even remotely possible.

But who else would show up at her door asking to see Bucky? She tried to think if she had ever told anyone else those stories. Her parents knew, of course, but they were so embarrassed by her appearance when she was young that they had actually forbidden the word's use in the house.

The more she thought about it, the more she was convinced that her Piggy had arrived at her door to see her and she had turned him away. She dropped her head down and let the tears explode from her eyes. *What an idiot I am! Why couldn't I have at least shown the courtesy to go downstairs and see who it was? Have I become so damned important that I can give a queenly flick of the wrist and say, 'off with his head'?* She sat and let the tears soak her fancy satin quilt for twenty minutes. *All these years! All my dreams and I threw it all away by just being rude!*

When she finally ran out of tears, she laid back down and knew what she would do. She'd put on her riding outfit and take her buckskin mare and go see Mister Bickerstaff at Pinkerton's. He might know where Stan was. She'd go right after breakfast.

CHAPTER 6

Stan was already on the road back to Boulder by seven o'clock. He had left his Sharps in his weapons room and kept his Winchester and the shotgun in the two scabbards. He arrived at seven thirty and went to his office, unlocked the door and brought the modified shotgun inside and hung it on the rack.

After leaving the black gelding at the livery, he headed down to the diner for his breakfast. When he entered, Laura saw him and almost plowed into a customer standing to leave in her anxiety to see him. Stan noticed and thought he might be starting a problem with Laura. She was a nice girl, pretty and well formed, but she wasn't Ellie. *Was there another Ellie anywhere?* Besides, he knew it was still too soon. It was almost as if he was in mourning, which he really was.

"Good morning, Stan," she said as she smiled so hard her face looked ready to split in two.

"Good morning, Laura. Just the usual today," he said as he returned her smile.

"I'll be right back," she said as she hustled back to the kitchen.

'The usual' was the same for all the men he knew: four eggs over easy, four strips of bacon, biscuits and coffee.

She returned with his coffee and poured it for him. She smiled again and left, leaving a strong lilac scent wafting over the table…too strong to suit him.

FINDING BUCKY

Stan knew he was in trouble now. He'd probably start eating more at home and bring something to the office which would save the county some money at the same time.

There was something else he needed to do today. He'd buy a couple of vests. He knew that the badge in some situations was a target. Harry Hastings had been wearing his badge, probably the one he was wearing now, when he left the office. Maybe if he had it behind a vest, the lookout man wouldn't have noticed so quickly. He should have gone out the back door anyway. When Harry had exited the office from the front door, he put himself right into that man's field of fire. It was a horrible and fatal mistake and was surprised that an experienced lawman like Harry would have made it. He must have been too anxious to stop the bank holdup.

Laura brought him his breakfast, smiled once more, and wafted away.

Stan made short work of the food and left a tip after signing the bill.

He headed for his office and walked inside, then decided that he'd go through the wanted posters and memorize the bad guys before he finished reading his ordinances, but he was interrupted ten minutes later by a messenger.

"Sheriff, you have to go down to the office. They have something for you."

"Oh. Thanks, Danny."

He tossed Danny a nickel, who didn't expect a tip because he didn't give the sheriff a telegram.

"Gee! Thanks, Sheriff."

"You're welcome, Danny."

He followed Danny out the door and down the boardwalk to the telegraph office. When he opened the door, the telegrapher saw him enter.

"Stan, I got a few vouchers for you. They oughta make you a happy man. I know I'd be happy if I got 'em."

"I'd totally forgotten about those things. It's been a while."

"Here you go."

There may have been only three bad men, but there were nine vouchers. Three different agencies had offered rewards on the men. Two were banks and one was a railroad company. The total was an astonishing twelve hundred dollars.

"That's a load of cash, Joe," he said as he looked at them.

"Most I've seen come through here."

"I'd better run these over to the bank and get them in there."

"See you later, Stan."

"You take care, Joe."

Stan walked to the bank with his vouchers, stepped inside and headed for the cashier.

"I need to deposit these things, Henry," he said as he began to sign them.

When he finished signing the last voucher, he slid them across the short shelf and said, "Here you go."

"That's quite a bit of reward money, Stan. But you earned every penny."

"Still wish I could have shot them coming into town rather than leaving."

Henry filled out the deposit slip and gave Stan a receipt with his current balance. It was back to a healthy $3274.14.

"Thanks, Henry," he said as he stuffed the papers into his pocket.

He returned to his office and began going through the wanted posters, taking his time reviewing each one closely and committing the drawings to memory.

———

Ellie left the house at eight-forty that morning wearing her riding outfit, walked to the stables and saddled her mare. She wasn't supposed to do such menial tasks, and in fact, she was discouraged from doing anything as plebian as even riding a horse. She was supposed to use the carriage.

But she wanted to ride for many reasons, so she mounted the mare, left the grounds, and reached the offices of the Pinkerton Agency just a minute later, dismounted then tied off the mare and entered the office, but didn't see Agent Bickerstaff anywhere.

She approached another agent and asked, "Excuse me, is Agent Bickerstaff available?"

"No, ma'am. He's off today. He went to Boulder to see a friend."

"Did he say what the friend's name was by any chance?"

"Not that I recall. He said it was somebody he knew in the war. Mumbled something about some woman wounding him more than any rebel ever did."

"Thank you," she answered, then turned and quickly left the offices.

She stepped onto the boardwalk then stopped and stared at her mare. She knew who Agent Bickerstaff was going to see. Stan was in Boulder and she must have wounded him horribly. She didn't give the possibility of danger for a young woman to ride unescorted all the way to Boulder a second thought. She stepped up onto her mare and set her off at a medium trot north out of Denver. She'd miss lunch, but she felt like she deserved some punishment for being so callous when he had shown up at her door.

She thought she'd arrive in four and a half hours, which would get her into Boulder around two o'clock in the afternoon.

————

Stan left the office and had taken a few steps toward the livery to saddle the black gelding when he saw a lone rider entering the town from the south, then stopped to see if he could be any trouble. Any cause for concern was eliminated when he recognized John Bickerstaff.

Stan waited for him to get close and waved to get his attention. John recognized Stan, waved back, then saw the badge on his chest and was immediately curious about why he had taken the job.

He pulled up and stepped down, tying his horse at the hitching rail in front of the jail.

"John! Good to see you again. What brings you back to Boulder? Nothing bad, I hope," Stan said loudly as he approached his friend.

"No. You did. Can I talk to you for a minute?"

"Sure. I was going to get something to eat. Can I buy you lunch?"

"Now, you're talking."

He and Stan turned back toward the west end of town and began walking toward the diner.

John asked, "So, why the badge? You sure don't need the money."

"You're right, it wasn't about the money. There was only one reason I would take it. There was no one here, John. The only ones who wanted the job were either unqualified or wanted the badge as a license to do what they wanted. I guess the sight of the previous sheriff getting gunned down in front of his office scared off the good ones. There was no one to protect the innocents."

"Good reason. How much does it pay, anyway?"

"Fifty dollars a month and found. I don't need a room at the boarding house, but I do get free meals at the diner, and they said they were going to build an apartment behind the jail soon. At least that's what they promised."

"That's a good deal, Stan. I'm only making forty a month at Pinkerton's and wind up spending a lot of time on the road."

"You should take this one and I'll be your deputy during daylight hours."

"You're kidding. Aren't you?"

"Not at all. Think about it."

"I will. Trust me, I will."

They reached the café and Stan held the door open, letting John enter first.

Once inside. They found a table and as each man took a seat, Stan spotted Laura waltzing their way.

"Good afternoon, Stan. What can I get you?" she asked.

"Hello, Laura. Laura, this is my good friend John Bickerstaff. John, this is Laura Price."

John looked at Laura, smiled and said, "Well, it's my pleasure to meet you, Laura."

Laura beamed back at John, saying, "It's very nice to meet you, John."

Stan said, "I'm trying to convince John to take this badge, so I can get back to my ranch."

"I think you'd do a marvelous job, John."

Laura hadn't slowed down her smile since she set eyes on John, and Stan felt a huge sense of relief. Obviously, Laura had sensed his discomfort.

"What can I get you, John?" she asked.

"I'll have the special. Stan?"

"I'll have the same, Laura."

"I'll be right back," she said before flashing an even bigger smile at John, then turned and walked back to the kitchen.

After she walked away, John looked at Stan and asked quietly, "Does Laura have any gentlemen callers, Stan?"

"Nope. I had to escort her home last night because a couple of local thugs were harassing her. I think if she'd been spoken for, she would have had protection."

John nodded and smiled before saying, "Thanks for the information. Your job offer is looking better all the time."

Laura bought them their food and gave John one more grin before leaving.

"So, John, what brings you to Boulder?"

"The woman you went to see, Ellie Rafferty. After you left, I got really mad and was going to go over there and chew her out, but it would have gotten me fired, so I did what I do best and did some background investigating. I found out some interesting things from the neighbors.

"It seems that hubby is rarely at home. They told me rumors that they almost had to share. People love to pass gossip, especially to Pinkertons. Anyway, they seem to think he doesn't like women at all, and his wife spends most of her time alone."

"Then why wouldn't she see me?" Stan asked in frustration.

"It may not be what you think it is at all, Stan. Mrs. Farmington, her next-door neighbor, has had some incidents with her maid. She used to be the father's maid. She's Mexican and English isn't her strong point. She botches words that she never heard before. I'm beginning to think she did that and your Ellie didn't get the right message.

"The way you'd been going on about her, for her to act this way was totally out of character. Plus, when she came in to ask me to search for you, you had to see her face. She was anxious and hopeful, Stan. She wasn't in the least pretentious. I think you got it all wrong and need to try one more time."

Stan sat back in his chair, forgetting to eat. He'd told himself that he was shocked she had made such a momentous change, and maybe she hadn't. He tried to remember how he had asked to see her. If he had just asked to see Mrs. Rafferty as an old friend from her childhood, that would have been easily understood. But he had said that Piggy wanted to see Bucky, which would sound odd to anyone other than him or Ellie. Even someone with a good grasp of the language would have looked at him as if he was growing antlers from his belly button.

"I think I may have screwed this one up myself, John. I told her that Piggy wanted to see Bucky. That sounds odd even to me when I think about it."

"I have no idea what it means, either. Why don't you head down there right now? You can get there before five o'clock."

"Let's finish eating and I'll think about it while I'm eating."

Stan ate quickly, having decided right after John finished talking that he would go to Denver again. The only question was when. He wanted to race down there right now, but it would leave the town unprotected again. Then, he had an inspiration.

"John, when do you have to go back?"

"The day after tomorrow. Why?"

"If I swear you in as a deputy sheriff when we get back to the office, can you take care of the town for me while I run down to Denver? I'll be back as soon as I can."

"I could use the time to get acquainted with the citizens," replied John as Laura dropped off the bill and smiled warmly at him.

"Exactly," Stan agreed, but didn't sign the check. He just dropped a silver dollar on the table.

"Let's go, John. I want to be on the road in ten minutes."

"Then let's go."

They left the diner, and John tried to keep up with Stan, but Stan was already making clouds of dust on his fast pace toward the jail, and with Stan's longer legs, John had to jog to stay close.

Stan reached the office just a few seconds before John did, went inside and pulled one of the two deputy sheriff badges from his drawer and handed it to a heavily breathing, but smiling John Bickerstaff.

"Consider yourself sworn in, John," Stan said as he grinned and flew out of the office, his feet barely touching the floor.

He trotted down to the livery and went inside but didn't wait for Arnie. He began saddling the black gelding, and five minutes later, he was heading south at a brisk pace.

———

Ellie had maintained her fast trot since she left Denver and was just ten miles short of Boulder, so in another hour and a few minutes, she'd be there. She was getting excited about finally being able to see Stan and explain the horrible mistake she'd made, and knew he'd forgive her.

She was so wrapped up in her thoughts of Stan that she hadn't been paying too much attention to the two riders heading out of Boulder just two miles ahead. They weren't going to Denver though, they were going to take a cutoff to their ranch a couple of miles away. The ranch, and it was barely that, was a poor piece of land with limited water and a sorry excuse for a ranch house. It had a corral but no barn, and they used the house as a retreat of sorts. It wasn't even on the lists as a separate property on the county tax records any longer.

Bert Pritchard and his brother Oscar had grown up there. It didn't have to go to seed as badly as it had, it was just that both men were lazy. They weren't active criminals; they just took whatever was available. Local residents were aware of their tendencies to relieve them of almost anything that wasn't nailed down, so they watched them whenever they entered the town.

They were in a bad mood because this trip into town hadn't resulted in any booty at all, not even some day-old bread from the bakery.

They were riding south talking to each other about possible future targets.

Ellie had just passed the entrance to their ranch and hadn't even noticed that there was an access road as did most passersby.

———

Stan had the black moving at a fast trot, and for the long-legged horse, that was a good pace. He knew the Pritchard brothers, but hadn't had any dealings with them since he'd accepted the badge the day before. He was two miles behind them when they spotted Ellie riding toward them.

"Will ya look at that!" exclaimed Oscar as he pointed at Ellie still riding their way.

"Why's she out on the road all by her lonesome, you reckon?" his brother asked.

"Beats me. But she's gettin' along right quick."

Ellie still hadn't seen them, and they were less than a mile in front of her.

"She's still comin' right at us. Whaddya think, Bert?"

"She sure is dressed nice and lookit that horse. He sure is fancy. She's probably got money on her, too."

"Could turn out to be a good day after all. We grab her, run her back to the ranch and see what she's got. And I ain't talkin' just money, Bert."

They both snickered as they picked up the pace.

Then Ellie finally spotted them. She didn't like the looks of them but thought she could just shoot past them when they were close.

———

Stan had closed the gap to about a mile and had seen the two riders he easily identified as the Pritchard boys. But he saw another rider approaching them. *A woman all by herself on the road?* That was begging for trouble. He kicked the gelding up to a canter and pulled the Winchester out of its scabbard. What made him feel better was that he was the county sheriff and they were in his jurisdiction.

Ellie was gearing up to accelerate past the men when they pulled their pistols, shocking her, so she dropped the idea and thought momentarily of turning around, but they were too close.

"Where you goin' all in a hurry, little lady?" shouted Oscar, "You turn that pretty horse of yours around and start him trotting back the way you come. You hear?"

She didn't reply but began looking for an opportunity to run, not knowing how good they were with those shooters. She felt like an idiot again. She didn't even have a gun, not that she knew how to use one. There wasn't even one in the house, but she wished she was armed now.

She turned her mare around, then rode with one of the men riding beside her and the other on the other side, and both had their pistols trained on her.

"Turn left on that access road. That's our place," said Oscar.

Ellie imagined it was as foul as its owners, and after turning, it didn't take long for her to realize the accuracy of her assessment.

The brothers had been chatting loudly since getting Ellie under their control and were getting excited about what would soon be happening in their ranch house.

Ellie slowed her mare once they were on the access road. This was going to be bad. She was going to be deflowered by these two poor excuses for manhood and was pretty sure that she wouldn't be alive much longer. Then she sunk into a depression and began to think she was cursed, never to have found her Piggy, never to have found happiness. They were one and the same to her. She was going to die and so close to finding him.

FINDING BUCKY

Piggy was a lot closer than she or the Pritchards knew and was surprised that none of them had even noticed him, especially as big as he and his horse were, but he was grateful that they hadn't. He slowed the black to a trot as he reached the access road, just a couple of hundred yards behind them. He could see their pistols drawn, which would be a problem. The young woman was riding a pretty horse that resembled his buckskin mare, and she was dressed well, too. *Why would she be this far out of town?*

He was still closing the gap as his fast walking horse's long legs kept him moving quickly. Stan saw that they were approaching their dilapidated ranch house and recognized an opportunity as they'd have to dismount soon. He hoped that they wouldn't be smart enough for one of them to keep his revolver aimed at the woman when the other dismounted. They hadn't impressed him with their intelligence before, so it was a real possibility.

He cocked the hammer of his Winchester and kept moving, surprised that they hadn't heard his horse's hoofbeats yet.

The reason none of them had noticed him yet was that the brothers had been concentrating on Ellie and she'd been trying to come up with a way of making her escape.

"Hold it right here, lady. Now you step down and tie up that pretty mare of yours. You got a nice saddle, too. I kinda like your saddle better though," Bert said as he laughed.

Oscar joined him, but with more of a giggle than a laugh as all three of them dismounted at the same time, and Stan had his window of opportunity.

They were laughing so hard they didn't hear Stan get within thirty yards. They just never suspected that anyone could be there.

"Bert! Oscar! Drop those pistols! I've got a cocked Winchester pointed at your backs! Drop them now!" he shouted.

The sound of Stan's commanding voice startled them both, and Ellie felt a wash of relief that almost made her pass out but kept facing away until she knew it was safe.

"How do I know you got that Winchester, Mister?"

"It's not mister, Oscar. I'm Sheriff Murray and you know how good I am with my rifles."

Ellie heard the name, felt her knees weaken, then her eyes rolled back, and she simply melted to the ground.

"Drop them, boys! Right now, you won't hang. Don't make me shoot you, but if you don't drop them, I will shoot you both, just like I shot those outlaws who robbed the bank."

They both dropped their pistols at the same time and popped their hands into the air.

"Alright, now step away from the woman."

They complied, keeping their hands in the air. Stan stepped down and walked quickly behind each man. He tapped Oscar on the back of the head with his Winchester's barrel as he kicked Bert's pistol thirty feet away.

"Turn around, Bert. I need to tie your wrists."

Bert turned around and Stan popped him on the head with the barrel. He had to remember to get some handcuffs, or at least some pigging strings.

With both brothers down and out, he grabbed his canteen and jogged over to the fallen woman. He guessed the fear of being captured followed by the relief at being saved was too much for her. He rolled her over onto her back and was stunned how beautiful she was. She was exactly how he pictured Ellie would look when she was older. Her hair was even the same shade as Ellie's had been, only now it was silkier and longer.

He lifted her head from the ground, laid her back on his right knee, then held her head in his hand, and as he poured a dribble of water onto her forehead, he asked, "Ma'am?"

Her eyelids flickered, then slowly opened before her eyes focused, seeing a handsome face just inches from hers, but it was his kind, compassionate eyes that announced his identity.

"Piggy?" she asked quietly.

Stan felt his heart stop beating before he asked just as softly, "Bucky?"

She was so close, and even though he knew she was married, he didn't care. He leaned over and kissed her softly.

Ellie felt his lips touch hers and she wanted to cry, but instead put her right hand behind his neck and turned the soft kiss into a deeply passionate kiss releasing as much of her stored love as she could. She wanted this for so long, and now it was happening, and she didn't want it to end.

But it couldn't last forever, and when it ended, Stan looked down at his Ellie without saying a word.

Ellie was still sitting on the ground, her back on Stan's knee with his smiling face so close.

"Can you stand up, Ellie? I think my leg's falling asleep," he said softly.

She laughed at the thought that among all that had happened, Stan's leg falling asleep is the first thing he said to her other than her nickname.

She nodded and sat straight up as Stan stood, then took Stan's offered hand and let him help her rise to her feet. She didn't even look down at the two men who were going to cause her harm. She just grabbed hold of Stan as if she was never going to let go, because that was her intention.

"Ellie, do you want to press charges on these two yahoos?" he asked as she clung to him with his arms wrapped around her.

"What do you think, Stan?" she replied, just getting a thrill saying his name.

"I don't think a trial will do anything. I just want to leave them here."

"That's what I thought, too."

"Let's get you to Boulder. I have so much to tell you."

"I need to apologize first, Stan. I sent you away. I didn't even bother going downstairs to find out what was going on."

"No. Don't apologize. I should have just asked a simple question instead of trying to be cute. Let's forget that and start over. Okay?"

"Okay," she replied as she smiled.

Stan picked up his Winchester, slid it into his scabbard, then they mounted their horses and rode out of the access road and headed north toward Boulder, keeping them at a walk so they could hear each other.

FINDING BUCKY

"How did you find me, Stan?"

"John Bickerstaff told me that I had made a mistake and he told me about your maid's problems with odd English words, so I was going to ride to Denver to talk to you, rather than the maid. Why are you even up here?"

"I finally figured out what had happened. I was afraid you were going to go away again."

"I have a small ranch now, Ellie. I can't go anywhere."

"You have a ranch, Stan? That's wonderful. Will you show me?"

"I'd love to show you, but Ellie, you're married. Won't that cause a problem?"

"I don't care, Stan. I just want to be with you. Ever since we left Michigan, you're all I thought about."

"And you've been the focus of my life since we were in school. All through the war and the long journey down here, you were everything to me, Ellie. I love you so completely, and always have. You're the same wonderful person that I remember from those early days when we had to huddle together for comfort."

"You've changed remarkably in the way you look, Stan. But your eyes and your soul haven't changed at all, and for that, I am deeply grateful."

"What is your marriage like, Ellie? John gave me all sorts of ideas, but I'd rather you tell me."

"Stan, I'm still a virgin. George doesn't even touch me. I'm just a showpiece wife. I'm at his side for parties, and everyone thinks we're a handsome couple, but it's all phony. If I were to die tomorrow, he'd shed a few crocodile tears and tell his parents that he gave it the good old college try and continue on happily as he is."

"John said something along the lines that he lived away from you and that he didn't like women at all."

"You like women, obviously," she said as she smiled, remembering the effect she had on him as he held her close.

"I most assuredly do like women, but I love you even more, Ellie."

"I've never stopped loving you, Stan."

They reached Boulder sooner than they expected, and Stan turned at the sheriff's office, then asked, "Did you want to come in? John should be inside."

"Why?"

"I made him a deputy really fast, so I could race down to Denver."

She laughed, and Stan reveled in the melodious sound. His Ellie was with him at last.

They dismounted, tied off their horses, then crossed the boardwalk before Stan opened the door to let Ellie enter.

John was behind the desk and stood quickly when Ellie walked in followed by Stan.

"Guess who I found on the road?" Stan asked as he grinned.

"How are you, Mrs. Rafferty?"

"It's Ellie, John," she said as she offered her hand.

John smiled as he shook her hand.

"John, I'm going to show Ellie the ranch. Can you handle it?"

"It's really quiet, Stan. I'm fine."

"We'll see you shortly."

"I'll believe that when I see it," he replied as he laughed.

Stan just waved as he and Ellie returned to their horses.

"Ellie, how did you handle riding so far? Aren't you sore?"

"Very. But it was worth it. It's not too far to your ranch, is it?"

"Less than five miles. Another half an hour."

"Good."

Stan helped her up this time. Assistance that wasn't required but appreciated, nonetheless. Ellie was still beside herself with unrestricted joy at finding Stan.

They left Boulder and thirty minutes later, Stan showed her the entrance road, and the sign for the ranch overhead.

"The B-P connected, Ellie. I had to name the ranch and register the brand."

"Does that mean what I think it means?" she asked, looking at the large sign above the access road.

"It does. When I bought it, I thought if I gave it that name, it would mean that I'd find you at last."

"Well, you did, and I couldn't be happier."

As they rode toward the house, Ellie commented on how beautiful the house and barn were in their new paint. They stopped at the hitchrail and Stan tied off both horses and helped Ellie down. He took her hand and led her up the steps to the porch, unlocked and opened the door and held it for her as she entered.

Stan closed the door, and Ellie turned and looked at him. He took off his Stetson and tossed it on a chair, then unbuckled his gunbelt and set his guns on another chair, all with his eyes fixed on Ellie's. She took two small, slow steps toward Stan and tilted her face upwards ever so slightly.

Stan put his big hands on either side of her chin and kissed her softly at first, but gradually turned it into a much deeper kiss. Ellie felt a warm rush flow through her. She had never been kissed like this. She had never been kissed at all, except for that vapid slobber of George's when the minister had said, 'you may now kiss the bride'.

This was heaven, and the emotions that had been held in check for more than a decade were finally released along with all of the suspended passion that she'd been storing away each night that they'd been apart. Passion that had been released each night as she dreamt of her Piggy.

Stan stepped back and said quietly, "Ellie, I know you're a married woman, but I know that I love you so much that I can never let you go. How can we make it work?"

Ellie answered in a husky voice she didn't know she had, replying, "I don't give a damn about anything right now, Stan. I want you to make love to me so badly. I want your love. All of it. I need your love. Please, Stan."

Stan didn't answer, but he knew above all else, he wanted Ellie to realize just how much he loved her.

He took her hand and led her to his bedroom as she trembled in anticipation. For so long, she had waited and fantasized about this moment. She wouldn't ask Stan to be gentle because it was her first time, she just wanted him, and however he made love to her would be what she wanted.

Stan began kissing her again, and she held him tightly as he did. As she felt him press against her, she knew he was ready, and thought it would be a short, but passionate few minutes of frenzied lovemaking. She simply had no experience in the passions of lovemaking and hadn't even talked to her mother or any other woman about it…especially not her mother. She was truly innocent, but at the same time, felt an enormous sense of freedom.

Stan pulled her flush against him, feeling her body against his, kissed her once more before moving to her smooth, perfect neck. He slid her silky, light brown hair aside and continued to slide his lips on her neck. Ellie as already aroused beyond what she thought possible and they'd only started. *How much more excited could she possibly get?*

Stan slid his left hand behind her knees and lifted Ellie onto the bed, laying her softly with her head on the pillow. Ellie made a mistake in thinking that it was time, and knew she was ready, or thought she was, but Stan knew she had a long way to go. He took off her riding boots and tossed them aside as she stared at him anxiously.

Then he sat on the bed beside her, leaned close to her ear and whispered, "I'm going to make you as happy and as excited as I can make you, Ellie. Tell me what you want me to do to make you more excited. Show me. Talk to me. You are my one love, Ellie, and I'm going to show you that."

195

"Then show me, Stan. Be my teacher," she whispered in reply.

Stan sat on the edge of the bed, just looking into those loving, hopeful eyes. The same eyes that has made him feel warm and wanted when no one wanted to do anything more than humiliate him. When he was Piggy, he wanted to hear her voice and just to have her near. Now, he wanted her as a woman...his woman.

He started kissing her again as he said in a normal speaking voice, "Close your eyes, my love, and just enjoy my touches and kisses."

Ellie did as he asked, closed her eyes and spread her arms wide, and let him touch her with his fingers and lips. She wanted him to touch her everywhere, and at first, all she did was hope he'd touch her where she wanted his soft caresses.

But then, she began to talk to Stan, saying, "Here...please. There...just there," and he did as she asked. Then she felt his fingers unfastening the buttons on her blouse and grew even more excited at the prospect of feeling his kisses and his gentle touches on her bare skin.

He opened her blouse, kissed her perfect breasts, then pulled her back to her feet before he undid her riding skirt and let it drop to the floor. Then, he took off her blouse and let it float to the wood.

When she realized that she had done nothing yet, she understood that she could no longer just be an object of his love, she had to be a full partner in their lovemaking.

She opened her eyes and smiled at Stan as she began unbuttoning his shirt and pulled it back. She was stunned just how masculine his body was. She had never seen a man like this, admitting that she had never seen any man without his shirt. But this was more than she had expected. She ran her hands over his chest and stomach, finding it almost as arousing as when he was touching her, and was glad she had decided to be an actor in their passionate drama.

Stan pulled her camisole over her head, and Ellie reveled in her nakedness as he began to touch and kiss her breasts again. Stan then pulled off his boots and his pants and underpants, as she just looked at him. Inwardly, she smiled as she thought of him as a fat boy back in school. *But this! He was all man!* Her man.

He stepped back to Ellie and began kissing her again creating goosebumps across her entire body. She ran her hands all over him now that he was naked. *It was all so new and so exciting!*

Stan again picked her up and laid her on the bed. She knew this had to be the time. *It had to be!* She couldn't wait any longer, but she would be disappointed, but definitely not disappointed at the same time.

Stan knelt on the floor next to the bed, momentarily confusing Ellie. Then he leaned his head over her and kissed her lips. She grabbed his head and pulled him closer. She was losing control of herself and was grateful that she was. Stan was taking his time, and she began talking to him again. Asking him to touch her, to feel her.

Stan not only touched her, he began to kiss her everywhere, or just gently slide his lips across her skin. It was driving her insane. *She had been missing out on so much for so long!*

Stan was just as enthralled with his Ellie as she was with him. She was so much a woman. *Who could deny her anything?* He was doing everything he could imagine that would raise her level of excitement. He may have dallied with other women, but he needed to let Ellie know how much he loved her.

Ellie felt her toes curl as he would kiss her. She was grabbing anything nearby to stay on the bed, writhing like a snake and making noises she didn't know she was capable of making. Then she began demanding that he take her. She was becoming vulgar and whore-like, but she didn't care. Stan was telling her what he was going to do next and she begged him to do it.

This was beyond anything she had ever imagined. Her hips were moving everywhere as Stan kept kissing and touching and sliding his fingers along her skin, sometimes gently and other times much harder because she asked him not to be gentle.

Finally, she knew she was beyond ready. She began to believe she would die unless he ended this.

"Stan! Please! I need you! Now!" she shouted.

"Now, Ellie," he said quietly as he joined her on the bed.

Ellie had vaguely remembered when this had all started how the first time was supposed to be painful, but it wasn't. To her it was a combination of blessed relief and overwhelming ecstasy. She clawed at Stan's back as he continued to kiss her neck and had her wrists pinned back against the pillow. Her eyelids were fluttering like crazed butterflies as he continued. She pushed up with her hips and cried out as they finished at long last.

As they receded from nirvana, Stan and Ellie slowed and then finally lay quiet, holding each other tightly still. Stan was still kissing her softly and she didn't want to talk. Ellie just wanted to simmer in the experience, to keep the passion alive.

FINDING BUCKY

After a few minutes of contented closeness, Ellie finally asked softly, "Stan, what happens now? I can't go back. If I have to stay in this bedroom for the rest of my life, I will."

Stan kissed her softly on her forehead and replied, "No, sweetheart. You won't have to stay in the bedroom all the time. Granted, I'll be with you here often, but in a little while, I'll show you your new home. Then tomorrow, I'll go to Denver and make everything better."

"But Stan, George and his father are very powerful men."

"Ellie, I'll take care of everything. I'm never going to lose you. You're mine now, and I'm yours. Nothing will ever separate us again. You're my wife now, Ellie, and we just consummated our marriage."

Ellie suddenly believed that somehow Stan would make everything right. She didn't know how. She just knew he would.

"I feel like your wife too, Stan, and I trust you. I'll stay here and wait for you," she said softly, then paused, before asking, "Stan, could I ask you something? You know that was my first time. Is it always going to be like that?"

"No, Ellie, it won't."

"Oh. I didn't think so. It was because it was all new to me that it was so exciting."

"No, I meant the next time will be much better. I'll be able to go a little slower and make you much more excited."

"You don't mean that!" she exclaimed as she looked at him with wide eyes.

"I do. I could prove it to you right now, but I'd like to show you the ranch first."

"You could do that? I mean, right now?"

"With you? Anytime, Ellie."

Then she asked, "Stan, did I embarrass you with some of the things I said?"

Stan laughed softly and replied, "Hardly, Ellie. It makes it more exciting, doesn't it?"

Ellie was relieved and pleased, because that's exactly what it did.

"Yes, it did. Stan, would it embarrass you if I asked you how many women you've been with?"

"No, it wouldn't. I've slept with six different women in the past ten years. That's how I learned to make love to you properly, Ellie. One of them was like a teacher, explaining exactly what she wanted. Now I know how to make you feel every bit of pleasure I can give you."

"Then I'm glad you did."

"But I never told one of them that I loved her because I couldn't lie, Ellie. I knew I could only love you."

Ellie sighed and pulled in even closer. This was bliss.

After a few more minutes, they mutually agreed to go and see the ranch. They dressed, and Ellie learned the pleasure of mutual voyeurism. That, coupled with some kissing and fondling, stretched the process. Stan had to finally dress quickly to prevent the inevitable.

FINDING BUCKY

They finally mounted their horses again and rode the perimeter of the ranch. Stan showed Ellie the spring and creek. When she asked about the rock patio, she was intrigued with the idea of swimming in the pool naked with Stan. She was surprised how easily she had fallen into the idea of making love in new places. She wasn't surprised at all how easily she and Stan had meshed after all these years. They knew each other much better than couples who courted for a decade. They knew each other better when Stan was ten and she was nine.

They returned to the house and Stan began to cook, but Ellie shoved him aside and enjoyed the chance to cook a full meal. She asked Stan to tell her about the ride from Fort Union. So, as she cooked, he narrated.

He ended the story with the bank holdup. She was surprised that she hadn't heard about it when he had told her that he hoped that his name appearing in so many newspapers would lead her to him.

When she served him dinner, he was impressed with how well she cooked.

"When did you learn to cook? I thought you had a cook."

"I do. But I sat and watched her cook and talked to her. She let me cook sometimes when my husband wasn't around, and I really enjoyed it."

"Well, this is great. I'd like to keep you around."

"I'd like to stay around. Stan, this is the life I wanted. I wanted to be loved and live in a nice house with my husband and have his babies. I wanted to be able to go riding and feel the sun in my face and the wind in my hair. This is heaven for me, Stan."

"It's only heaven because I have you here with me. Ellie."

After dinner, Stan helped Ellie clean up. They stood at the sink washing dishes and pots and pans, talking of what had happened to each of them over the years. Ellie learned about his wartime experiences and was so amazed he had come through it with so little in the way of damage to his wonderful heart and personality.

After they finished cleaning, Stan took Ellie's hand.

"I have some things to show you, Ellie."

She thought they were going to the bedroom for more instruction, but they stopped in the last bedroom, his weapons room.

He sat her on the bed and opened a pannier that was in the corner that contained all the ammunition and a few other things and pulled out the Cheyenne war axe.

"What is that?" she asked with wide eyes as he handed it to her.

"This is a Cheyenne war axe. It was given to me by the last Cheyenne warrior in the first attack."

"It's awfully heavy."

"It's meant to crush enemy's heads."

She gingerly put it down on the bed as Stan reached in and took out the two Arapaho war tomahawks and handed them to Ellie.

"These are like the war axe only smaller."

"Those are Arapaho war tomahawks. I took those off the Arapaho warriors who were trying to recapture Mary, the Ute woman who I told you about."

"These aren't as frightening as the war axe."

"The reason I showed you these was to lead up to something else. I had four of the war axes when Mary brought me to her village. I gave two to her husband, Red Hawk, who presented them to his two sons. Mary was grateful and presented me with something to ensure my safe passage anywhere in the Ute nations."

Ellie knew it wasn't going to be an instrument of war.

Stan pulled the shawl from the pannier and showed it to Ellie. Then he stood and spread the shawl out to its full length on the bed next to her.

"Stan, that is so beautiful!" she said as she ran her fingers across the woven cloth.

Stan had her stand facing away from him, then picked up the shawl and gently placed it over her shoulders. When he did, Ellie felt a rush of warmth.

Stan looked into her eyes and said, "When I saw it, I thought the blue was the same shade as your eyes, but Mary told me something else about the shawl. It means more than just to tell Utes that the bearer is a friend and to grant him safe passage and protection. She said it also is a sign of perfect love, and to give this to the woman I love to give her safe passage to my heart. You've always had that passage, Ellie, and now you've reached your destination."

She turned around and pulled the shawl closer. She wasn't sure if the warm rush she was experiencing was from the shawl or from Stan's eyes.

She spoke softly, "Stan, show me perfect love."

Ellie put out her hand and led Stan into what she already considered their bedroom to experience the immense love they already knew they shared.

CHAPTER 7

The next morning, after they finished the breakfast that Ellie had prepared, they walked out to the barn where Stan saddled the black gelding while Ellie watched.

He had come up with his daring plan last night and thought of it as a strategic plan that was built on sound intelligence and all he needed to do was follow the tactics.

He finished saddling his tall gelding, then smiled at her and said, "You make me want to stay home, Ellie, but I'll do what needs to be done. I'll tell John, too. I'll be back late this afternoon. Ellie, did you want anything from your house at all?"

Ellie had to think for a minute, then replied, "No, I don't think so."

"You don't want your clothes or jewels or anything?"

"Not really. I'd probably just give the clothes away."

"Alright. Let's hope this happens the way we hope it will."

"With all my heart, Stan, I want this."

"Me, too," he said, pulling her into another hug and kissing her.

"I'll be back as soon as I can," Stan said as he looked into her eyes.

She just sighed and watched him turn to leave.

He mounted the black horse and rode out of the barn. When he turned off the access road toward Boulder, he could still see Ellie on the porch waving. He waved back and headed into town. It was a sight he knew that he'd never tire of seeing.

When he arrived in Boulder, he went to his office and found John waiting. John greeted him with a giant grin, and Stan wasn't sure if it was for him or for himself.

"John, I'm going to have to run to Denver again."

"I figured as much. Taking Ellie with you?"

"No. I left her at the ranch. This is going to be a mad dash, a little bit of blackmail followed by a return sprint. I told Ellie what I was going to do almost as a battle plan."

He smiled and asked, "Can I guess this involves chatting with her husband?"

"Nope. My first target will be her father-in-law."

Understanding Stan's plan, or at least thinking he had, caused him to nod his head and say, "That might work. I've been thinking, Stan, and I think I'll take you up on your offer, if it's still open. I really like Boulder, and I'd like being part of a community."

"You like having Laura around," Stan said with a grin.

"Yeah, well, there is that."

"I'll be back around four or five o'clock, John. Tomorrow, we'll talk to the county commissioners."

"Sounds good. If you have time, can you swing by my office and tell them I've found a better job?"

"I'll do that. Well, I'm off."

"Good luck, Stan."

Stan waved and jogged back to the gelding and was out of Boulder five minutes later, burning up the road to Denver. He had the gelding at a fast trot and watched him for any signs of fatigue, but not finding any. He'd be in Denver by noon at this rate.

He reached Denver faster than that, arriving at 11:50. He was about to initiate his first phase of his plan and was convinced that he'd be returning with the enemy's colors when he rode back.

He made sure his badge was prominently displayed as he rode to the First Colorado Bank, tied the reins around the hitching post and walked inside. He felt a little out of place when he arrived. He was dusty, and the bank was immaculate, but that didn't impact his opening thrust.

He stepped up to a clerk and said, "Excuse me. I'm Sheriff Stan Murray from Boulder. I need to see Mister Geoffrey Rafferty."

"You need to see the bank president?"

"Please."

"And what does this regard?"

"It's of a personal nature involving a family member."

"Very well. I'll see if he's busy."

As the clerk walked away and disappeared into a long hallway behind a frosted glass door, Stan wondered what the scion of a banking family looked like. He also wondered where Ellie's fake husband was, but this visit was going to be with his father.

The clerk came out of the door, made eye contact with Stan and waved him through the private doorway. When Stan passed through, the clerk closed the door and led Stan to the end office. He rapped on the door and opened it after a few seconds even with no response from behind it.

Stan entered, the clerk closed the door and Stan met Mister Geoffrey Rafferty, father of George and father-in-law to Ellie. He was a lot smaller than Stan expected, around five and a half feet tall and was showing the signs of a lifetime of living well. He had large jowls, sported a full beard, which made him seem even thicker, and had bushy gray eyebrows above his piercing brown eyes, his most noticeable feature.

Mister Rafferty indicated a chair in front of his desk and Stan took a seat, removing his Stetson as he did.

"What can I do for you, Sheriff? Percy tells me this is a personal matter involving a family member."

"Yes, sir. It's somewhat awkward, to be honest, but I have your daughter-in-law in custody in Boulder."

"*What?* My son didn't say anything about her being gone! Are you sure you don't want to talk to my son?"

"No, sir. I thought it was better to talk to you. You'll understand why when I'm finished. I'm not surprised that your son was unaware of her disappearance from what Mrs. Rafferty said, sir. Again, this is very awkward, and it has been kept in the strictest confidence. Only I and Doctor Henry Ainsworth know about it."

"Yes, yes, get on with it," Mister Rafferty said, beginning to sense a scandal in the making.

"Very well. It seems that Mrs. Rafferty arrived outside of Boulder late yesterday afternoon. I was on the road south of Boulder and spotted her being abducted by two local men, Bert and Oscar Pritchard.

"I got behind them and forced them to let her go. She passed out and after I gave her some water, she asked me to take her away from there, and I assumed she meant the Pritchard ranch. When we were leaving and reached the end of the access road, I asked her where she was from because I didn't recognize her at all, and she isn't the kind of woman one would forget."

"No, that's true."

"Well, sir, she told me that she was Mrs. George Rafferty from Denver and I asked if she needed a carriage with an escort to take her back home, and she surprised me when she said that she'd never go back. She said she was tired of being a showpiece wife."

Geoffrey was shocked and exclaimed, "*Why would she say such a thing?* That girl has been given everything! She has no right to complain."

"I could see that, sir, just from the high quality of her clothes and her beautiful horse. But that wasn't the problem, you see. It's why I came to see you rather than your son."

"Go on."

Stan looked around as if someone might be listening.

Then he leaned forward conspiratorially and said in a low voice, "She said she's not going back to live with a man who has never even touched her since they were wed, and that she was, um, still intact."

That news stunned the elder Rafferty, who had always suspected that of his son, but adamantly refused to believe it.

"She's lying! My son is a handsome, virile young man."

"Well, sir, that's what one would think because I thought no man could refuse a young woman as perfect as she, but she demanded that the local physician examine her to verify her claim. I was somewhat embarrassed to comply with her request, as you can imagine. I mean, I don't have a problem facing hardened criminals, but this was very different and made me very uncomfortable. But she was adamant, so I did as she asked.

"I left her with the doctor and as I waited, I knew I had a problem regardless of what his examination discovered. You and I both know that her husband has the right to come to take her back to Denver, even if she doesn't want to go.

"In fact, that was why she told me that she ran away, to get to someplace where an independent doctor could confirm what she claimed. She said that if the doctor verified her claim, she could file for an annulment on the grounds that the marriage had never been consummated."

Rafferty's bushy eyebrows were almost to his hairline as he asked, "Did he confirm her unsullied condition?"

Stan sighed loudly, nodded, then said, "Yes, sir, I'm afraid so. When Mrs. Rafferty arrived in Boulder, she was in fact a virgin."

Geoffrey Rafferty was rocked. *How could his son not bed that gorgeous woman two or three times a week?*

He recovered from his shock, then replied, "As I'm disappointed that she's gone, it's not important. My son will let her have her annulment and remarry."

"No, sir, it's not that simple. You see, she is demanding more than just an annulment. She was angry and frustrated, so she had already contracted with the Pinkerton Detective Agency to find out where your son spends his nights, because it wasn't in her bed. Did you want the details of where he spends his nights?

"I don't have the report with me as she wouldn't let it out of her sight, but between you and me, man to man, reading it kind of made my stomach turn. She said that she was going to make the report public unless she was allowed to keep her current lifestyle and asked me to come here and talk to you. I was going to object, but she made one valid argument which forced my hand. This whole affair is very awkward for me as I'm really out of my element here, sir."

He leaned back and closed his eyes. All those rumors over the years were true after all. *This can't come out!*

"What do you think she wants to keep it quiet?" he asked quietly.

"She told me that she wants the carriage with all of her possessions, a quiet annulment of the marriage, and a financial settlement to ensure her way of life, whatever that means."

"This is blackmail! You can arrest her for that, can't you?"

"Yes, sir, it most certainly is, and I most certainly can arrest her, and in fact, I even threatened her with serious jail time for the crime, but she just laughed and said she'd rather be in jail than living in that gilded jail she's been living in and that it would be fun spilling all the dirt during the open trial. That was the argument she used to persuade me to come here, when she said you wouldn't want to read about her revelations in the newspapers. But if you'd like to press charges for attempted blackmail, I'll talk to the prosecutor. I know I'd like to press her."

Mister Rafferty missed Stan's double entendre. He was just trapped, and he knew it. If he pressed charges and went to trial, it would all come out, and if he let it go, that woman would still make that report known. The public humiliation would be immense, and he couldn't allow that. He had to give in to her demands, but would need some proof that she wouldn't release the report.

"How can I be sure the report is destroyed?"

"I will handle it, sir. As a third party, I can guarantee that no report will exist when this whole episode is over."

"How much compensation will suffice? Or did she not name an amount?"

"She didn't, sir. She just said she wanted to keep living as she does now and reminded me that she is still a very young woman."

"Do you think ten thousand dollars is enough?"

"I have no idea, sir. Do you think this greedy woman would be satisfied?"

"Honestly? No, I don't believe that it would. If I were in her shoes, I wouldn't settle for less than twenty thousand. But that's as far as I'll go."

"She mentioned a personal account as well."

"I'll have the money placed into her personal account today. I have an attorney for private affairs who will have the marriage annulled quickly, but I want your word as a peace officer that she will destroy the report and never say another word about the marriage."

"I'm sure she'll agree, sir. And I will watch her burn that report as if it never existed. I'll even threaten her with incarceration if she has a second copy, but I don't believe she does because this one was signed by the agent and they don't make a second copy. I believe that she was just happy to be out of Denver. I think she said something about moving southwest."

Her soon-to-be ex-father-in-law nodded, then said, "Probably all the way to California. I'll make it all happen quickly. Are you going back to Boulder today?"

"I had planned on it."

"Could you do me a favor and drive their carriage with her personal effects? I'd just as soon get them out of the house."

"I can do that, sir. Is the carriage and team at the residence?"

"It's in the carriage house in back. Here, let me write you a note. Just give it to Maria Elena, the maid. She can help you empty the room."

"That's fine, sir. I may not be able to return the carriage and team for a few days, though."

"Tell her to keep them as part of the compensation. My son can use my carriage if he needs one."

"Sorry to be part of all this, Mister Rafferty. I would much rather have preferred to spend the day in Boulder," he said, meaning every word.

The bank president then reached into his pocket, pulled out three double eagles and handed them to Stan.

"This is for you to let you know that I appreciate your help."

"Why thank you, Mister Rafferty," Stan said as he accepted the money.

Rafferty wrote out the note and handed it to Stan.

"When you leave, send Percy back in here and I'll take care of the other parts of the arrangement. She'll be able to transfer the money to whichever bank she chooses."

"I think she'll transfer it to our bank in Boulder and then decide where she goes from there."

"That's wise. Thank you for your help, Sheriff. I'll send the annulment to your office and you can give it to her after she burns that report," he said as he stood, and reached out his hand.

Stan rose, shook his hand and felt a little guilty for what he just did, but the feeling passed quickly.

Stan rode to #14 3rd Street and dismounted, thinking that this should be interesting. He stepped up on the porch, pulled the doorbell cord, and Maria Elena answered the door a minute later.

"Good afternoon, ma'am."

"Mrs. Rafferty is not here," she said quickly remembering Ellie's last instructions to the stranger with the odd request.

"I know, ma'am. She's in Boulder, and Mister Geoffrey Rafferty gave me this note for you. I'm to take the carriage and all of her things from her room, including her clothing and jewelry and everything else, put it in the carriage and take it to her."

Maria Elena nodded and left the door open without even reading the note. The man was wearing a badge, so he must be telling the truth. She knew that Mrs. Rafferty was unhappy and understood the reason. She just hoped that Mrs. Rafferty would find a real man and maybe the handsome lawman would be the one she chose. Despite her professional indifference, she was impressed with the young sheriff.

"I'll go and get the carriage ready," he said.

"Alright," she said, then smiled, and walked away, her voice echoing in the large, empty house.

Stan walked around outside the house and found the carriage house easily enough. The carriage was very impressive, and not as ornate as he expected, but very voluminous. He found four carriage horses, but had been expecting two, failing to realize that two-horse teams were for the semi-wealthy, and the Rafferty family was well past that level. Maybe he should have pushed for a higher settlement, but he knew that the amount she was getting didn't matter. His Ellie would soon be free and would become his Ellie in every way possible.

The team was a matched set of gray geldings, and he soon had them in harness and led them to the back door.

Then he began to move Ellie's possessions. He was taken aback by the amount of clothing she had. She had several furs, two boxes of jewelry, and he took her beauty items as well: her silver hairbrushes, fancy combs, perfumes and soaps. He didn't bother with the makeup, though. Ellie was too beautiful without it. The oddest thing he found was a blonde wig. He was going to leave it, but on a whim, added it to the stacks, curious as to why she would even have it.

It took almost two hours to empty out her room before he finally rolled the carriage to the front of the house and walked his gelding to the carriage house and let him eat his fill of oats and drink before the trip back to Boulder. He then hitched the gelding to the carriage.

Before he left Denver, he remembered to stop at the Pinkerton Agency where he told the boss that John was leaving.

The boss asked why, and Stan told him he got a job offer and he was smitten with a local girl, which he understood, so the chief Pinkerton agent told Stan to pass on his best wishes to John. Stan shook his hand, waved and left the office.

Stan trotted across the boardwalk, climbed up onto the driver's seat and left Denver. It was later than he expected, but he had a lot of things stuffing the carriage and wondered what Ellie would say to all this. He knew she'd be happy about the annulment, because he was ecstatic. He and Ellie could finally be married as they had been teased about doing when they were Piggy and Bucky. But there would be no laughter or joking when Mr. and Mrs. Stan Murray were joined in marriage.

He had the carriage moving at a nice rate with four horses. It had a very smooth ride, and as high as he was in the driver's seat, he had a commanding view of the surrounding area.

———

Stan pulled into Boulder shortly before eight o'clock, stopped at the livery and had Arnie trail hitch his buckskin to the carriage with the big black.

As he was hitching the buckskin to the back, Arnie said, "Those are some mighty fine carriage horses, Stan."

"They are. You should come out to the ranch sometime and check out my other horses. I think all eight of those mares are in foal."

"I'm not surprised."

He climbed back onto the carriage and drove to his office, stepped down and hadn't hit the boardwalk when the door opened, and a grinning John Bickerstaff stood looking at him.

"Good God! Stan, what do you have?" he asked as he stared at the stuffed carriage.

"I have Ellie's stuff from Denver. I'm going to run out to the ranch now. I told your boss that you were resigning, and when he asked why, I told him you were smitten by a local girl and he said he understood that and wished you well."

John laughed and said, "Thanks a lot, Stan."

"I'll see you in the morning."

John waved as Stan climbed back on the carriage and left Boulder heading west, wondering how the hell he'd pulled this off.

Twenty minutes later, Stan reached the access road and saw Ellie on the porch waving at him. He waved wildly back and couldn't wait to tell her what had happened, although she might have already known something had happened as he was driving the family conveyance.

He pulled the carriage up to the house and clambered down, trotted up to her, pulled her off the ground in a hug, kissed her and kept kissing her as he swung her around in a circle.

When she started laughing, he let her back down.

"What did you do, Mister Murray?" she asked as she looked at the carriage.

"Come and sit on the porch and I'll tell you the whole gruesome story."

She was almost giggling as she took his hand, walked to the porch and they sat on the top step.

"We need a pair of rocking chairs, I think," he said.

"Enough delay. What did you do?"

"Just as I told you, I went and visited Mister Rafferty."

"You saw George?"

"No, I visited Geoffrey."

"And he didn't throw you out?" she asked in surprise.

"No, I arrived with my badge on and told him I needed to see him as the Sheriff of Boulder in my official capacity because of a personal matter. When I saw him, I acted like I was embarrassed to be seeing him and then I confided that I had his daughter-in-law in custody."

"*You said I was arrested?*" she asked with wide eyes.

"No. I said you were in custody, and you are, by the way. You are in my personal custody and will be that way for the rest of our lives. Anyway, I told him that you were trying to get away from Denver, and I said that I had told you that your husband could take you back if he wanted, no matter what you wanted. Then I said you had told me that he wasn't your husband because he had never consummated the marriage."

"You didn't!" she exclaimed with wide eyes and raised eyebrows.

"I did. Now, you need to understand that I only told one fib during this whole process, well maybe two. After he said that was nonsense, I told him I had it medically confirmed."

Ellie almost choked when he used that term to describe how he'd confirmed her condition.

"I told him that when you arrived in Boulder you were intact. He was stunned when I told him that, too. Luckily, he didn't ask if you still were virginal. He said he was surprised your husband wasn't taking you to bed two or three times a week, which I thought was too infrequent as I'm planning on two or three times a day.

"Anyway, then I mentioned that you had contacted the Pinkerton Agency and had a report made, and I implied that you knew where George was going at night. I did say that when I looked at the report, it made me sick. My guess is that he had heard the rumors of his son and refused to believe them until I told him about the fictitious report, which was the fib.

"Then I told him that you wanted to be free to go away but wanted to keep your current lifestyle. He asked what you wanted, and I began making things up. So, here's what you wind up with after everything is all said and done.

"You get the carriage and horses, all your clothes, furs and jewels, and I even took your toiletry items. For some reason, I even brought your blonde wig, but I have no idea why. I was getting silly by that point. You'll be able to transfer your bank account money to a new account here. Oh, and it'll be twenty thousand dollars more than what you had before."

"*What?*" she almost shouted.

"I told him that you wanted to live the way you wished, and he must have thought that it meant you wanted to live lavishly. So, he started with ten thousand dollars, and I asked him if he thought the greedy woman would take that, and he doubled it. So, you have a lot more money than I do."

"Stan, what can I say? You're amazing," she said before she leaned over and kissed him.

"Oh. I almost forgot, in the next few days, I'll receive your marriage annulment in my office. And I'll have to watch you burn that fictitious Pinkerton report before I give it to you."

Ellie squealed, then bounced into the air and began dancing around the front yard. Stan was smiling as stood and watched his future wife. When she saw him smiling at her, she reached over and pulled her to him to join her in her dance, which he was only happy to do.

After almost a minute of dancing in the dirt of the front yard, Stan finally pulled his still grinning Ellie to a stop.

"Ellie, I think we need to empty the carriage, so I can get the horses put away."

"Okay. Did you eat anything today after I fed you breakfast?"

"No. I was too anxious to come back and give you the good news."

"You can start taking things inside and I'll get something for you to eat."

"Thank you, Ellie."

Stan began unloading all of Ellie's things, putting them in the spare bedroom. It took a lot less time to unload because the ranch house was much smaller and didn't have a long, winding staircase to navigate. Once it was empty, he led the carriage to the barn, unharnessed the four carriage horses and his two horses and put them in the corral. He decided right then that he'd add a carriage house with at least six more stalls for horses. He might make it bigger with all those mares in foal.

After the horses were all cleared, watered and brushed down, Stan felt the energy just drain from him as all of the tense drama of the day was over.

But Ellie was in the house making him dinner and would share his bed tonight. His Ellie was home for good now.

He walked into the house, closed the front door and could smell Ellie's presence. It wasn't the lilac toilet water that Laura Price used. It was much more delicate and subtle. He walked back to the kitchen and stopped before entering and watched as Ellie cooked. She had a gentle smile on her face, a look of total contentment, and he hoped he could keep it on her face permanently.

He stepped quietly behind her.

"I can hear you back there," she said loudly.

Stan laughed and said, "Just admiring the view, ma'am."

She wiggled her behind and replied, "There. That's just for you."

"I appreciate it, ma'am," he replied as he laughed.

Lord, he was going to enjoy having Ellie around!

He reached over and took the coffee pot and poured himself a cup. It was pretty strong after sitting in the pot for a few hours, but he'd had worse, especially in the army.

He sat down and continued to admire Ellie, not just because of the way she looked, but the way she simply was.

Ellie brought him a plate of food and sat down.

"Now, what do we do, Stan?" she asked as she sat next to him.

"That is entirely up to you, Ellie. If you would do me the honor, I would like to marry you and live here with you on our ranch. I love you, Ellie, and I want to spend the rest of my life with you."

Ellie rubbed a tear from her left eye, and replied, "I want to marry you so much, Stan. It's all I've dreamed of for the past ten years."

"Then as soon as those annulment papers arrive, we'll go see Judge Whitaker and get married."

"Will it be that easy?"

"It will."

After they finished eating and cleaning up, Stan and Ellie had some fun going through all of her things. He asked about the wig and she told him that George had insisted for a costume party.

"I was humiliated. I was supposed to be Little Bo Peep," she said as she stared at the wig.

"Want to burn it?" he asked.

"Could I?"

She clenched the wig in her fist and trotted into the kitchen where Stan opened the firebox door and Ellie dramatically tossed the wig into the fire. It flashed in a crackling blue blaze and vanished in seconds.

"*What was that made of?*" Stan asked, surprised at the almost fireworks nature of the flames.

"It was supposed to be human hair, but I don't know how they glued it altogether."

He closed the door and they returned to the bedroom, but not the one with the clothes.

———

While Stan and Ellie were enjoying their new relationship, George was sitting in the parlor with his father.

"Your wife won't be coming back, George. It's better this way. Trust me."

"Why did she leave in the first place? I bought her everything she wanted."

"Who knows? Women are just that way."

"Will I have to marry again?"

"No. You've done your duty. We'll just say she had to return home to Michigan because of her grandparents."

"That's good. What about that annoying father of hers? He's not worth having around."

"Fire him."

"I'll notify Charles with the store. He'll handle it."

"Can I ask you something about your wife?"

"Of course, you can, Father."

"Was she acceptable as a bed partner?"

George Rafferty didn't quite know how to respond to the question. He didn't think his father knew about his personal life.

"She was all right. She was kind of boring, really. I like them more active."

"Ah. I thought so. A regular prude, would you say?"

"That's it. She wanted to keep all her clothes on."

"Too bad. She must look spectacular without any," he said as he smiled.

George was getting nervous. This topic was unsettling.

"I don't know. She stayed dressed all the time."

"Getting that corset off must have taken time, though."

"She never let me take if off."

Geoffrey was looking for the confirming answer to what he suspected was true.

"Did you know what she did before she left?"

"No. Who knows?"

"She hired the Pinkertons to follow you."

George stuck his finger behind his celluloid collar and pulled it out to give him some breathing space.

"And what did they find?" he rasped.

"What do you think they found?"

"Nothing worth noticing. I spend a lot of time at the club."

"You don't go anywhere else? Would you like to read the report?"

"No, I don't need to. What do you want me to do? I just didn't want her. You made me marry her."

His suspicions were confirmed, but he still asked, "Would you marry a different woman?"

"No. I won't."

"Do you have any idea how much your activity has cost me?"

"No."

"You don't want to know. You have no idea how costly this incident was. She's up in Boulder now waiting for the annulment papers that will be sent tomorrow. Judge Carrington signed them this afternoon twenty minutes after that sheriff left. Now, there was a real man, George. Hell, I wouldn't be a bit surprised if he wasn't deflowering her already. If I knew you weren't touching her, I'd take her."

"But mother…"

"Your mother is a dried-up prude. How we ever had you is beyond me. I've been enjoying the pleasures of other women for years. That wife you just lost was better than any of them."

"Why is she in Boulder?"

"To get away from you. She probably wanted some loving that you didn't provide. The sheriff said she'd probably be leaving as soon as she gets the papers tomorrow, but I wouldn't be surprised if she stayed with that sheriff, either. Now, go home and stay there."

"Yes, Father."

George stood and left his father's house after hearing all of the revelations. But that woman was ruining his life and she was in Boulder, which was just a few hours away She was costing them money, too.

Well, George thought, she'll never get to spend it. He walked into his dark house and went to the library, pulled out the bottom drawer of the desk and removed a Colt 1862 Model Pocket Navy pistol. All five .36 caliber cylinders were filled, so he slid it under his belt and went to his room.

———

Ellie sighed as she clung to Stan. She felt so complete after just two days with the man she already knew was her husband for the rest of her life. She was free of her prison and living her life as she wanted with the man she wanted.

She felt Stan's left hand stroking her head softly and asked, "Stan, what will we do with all those gowns? They're a bit much, don't you think?"

"I think you might want to find one or two that Laura Price would like to wear."

"Who's she?"

"The waitress at the diner. I think John will be calling on her soon."

"Already?"

"It's been known to happen. Besides, they're yours to give away. You can do anything you want with them. I wouldn't throw them out, though. Some women could make a few alterations and make them into nice dresses. Now, the jewelry is interesting. I only took it to make sure they didn't get some of their money back. Some of them are a bit outrageous, but there are a few pieces that were very elegant."

"Thank you for noticing. I picked out the simpler designs myself. Mrs. Rafferty picked out the others."

"Tomorrow, I'll go to town and talk to the county commissioners about John. You can go through your things and decide what you want to do with them. Maybe your annulment papers will arrive tomorrow."

"Is that even possible?"

"When you have money, you can get things done very quickly. He probably has a good friend who's a judge."

"He does."

"Then he'll get it done. Men like Rafferty don't like to linger. He wants this done quickly and make it seem as if it your marriage never happened in the first place."

"What happens when he finds out you married me?"

"Nothing. He'll still want to avoid the scandal. As long as we don't say anything, he'll stay out of it."

"I'm a bit worried about George, though. He has a bad temper when he feels slighted."

"I'll keep an eye out for him. What does he look like, anyway? I've never seen him."

"George is about five feet and eight inches with dark hair. He's quite handsome, and his most notable feature is his beloved moustache. It's a handlebar moustache that he waxes constantly. He has a nervous habit with it, too. He always twirls it with his fingers or just slides his fingers over it."

"I'll tell John. John may recognize him anyway."

"I don't think so, unless he met him recently. When I first saw John, he mentioned that he had never met him."

"Well, I'll pass along the description, just in case."

"I want things to always be like this, Stan. Just us on our private paradise."

"Don't forget those babies you want to have."

"And our babies," Ellie said softly.

"I think we should make sure that happens, Ellie."

Ellie slid closer to Stan and kissed him, saying, "With pleasure," in her husky voice that Stan liked at moments like this.

CHAPTER 8

James McCormick walked into Rafferty's Emporium with a spring in his step. *Why not?* He was an important man now. He was one step down from running the store and knew he would soon take that last step. He would be the Big Man in the business soon. All because he and Ida had taken that risk ten years ago to leave Michigan and come to Denver, but he had never confided in his wife what the true reason was for their abrupt departure.

He had to leave suddenly because of the liaison he'd been having with Maude Murray. They had met when they had to see the schoolmarm about the behavior of their children. It seemed that Ellie had been seen giving Stanley a kiss on the cheek and such contact could not be allowed.

He had given Maude a big smile and it had evolved from there. He had thought they had been discrete, but then she told him in March of '57 that her husband suspected something, so he had to hastily sell the farm and move. He was horrified to find that Ellie had wanted to stay and be close to Maude's horrid son. That made the move even more urgent.

His shrew of a wife hadn't been at all pleased, and for once, he had put his foot down, but had only convinced her to go when he told her that their now pretty daughter wanted to marry that fat boy she had kissed in school.

He had planned on going to California, but their wagon wasn't doing well, and they had stopped in Denver. They had plodded along in their lives until that miraculous day when George Rafferty had fallen head over heels in love with their beautiful daughter, who was still mooning over that obnoxious Murray boy. It had taken quite a few threats to convince her to go through with it, but once that happened, the family's entry into a higher rung of society was assured.

Now he was near the pinnacle of success, and could almost hear the staff wishing him a good morning, sir, when he strode across the floor.

Oh yes, James McCormick definitely had a spring in his step this morning.

He gave casual waves to his workers as they began setting up for the day, then he reached the administrative offices and was headed for his own well-appointed office when his secretary, Will Litton, told him that the store president, Mister Carlisle, wanted to see him right away.

"Of course," he said, his heart suddenly racing.

This was it. Carlisle was going to let him know that he'd be taking over the store, probably with a substantial increase in salary.

James McCormick practically floated to Henry Carlisle's office. Henry was almost sixty. He should have retired years ago, but now he was leaving and he, Mister James Elrod McCormick would take the reins of command.

He opened the door to the president of the store's office and walked in. Vice presidents could do that, he thought with a smile.

"Good morning, Henry. You wished to see me?" he asked as he took a seat, uninvited.

"Yes, James. Don't bother sitting down. I've been notified by Geoffrey Rafferty that your services are no longer required. You may take any personal items from your desk," he said conversationally, as he handed McCormick an envelope.

"This is your salary payable to this date. Good day."

James McCormick stood there in stunned silence. *What had just happened?*

Mister Carlisle repeated in a firm, hard voice, "I said good day, Mister McCormick. You may leave my office."

McCormick picked up the envelope, then turned slowly and walked mindlessly out of the president's office. He was going to go to his office to retrieve his personal effects but realized he didn't have any, so he just continued walking until he left the store and kept going, leaving his buggy at the store's livery.

He reached his fancy home fifteen minutes later, walked inside, and Ida saw him enter.

"James, what are you doing home? Are you ill?" she asked.

He looked at her and said in a monotone, "I've been fired, Ida. They didn't say why. They just fired me."

Ida knew the horrible situation this was. When Ellie had married George Rafferty and they'd given James the job, they had bought the large, well-appointed house and taken out a mortgage; a mortgage happily financed at George's bank. They had been spending his salary buying things that allowed them to move in the elevated social status they now enjoyed.

Ida loved her new clothes and jewelry, and she thoroughly enjoyed being accepted by what she considered her peers. This would all be gone in an instant if James lost his job.

"This must be some kind of mistake. I'll go over to see that daughter of ours right now! They can't do this! She's got to have her husband straighten this out!"

Ida McCormick then grabbed her waistcoat and stormed from their house, leaving her speechless husband behind. It took her less than five minutes to reach Ellie's house where she stomped up the steps to the porch and was about to pull the cord for the bell when the door flew open and George Rafferty charged out the door, running into Mrs. McCormick. They both fell to the porch with George landing on his ex-mother-in-law. He pushed himself back to his feet and did not offer a hand to Ida as she lay sprawled on the polished oak wood, her dress having been thrown to her thighs, revealing her legs.

George just straightened out his jacket and began to pull on his moustache.

From her position flat on her back, Ida proceeded to dress him down for his crude behavior as she pulled her skirts back to cover her legs.

"George Rafferty, you have knocked me over, now help me up this instant!"

He looked down at Ida, and snarled, "I'm not helping you up, you cow. That bitch of a daughter of yours left me, and now I'm going to Boulder to straighten her out."

He turned and marched down the steps, then headed left and back to the carriage house, but then swore when he realized that it was empty. He marched off to his father's house, two doors down, to borrow his father's horse.

Ida still lay on her back, totally shocked by not only George's manner, but by his statement. *Ellie had left him? Whatever for?* She had everything: beautiful clothing, jewels, servants, and a handsome husband who had idolized her. *What more could any woman ask for?* But if she had deserted him, that was the reason behind James' termination.

She sat up, then stood and brushed herself off. She'd go and tell James about this incident, so they could correct their misbehaving daughter. George had said that Ellie was in Boulder, of all places, so they'd go to that town, find her, then set her mind straight, get her back to her husband, and James back on the job.

George was saddling his father's black stallion, still with no idea why his father rode such a brute of a horse. He preferred the smooth ride of a carriage, but he needed to get there quickly, but before he climbed on board, he moved the pistol to his jacket pocket.

He stepped up and rode the horse out of the carriage house and onto the street before heading north.

Forty minutes later, a courier carrying Ellie's annulment papers took the same road.

———

Stan was finding it hard to leave the house.

"Stan, it's almost nine o'clock. I think John will be worried," she said as she smiled.

"No, he won't. He's seen you," he replied still holding onto Ellie.

"One more kiss and then you need to go."

Stan made it a good one, with a minor fondle at the end.

"I suppose one of these days I'll get used to having you around, Ellie. I hope not, though."

She laughed and waved him on his way.

————

Stan had the big black gelding saddled quickly now that he had finally decided he needed to get to town. He had to meet with the county commissioners and get their approval for John to take over. It would be a no brainer, as he had decided to be an unpaid deputy. They'd be getting two lawmen for the price of one.

Thirty minutes later, he opened the door to the sheriff's office and found John sitting at the desk, the soles of his boots visible as he leaned back.

"So, there you are. Earlier than I expected, really," he said as he grinned, then pulled his feet off the desk and sat the front feet of the chair back to the floor.

"John, let's round up the county commissioners and get you appointed sheriff."

"You sure they'll buy it?"

"I'm going to make it too sweet an offer to pass up."

"Then let's go."

It took forty minutes to find all three commissioners, and rather than getting them all together for a meeting, Stan just explained what he wanted to do and introduced each one to John. His background and Stan's offer to stay on as an unpaid deputy did make it a no-brainer.

FINDING BUCKY

An hour later, John and Stan sat in the office, having exchanged badges and John was finally able to hear how Stan had 'convinced' Geoffrey Rafferty to part with everything so willingly. He laughed through most of the narration.

Stan was filling John in on the different businesses and some of the malcontents that he knew of when Phil Harper, the baker, walked through the doorway.

"Stan, that damned Jimmy Ryder and his partner Ed Crenshaw just walked off with a dozen doughnuts without paying."

Stan looked over at John and said, "I'll take care of this one, John. I have a deep personal relationship with Mister Ryder and his pal."

"Go right ahead, I need to read up on the local ordinances anyway."

Stan stood, and asked, "Where did they head off to, Phil?"

"Out in back of the feed and grain. I don't know if they're still be there, though."

"I'll find them and wish they never see another doughnut in their lives."

He followed Phil to his shop and surprised him by buying another dozen doughnuts. After he handed the paper sack to Stan, he had an idea what Stan was planning on doing and grinned.

Stan passed his black gelding that was still standing at his last stop, reached into the bag, took out a sugary doughnut and handed it to him.

"Sorry, big fella. I'll get you taken care of as soon as I handle our doughnut thieves," he said then followed it with a snicker.

He left the gelding and walked to the feed and grain store, then turned down the space between it and Richard Looper's hardware store. It wasn't hard to follow the boys' trail. They must have been eating doughnuts along the way leaving a Hansel and Gretel-like trail of crumbs. Stan entered the line of trees behind the stores and found Jimmy and Ed finishing off their doughnuts. They were sitting down and already were looking a bit out of sorts. Six doughnuts could have that effect.

"Howdy, boys. Having a picnic?" he asked loudly, startling the two overeaters.

"Kinda," replied Jimmy, "We just figured we'd take a break."

"Looks that way. You know, if you're working hard and need to take a break, nothing tastes better than a warm doughnut. I just bought some and was heading to the office when I saw you guys relaxing. So, I figured, why not share?"

Stan reached into the bag, pulled out a doughnut, then as he took a bite, he offered the bag to Jimmy. Jimmy thought he'd pass, but the sheriff seemed insistent, shaking the bag at him. He took one and then the sheriff offered one to Ed, who followed Jimmy's lead.

Both men nibbled on their doughnuts before Stan said loudly as doughnut crumbs flew out of his mouth, "Come on, boys! You can do better than that! You aren't sissies, are you? Girls take bigger bites than that."

Reluctantly, they both began taking bigger bites, despite their stomachs' protests.

This went on for all of three minutes before Ed finally leaned over and hurled his morning's doughnut intake across the gap and onto Jimmy's pants and boots. Jimmy reciprocated seconds later. Even Stan felt his stomach dance, but he held on.

"Now, boys, I don't want you stealing from our hard-working merchants anymore. This lesson just cost you a stomach revolt. I won't be so kind next time."

There was no response, and Stan didn't know if it would have any impact on either of them, but it might for a little while.

As he was behind the feed and grain administering his punishment, George Rafferty rode into town from the south. He had no idea where that woman was, but his father had said he was having the annulment papers delivered to the sheriff's office today. He doubted if the courier would have arrived yet, so he looked for the sheriff's office and found it quickly on his left.

He rode to the front of the office and stepped down, tying off the stallion. He walked inside and found John reading the ordinance book.

John looked up and asked, "What can I do for you?"

"I have some papers for Mrs. Ellie Rafferty."

"Fine. I'll take them and see that she gets them."

"No, I have to have her signature. They're very important papers."

It sounded reasonable to John, although he was wondering why a courier would be such a fancy dresser.

"She's at the B-P connected ranch. Take the road west out of town and two miles out, you'll see a cutoff to the southwest.

Take that and the ranch is around three miles further on the right."

"Thank you," he replied as he twirled his moustache.

He left the office, mounted his stallion, and was almost out of Boulder when Stan returned with his half bag of doughnuts smiling. He went inside and dropped the bag on the desk.

"Doughnut, John?" he asked as he grinned.

John opened the bag and took one, then said, "Good news for you, Stan. A courier just arrived with Ellie's annulment papers."

"Great! Where are they?"

"He said he had to have her sign for them."

"No, Rafferty said they'd just deliver them to this office."

"Why would he say she needed to sign for them?"

Stan felt a concern spiking in his mind and quickly asked, "John, what did this guy look like?"

"Average height. Good-looking fella with a big moustache."

"Damn! That's probably George Rafferty!"

Stan didn't wait for a response but turned and sprinted across the boardwalk then raced diagonally across the main street to where his black gelding still stood.

His left foot barely touched the stirrup when he and the gelding were tearing down the main street, heading for the ranch.

———

George had the stallion moving at a fast trot. He wanted to get this over with, so he could return to his job and pretend he hadn't been gone. He should be able to get back a little after two o'clock if he hurried.

He found the turnoff easily and continued at his rapid pace.

———

Stan was riding faster, letting the big gelding have his head. Stan was suddenly more frightened than he had been in his life. He'd been through years of war, faced killers, Cheyenne and Arapaho warriors and had never felt such terror. He finally had found Ellie and now this bastard was going to ruin it. He knew that George Rafferty hadn't come to Boulder to bring Ellie back to Denver.

———

George reached the access road and turned into the ranch. He had only slowed slightly.

Ellie was in the second bedroom going through her things when she heard hooves approaching and assumed Stan must have finished sooner than he had suspected. She smiled, stood, then left the bedroom and walked down the hallway to the main room.

George had reached the house just as Ellie reached the front door. She saw George then quickly slammed the door closed and ran back to the third bedroom, the weapons room. She had never fired a gun, so she grabbed the war axe in both hands and kicked the door closed with her foot, then stood with her back against the wall and waited.

C.J. PETIT

Stan roared toward the access road, and bypassed it, cutting diagonally toward the house. He saw the big black stallion tied at the hitch rail, pulled out his Winchester and cocked the hammer.

George heard the pounding hooves of a hard-running horse and turned to see Stan throwing up a massive cloud of dust as the big horse closed the gap.

George pulled his pistol, then aimed and fired at a hundred yards. There was no way he even had a chance at hitting a target at that distance with that weapon and his lack of practice, but he fired twice more as Stan closed the gap.

Stan didn't want to kill the bastard, as it would have ramifications. He had made the decision on the ride in, but he sure as hell didn't want to get shot again, either.

He began firing at his own porch, but a little lower.

As the .44 caliber rounds began hitting around his feet, George fired twice more at Stan before hearing that even more frightening click as his hammer struck an expended cartridge.

Stan had hauled the gelding to a dust cloud-creating stop and leapt from the saddle, dropping his Winchester as he did. George panicked and threw his useless pistol at Stan and ripped open the door. Stan was right behind him and just as George reached the hallway, Stan tackled him around the knees. Both men hit the floor hard, but Stan had George as a cushion to soften the blow and was both bigger and much stronger. George took the full brunt of Stan's weight as it drove him into the boards.

Stan gained some leverage by getting to his knees and then standing. He still had George Rafferty by the ankles as he dragged him out of the house, his arms flailing.

FINDING BUCKY

Stan got him outside and put his boot on George's back.

He almost shouted, "George Rafferty, I am arresting you for breaking and entering and the attempted murder of a law officer."

Ellie had heard all the shooting and gripped her war axe tightly. She was staring at the door when she heard the outside door slam open and then the loud crash of something hitting the floor. She felt it under her feet as the floor shook. That was followed by a scuffling noise that confused her, until she heard that glorious sound of Stan arresting George Rafferty.

She blew out her held breath and laid down the war axe. Her hands were shaking as she opened the door, then Ellie tentatively stepped down the hallway and through the open door, where she spotted Stan man-handling George to his feet.

"Look what you made me do to my house, you, stupid bastard!" he yelled, pointing down at the four holes from ricochets into his porch.

Ellie had to keep from laughing, as she stepped to the door and caught Stan's eye.

"Are you all right, sweetheart?" he asked softly, in contrast to his recent demanding voice.

"I'm fine. I had the war axe ready if he came into the room."

Stan looked at George, his temper cooling, and said, "Then you're damned lucky I caught you before you opened that door, George. She would have crushed that empty melon of yours."

Stan had picked up some pigging strings just a few days earlier in lieu of ordering handcuffs and soon had George's wrists bound behind him.

"Ellie, I'm going to take him into Boulder and lock him up. You stay here. I may be taking a ride down to Denver again soon, maybe tomorrow."

"Alright. Stan, sometime this week, can you show me how to shoot those guns?"

Stan smiled and replied, "I think so."

George had been following the conversation and it was immediately obvious why his wife had left him. *She was an adulteress!* He began to believe that he had won after all. He must have forgotten about the annulment papers that were now laying on John Bickerstaff's desk. The courier was already enroute back to Denver.

Stan put George on his stallion and stepped up to his gelding, took the stallion's reins, then trotted back down the access road.

"I'm going to have you brought up on charges of adultery and philandering!" snarled George after they had ridden for a mile.

"Good luck with that. She's not your wife anymore, George. You never consummated the marriage. You know why, I know why, and our father knows why, so drop all the pretenses. You are what you are."

"My father made me marry her, now she's costing us a lot of money and trying to ruin us."

"No, George. You've got that all wrong. She just wanted to get away. She wants her own life, not the one you and her parents want. Did you know we were best friends through school until the day she left to come here? Or that I left Fort Union, Montana to ride across six hundred miles of hostile territory just to find her? That's how important she is to me, George. To you, she was nothing but a showpiece."

"I bought her everything. I never abused her. I never even touched her."

"I know that, and that's part of the problem. You just don't know Ellie like I do. She hates the things you bought her. She's going to give them away. She wants nothing more than to be a loved woman and have children, my children, George."

"Then why didn't she just leave. Why did she demand all those things from my father?"

"She didn't. She would have been thrilled just to get the annulment. I asked for those things to compensate her for the misery she had been caused by being placed in this situation. You know, if you had loved her, shown her the respect she deserved, it's very possible that I would have lost her. But you didn't. Now you have a serious problem, George. You've been arrested for crimes that will send you to prison for twenty-five years."

"*Twenty-five years? For what?*" he asked in surprise.

"Attempted murder of a law officer. Twenty-five years is pretty much a given, from what I understand."

George suddenly realized that he was in a lot more trouble than he had believed as they rode along the cutoff.

"Do I have to go to trial? I could pay you."

"George, when will you learn? It's not about money all the time. It may surprise you that I'm fairly well off. Not as rich as you by any means, but enough to live comfortably in the manner that Ellie and I want to share. We won't go to balls or soirees, but we'll enjoy the company of our friends. We'll go riding across the ranch and feel the wind in our faces. We'll even go swimming in our spring. But most importantly, we'll have each other. You can keep your money, George. I'm leaning toward just letting you go back to Denver anyway and forgetting you ever came up here. All I need is a promise that you'll let Ellie live in peace."

"Are you serious? You aren't going to ask for anything?"

Stan looked over at him and said, "I'm asking for everything. Everything that Ellie and I want."

"Then I promise. I'll return to Denver and never bother either of you again."

"Alright," Stan said as he stopped the gelding, then leaned over with his pocketknife and severed the pigging strings.

"You're free to go, George," he said.

"Where are you going?"

"I'm going to the jail and tell John that there's nothing to worry about. Then I'll go back and tell Ellie that we can go on with our lives."

"Can I still ride with you for a while?"

"Sure. I'm heading that way."

"Doesn't it bother you that I'm, well, that way?"

"You are what you are, George. I'm sure you didn't choose to be that way just as I didn't choose to be a fat kid."

"You were fat?"

"As a pig. When we were growing up, I was picked on by all the other boys who called Piggy. Ellie, as hard as it may be to imagine, had big front teeth, and both the boys and girls called

244

her Bucky. That's what drew us together. We were outcasts, misfits. None of the other children wanted to have anything to do with either of us, so we hung together. When other kids called me 'Piggy' or called her 'Bucky', it hurt. But we could call each other those names and it made us smile because there was no meanness behind them. We used them as shields against the others.

"When Ellie was twelve, she suddenly morphed into a very different looking girl. Her face changed, and her teeth were no longer prominent. She became a very pretty girl, and it was a measure of her goodness that she didn't abandon me to seek the available popularity from the other boys. She stayed by me as my best friend.

"When her parents dragged her away from me when she was thirteen, I vowed to change and eventually I did. But it was a measure of Ellie that she never succumbed to the temptation to become someone she wasn't. Your fancy gowns and jewelry meant nothing to her because it wasn't who she was. It was what her parents wanted."

"We fired her father this morning."

"That will be interesting, don't you think?" he said as he smiled at George.

George smiled back. He couldn't believe the change that he felt come over him in such a short time. He had been shooting at this man just an hour earlier, yet now they were having a normal conversation.

"Do you mind if I call you Stan"

"Go ahead. It's my name."

"I'll tell you what, Stan, interesting doesn't quite cover it. They had a mortgage with the bank for their big house. I don't think they have much money either. He was being paid well, but they were spending it all on things to keep up the image. What did he do before he got to Denver?"

"He was a farmer. They sold the farm suddenly about ten years ago. I have an idea why, too."

"What was it?"

"I'm pretty sure James McCormick was having an affair with my mother."

George's eyes widened as he exclaimed, "*You're kidding?*"

"Nope. He was over the house a lot when my father was at work at the mill. I was too young at the time to know what was going on, but as I grew more knowledgeable in the way of the world, it dawned on me that they weren't playing checkers."

"Do you want us to be lenient with them?"

"Not particularly. You're in the banking business, not the charity business."

George smiled again, saying, "That's true."

They were reaching the outskirts of Boulder as a buggy carrying James and Ida McCormick rode in from the south. Both the buggy and the riders were headed for the sheriff's office, but the buggy would reach it first.

James helped Ida out of the buggy before they walked into the office. John Bickerstaff was still reading the ordinances, and like Stan, found some ludicrous. He was laughing at one when the door opened.

He looked up and said, "Good morning, folks. What can I do for you?"

"We're looking for our daughter. Her name is Ellie Rafferty. I was told she was in Boulder. Do you know where she is?"

"I do. She's at the B-P connected ranch waiting for these papers, I assume," he said, tapping his finger on the annulment papers.

"What is she doing there?" asked James.

"Beats me," John replied.

"How do we find this place?" asked Ida.

"Just head west, you'll find a cutoff after two miles that goes southwest, and it's three miles along the cutoff."

"Well, we'll be leaving. We've got to find out what's going on."

———

Just a hundred yards down the road, Stan and George were walking their horses side by side.

"George, did you want to get some lunch before you head back?"

"I rushed out so quickly, I didn't bring any cash."

Stan laughed, and said, "Now that's kind of funny, don't you think? With you being a banker, I mean."

George laughed as well and replied, "It is somewhat ironic."

"I'll take care of lunch. It's pretty good food, too."

"I don't think I've ever eaten in a café before."

"They're good folks in this town, George. All except a few troublemakers, but we keep them in line. I'll tell you about the doughnut thieves when we get there. Let's go and get John so he can join us."

"Okay."

George was still amazed at how comfortable he was in Stan's company. He didn't have to pretend anything, but he knew one thing, he wanted to be a friend to Stan and Ellie.

They saw the buggy parked out in front of the office just as James and Ida McCormick stepped out of the jail.

Stan recognized them both immediately, then looked over at George and said, "Well, it looks like interesting just got more interesting."

"This will be fun," George said as he grinned back.

As their horses stopped in front of the buggy, George and Stan stepped down, then tied off their horses.

Ida was the first to spot George with the tall lawman, so she grabbed her husband and pointed.

"It's George! Maybe he went and talked sense into Ellie!"

The McCormicks then stalked over to George and the big man beside him.

James quickly said, "George, it's great to see you! Did you go and straighten out our daughter? I don't know what's gotten into her."

"Actually, I went there to shoot her," he admitted.

"Did you shoot her, George?" asked Ida, not knowing which direction she should take.

If George did shoot her, they could sue him. If he hadn't, maybe this would lead to some form of leverage.

"No, I wound up shooting at Stan here."

"Stan?" she asked as she turned to the man beside George.

Stan pushed his Stetson back so they could see his face more clearly and said, "Yes, Mrs. McCormick. Stan. You might remember me. Stanley Murray from Southfield."

Ida looked at the tall, handsome man. Surely, he must be joking.

"No, you can't be him. You're just trying to have fun with us."

"You and just about everyone else called me Piggy and they used to call Ellie Bucky. Well, she's no longer Bucky and I'm no longer Piggy. We still call ourselves that because we love each other."

"You can't love her. She's married to George Rafferty. He's our son-in-law."

"No, I'm not, Mrs. McCormick. The marriage was annulled yesterday, and she'll probably marry Stan today or tomorrow. Is that right, Stan?" he said before turning to his new friend.

"As soon as we can."

"But she can't do this to us! Where will we live?" James asked in a noticeable whine.

Stan replied, "It's a free country. You can live and go wherever you want to go. I think my mother is a widow now,

Mister McCormick, so she's available if you want to continue where you left off."

James McCormick was aghast. *How could this come out now? Ten years and a thousand miles from when and where it had happened?*

Ida turned to him. "James, what is he talking about?"

"I have no idea, Ida. Let's go and see if we can talk some sense into Ellie."

"Not yet. What did he mean, James?" she asked as she fumed, her voice rising two octaves and increasing noticeably in volume.

"I haven't got a clue. Now, let's get going."

"Yes, you do have a clue, and probably a lot more," she snapped, "You were having an affair with his mother, weren't you? I suspected something at the time but didn't say anything. Now, it's out, you, cheating bastard!"

As she screamed, she suddenly hauled back and then smashed him with her purse as hard as she could.

James felt the blow and stumbled back against the sheriff's office wall, almost exactly where the sheriff had fallen when he had been shot.

John, George, and especially Stan just watched with big grins on their faces, waiting for the next round.

James covered up as Ida lit into him and began pummeling him with her weighty purse before beginning to use her weaponized feet.

Stan looked over at John, mimed eating and thumbed toward the diner. He nodded and the three still smiling men left the scene of domestic violence behind them and headed down to the diner.

Stan held the door as George and John entered.

Laura caught sight of John and headed their way, even though they hadn't taken a seat yet.

"Hello, Laura. How are you doing?', asked Stan, already knowing the answer.

"I'm fine. John, how is your first full day as sheriff going?" she asked as she smiled broadly.

"Perfectly well, Laura," he replied, matching Laura tooth-for-tooth.

Stan sat down at a table and George joined him. Stan looked at George, raised his eyebrows and tilted his head toward John and Laura. George got the message and smiled. He knew that he had been accepted as a friend and felt better than he had in a long time.

"John, why don't you have a seat and let Laura do her job? Not that she's going to be doing it much longer," Stan said.

John and Laura snapped out of their infatuated conversation and Laura reddened, but still smiled.

A chagrined John took his seat.

Laura returned to doing her job and asked for their orders but was still flushed. After she took the orders, she headed back to the kitchen area.

"Feeling your oats today, Stan?" John asked to turn the tables.

"Just making an observation, John, or was I incorrect in my deduction?"

"No, you weren't. I've been talking to Thad Harkins over at the bank. I'm going to go over and look at a ranch up your way. It's a little bigger than yours, but it's been on the market for three years, so it's probably run down a bit."

"How much is the asking price?"

"Twenty-two hundred."

"After you settle on a price, come and see me. I'm sure Ellie would like to buy it for you. Maybe you can consider it a wedding gift."

"Stan, I couldn't ask you to do that!"

"You didn't ask. I'm just telling you what will happen. Use your money to fix it up. Are you planning on running cattle?"

"I don't know yet."

"Horses are better, I think."

"I'll think about it. Want to come over and see it?"

"Maybe. It depends on what happens for the rest of the day."

"Would Ellie really just give John the money?" asked George.

"I won't even have to ask. I'll just mention that John is looking at a nearby ranch and she'd tell me it would make a wonderful wedding gift."

"You're serious, aren't you?" asked John.

"Sure. I know Ellie. It's the way she is."

"Can I help?" asked George.

"Did you want to go and look at the ranch?" asked Stan.

"Sure. I think I've got to get back and see my father first, though. He's probably really mad at me."

"Tell him you came and talked to me. He'll be all right. Tell him you talked to Ellie, too. You can take it from there."

"I can do it."

"Good."

Laura brought their lunch, and as they began eating, Mister and Mrs. McCormick entered the diner.

Stan nudged John, who looked at Stan as he tilted his head toward the door.

"Maybe they're just hungry," joked George.

"Not Mrs. McCormick," replied Stan, "she already ate her husband's ass."

John had been sipping coffee, and some of it made its way out of his nose at the comment.

Ida pointed toward their table and almost dragged her husband toward them.

The other diners were staring at the couple as Ida marched across the room pulling her battered husband behind her.

C.J. PETIT

"You! Who do you think you are?" she demanded, pointing at the table.

Stan and George looked at each other, wondering who exactly she was trying to confront, so they both shrugged.

Stan decided he'd better try to control this, although he was thoroughly enjoying himself.

"I think I'm a deputy sheriff of Boulder and I believe you'd better calm your tone, or I'll arrest you for disturbing the peace, and I'm not joking," he said.

Ida did tone down her voice somewhat before she snapped, "You came here and disrupted our lives and stole our daughter. *How dare you?"*

"Now, Ida, you've got that backwards, haven't you?" Stan asked, his voice level, but loud enough for the entire diner to hear, including Laura who was standing fixed in place two tables away.

Stan continued, saying, "You and your husband stole Ellie away from me when she was thirteen. You disrupted our lives, then came here and tried to improve your lives by using her. I've loved Ellie since we were children, and after I left the army, I rode over six hundred miles of wild country, had to kill a dozen Indian warriors and two men who tried to ambush me to find her.

"Now you have the audacity to come into this place and make a scene because your pride has taken a blow. Well, that's just too damned bad. Ellie and I will be married, and I'll keep her happy for the rest of her life. If you want to come and see your grandchildren some time, that's fine. If not, that'll be your loss. I suggest you return to Denver and think about it."

Stan returned to his lunch and continued eating while Laura and the other diners all had varying levels of smiles on their faces.

There was no smile on Ida's face. She was about to say something when George spoke up, surprising Stan.

"Mrs. McCormick, I suggest you do as Stan said to do. Have your husband apply for his previous position as a clerk. I'm sure it will be accepted. As to your mortgage, the bank will buy back the house, giving you enough profit to buy a smaller, but still decent home. That's provided you do as he suggested. You can even have lunch before you go. I'm sure Stan wouldn't mind providing lunch for his future in-laws."

Stan glanced at George and tried to keep the smile from his face but failed.

Ida was doing quick calculations. As she was thinking, James pulled her to a table and pulled out a chair and almost pushed her down into it. He sat down, and Laura glanced over at Stan, grinned quickly, straightened her face and went to the table to take their order.

After taking their order, she swung by Stan and whispered, "You're paying," before she slipped back to the kitchen.

Stan looked over at George and winked. George just grinned and went back to eating.

The men finished their lunch and Stan left three silver dollars on the table. It would be a large tip for Laura, even after taking out the bill for his future in-laws.

They walked outside and headed back to the office.

"That was the most fun I've had in years!" exclaimed George.

"It was kind of enjoyable," agreed Stan.

They reached the outside of the sheriff's office and stopped before entering.

"Alright, here's where we separate," said John.

"Stan, do you think Ellie would be mad if I came to visit sometimes?" George asked.

"Not at all, George."

"Good. I did treat her rather shabbily."

"She's a forgiving woman. She sure doesn't get that from her mother."

They all laughed at the thought of Ellie getting anything from her mother.

"John, I've got to get that annulment paper and bring it to Ellie. Which ranch are you looking at? Maybe I'll take Ellie over there."

"The Bar L. It's another mile down that same road, but on the other side. I told Thaddeus Harkins that I wanted a place near yours."

"We'll go and look at it. Have you seen it yet?"

"Not yet. I have the keys, though. I'll probably swing by later if it's quiet."

"Alright."

George shook both their hands then mounted his father's horse. He waved happily as he set off south.

"That all worked out amazingly well," John said.

"Let me get those papers then I'll go and see Ellie. I'm kind of excited."

"I can understand that. Laura does the same thing for me."

"Good, John. It'll be great having you for a neighbor."

John opened the door and stepped inside, pulled the envelope with the annulment papers from his desk and handed them to Stan.

Stan almost hugged the papers as he mounted the black gelding, then waved at John as he turned north and rode out of Boulder.

Twenty-one minutes later, he was turning into his ranch. Ellie was sitting on the porch steps, and when Stan saw her, he easily made the mental leap of Ellie waiting for him on the school steps. Now, just as it did then, Stan felt the warmth of love wash over him as he saw her.

His Ellie, his Bucky, was waiting for Piggy to come and talk to her. The circumstances and their appearances were certainly much different, but the connection, that unbreakable connection that they had forged in those early days was still there.

He slowed down to keep the dust to a minimum and then hopped down and led the gelding to the hitching rail, tied the reins and stepped over to Ellie. He sat down on the steps and looked into those same miraculous blue eyes.

"Hello, Bucky," he said with a smile.

"Hello, Piggy," she replied as she smiled back with her perfect white teeth.

Stan reached into his vest pocket and pulled out the envelope and handed it to her.

Her hand was a bit shaky as she took the envelope and pulled out the official document.

"It's real, isn't it, Stan?" she asked quietly.

"Yes, my love, it's real."

"Can we get married tomorrow?" she continued just as quietly.

"We can, and we will, Ellie."

She turned and hugged him, the all-important annulment papers still in her hand. Stan held her tightly. She finally sat back and just looked into his eyes. There would be no more searching and no more waiting.

"Stan, what happened to George?"

"He's on his way home to Denver to talk to his father."

"He's not in jail?"

"Not at all. In fact, he's a very happy man right now."

She sat back and tilted her head as she asked, "He's happy? What happened on the way to Boulder?"

"We became friends."

Ellie's jaw dropped as she exclaimed, *"He just tried to shoot you and was probably trying to kill me and now you're friends?"*

"He was just mixed up, Ellie. His father kind of made him into what he was. He didn't even see how miserable you were. It started when he tried to bribe me to let the charges drop."

"He tried to kill you, and then he tried to bribe you, and now you're friends?" she asked incredulously.

"That's when I pointed out that he didn't understand what made you happy is that you needed to be loved and respected. I'm not sure when the realization hit about how wrong he'd been, but it must have hit him hard. By the time we reached the office, we were chatting amiably. He called me Stan and I called him George. Then we and John had an incident outside the sheriff's office with a couple who had driven their buggy up from Denver to come and talk sense to you."

"My parents showed up?"

Stan grinned and replied, "You might say that. The three of us, me, John and George, had a wonderful time with your parents, but it was all at their expense, except I did have to pay for their lunch."

"Alright. I suppose I can take this if I can accept you and George being friends."

"Well, your mother was a bit irate because your father had been fired that morning. They were going to blame you for all their troubles, you see. Anyway, I kind of let it slip that I knew that my mother and your father were having a long-term affair."

Ellie was shocked, then made a mental leap as her hand flew to her mouth and she asked in a terrified voice, "No! Stan! Don't tell me that you and I…"

Stan suddenly realized what he'd missed, then hurriedly replied, "No, Ellie, the affair was when we were in school. We're not brother and sister. I started noticing that your father was showing up at the house when I was about eleven. It went on for a couple of years or more. I was too naïve to know why he was there. It wasn't until I was an adult that it dawned on me what was going on. I think that's what spurred your father's sudden decision to go to Denver. I think my father might have finally figured it out."

"My father was in your mother's bed?" she asked, still stunned by the revelation.

"Scary, isn't it? Especially if you remember what my mother looked like."

"I wasn't going to say anything."

"Well, we left your parents outside the office with your mother flailing your father with her purse. We went to lunch and were eating when they came in. Your mother launched a diatribe at me for disrupting their lives and stealing you away. I told her she had it backwards. The whole diner could hear what was going on. Then George suggested that your father apply to get his clerk's job back and the bank would buy the house and give them enough profit to buy a comfortable but not grand house."

"George said that?"

"He did. Like I said, he's changed remarkably. He even asked if it would be all right if he came to visit every once in a while. I told him it would be fine and that you're a very forgiving woman."

"Oh? I am, am I?"

"Don't give me that fake heart of ice look. I know you, soft-hearted woman that you are. Trust me, this George will be so nice to you it'll make you wonder where the old George went."

"I can't believe all this has happened so quickly."

"And there's something else I need to show you. I'll have to go and saddle a horse for you first. Which one do you want to ride?"

"I don't think I can ride my buckskin mare right now. That randy stallion of yours seems to think he owns her and those other eight ladies."

"I know. He does seem to be that way, doesn't he? I'll find you a nice gelding soon for you to call your own. For now, I'll go saddle one of the nondescript geldings and you can go get changed into your pants and shirt. I like them better than the riding outfit."

"You are being demanding," she said as she smiled.

"Just a personal preference, sweetheart."

"Well, seeing as how tomorrow is our wedding day, I guess I can submit to your request."

Stan stood up and Ellie swatted him on the backside.

"Thank you, ma'am," he said as he walked to the barn.

Ellie giggled as she walked up the stairs. She felt so alive. Her annulment in her hand and her almost-husband was with her. She changed into her requested clothing as Stan saddled a brown gelding.

As he looked around the crowded barn, he realized that he really needed to get that carriage house built. He'd mention it to Ellie on the ride to the Bar L.

He led the gelding out to the front of the house as Ellie stepped down from the porch.

As she put her foot in the stirrup, she felt a hand 'assisting' her upwards. She was going to say something but thought it would be more fun to act as if she hadn't noticed.

Stan enjoyed the lingering assist and was waiting for a biting comment. When one didn't arrive, he took the challenge.

"Helping you up reminded me of an incident I had earlier with Jimmy and Ed. It involved doughnuts."

It had its desired effect when she asked, "Why would having your hand on my behind remind you of doughnuts?"

"Because they're both so sweet, my love," he replied as he grinned at her.

She laughed, and they were soon riding down the access road. She was getting ready to turn left toward Boulder when Stan turned right.

"Where are we going?" she asked.

"You'll see," he replied.

They rode for a mile and Stan saw the aging Bar L sign and turned down and overgrown access road.

"Is this what you're going to show me?"

"It is."

"You want to buy another ranch?"

"No. I just want to see it and ask your opinion."

FINDING BUCKY

"This sounds fishy, Stan."

"It's just me, Ellie."

"I know, and that's what scares me."

They rode until they reached the house. It was a little smaller than their house, but not by much. It was in decent shape but needed repairs. The barn was in similar condition.

Stan stopped and set down, but Ellie stayed in her saddle. Stan tied both horses to the hitch rail.

"Are you going to stay there?" he asked.

"I was waiting for you to help me down, because you obviously enjoyed helping me up."

"Yes, ma'am!" Stan said enthusiastically.

Stan jogged to her horse and she took his offered hand. She stepped down and Stan kept holding her hand and then pulled her into his arms and kissed her. She held him closely, and they kept the kiss for almost a minute.

"I suppose I'd better stop. I'd hate to have to ravage you in a dusty house, but I will if I have to."

"Like that would stop you," she said as she smiled before they walked up the porch steps.

The house was unlocked, so they went inside. There was some furniture, but not much, but the dust was everywhere.

"It's not bad structurally, but it'll need some serious cleaning and new furniture," said Stan.

"It has potential. Let's go and see the rest of the house."

The rest of the house was like the kitchen, dusty and incomplete. They left the house and checked out the barn. It had more inside than the house did, but the tools were all rusty, as Stan expected. But the barn itself was sound and the roof looked good.

"Not bad, Stan."

"Let's go for a perimeter ride."

"How big is this ranch?"

"Bigger than ours. I think it's six sections."

"How's the water?"

"We'll find out as we ride."

"Then let's go. Are you going to assist me in boarding my horse again?"

"If you'll grant me that privilege."

"Permission granted," she said as Stan took her hand as they left the barn.

Stan did provide the added leverage to Ellie as she intentionally slowed down her boarding process, letting Stan get a few extra seconds of behind time.

They rode to the western edge of the property and made their tour, finding a similar terrain to their ranch and two creeks crossing the property. They had finished their tour and were leaving on the access road when Ellie turned to Stan.

"This is a nice property, Stan, so now you can confess. Why are you showing it to me?"

"John will be coming out to look at it shortly. He's thinking of buying it. My guess is the plan is to have a home for him and Laura."

"That's just wonderful, Stan. Do you know how much they're asking for it?"

"I can't remember exactly, but I know it's less than what I paid for our place. I think he can get it for less than two thousand dollars."

Ellie looked back at the receding house and said, "Stan, I have an idea, but I want to check with you first."

"I think it's a marvelous idea. Furniture and fixing it up, too?"

Ellie laughed, then replied, "We do have all that money and we don't need anything."

"Want to buy it from under him?"

"What do you mean?"

"We go to see Thaddeus Harkins at the bank tomorrow right after we're married. We get your name on my account and transfer the money from your account in Denver. Then we buy the property and contract for the repairs and painting. We get the grounds cleaned up, then we give John the keys."

"And you wonder why I love you so much, Stan."

They made it back to their ranch before John could make his inspection.

———

George returned to Denver before the McCormicks, rode directly to the bank, walked in, and headed straight for his father's office. He didn't knock but just went inside and closed the door behind him.

"Where have you been, George? We thought you'd gone off to shoot your wife."

"I did."

Geoffrey's eyes popped wide as he asked, "You didn't shoot her, did you?"

"No. I didn't."

"Thank God!"

"I shot five times at the sheriff."

"You shot the sheriff?" he asked as he sat back, totally flabbergasted.

"No, I shot at him, but I missed."

"So, you're running from the law now," he said as he rubbed his forehead with the palm of his hand.

"No, not at all. In fact, I consider the sheriff to be a good friend already, and I believe he's going to marry Ellie tomorrow."

His father was totally lost as he asked, "Why would the sheriff marry her so quickly? He just met her two days ago."

"No, father. Let me tell you a story."

George then told his father the story of Piggy and Bucky and Stan's ride across hostile Indian territory to find her. He included everything, including what Stan had said to him and the McCormicks' arrival and dressing down by Stan. He even added the tidbit about James McCormick's affair with Stan's mother.

FINDING BUCKY

After he was done, he sat back and looked at his father.

"I asked him if I could visit from time to time and he said I could. He's a good man, Father. Maybe the best I've ever met."

"But he knows about you."

"I know he does. That's one of the reasons I think he's the such a good man. He knows and still treats me like he does everyone else."

"So, what do you think I should do? I've already transferred twenty thousand dollars to her account. Should I pull it?"

"Absolutely not. I was thinking of adding something from my own account, but that would be silly. They don't want the money. I think I know what I'll get for them as a wedding present."

"You're going to buy them a wedding present?" his father asked in disbelief.

"They're friends and that's what friends do. I think I'll buy a few mares for the ranch and a gelding for Ellie. Her mare is already carrying a foal, and she needs a good horse to ride."

Geoffrey suddenly got into the flow of the moment and said, "I know where you can get what you need. We'll take a ride over there if you'd like. It's not too far."

"I still have your horse saddled outside."

"You keep him. I've got another one."

George and his father left the office then the bank to ride to a nearby horse ranch.

———

The McCormicks arrived back in Denver as Geoffrey and George Rafferty were leaving to the west. Ida was driving the buggy as it slowed before the bank.

James exited the buggy and stepped into the street, and then assisted his wife to the ground.

"We have to take his offer, James," she said firmly as they stood beside the buggy.

"I am not going back to just being a clerk and listen to all those people make snarky remarks behind my back," he replied, his voice rising in anger at the thought.

"Then what do you propose we do?"

"We let him buy back the house and we sell the things we can, then we move."

Ida snapped back loudly, "Where? Back to Michigan, so you can return to Maude Murray's bed again?"

"No. I think we move to Boulder, and make Ellie take us in. She has lots of money now, and she can build us a house, too."

"I think you've lost your mind. That girl isn't going to build us anything. Maybe you forget what that sheriff said."

"It doesn't matter what he said. We're her parents, and she has to take care of us. It's the law or something."

Ida all but shouted, "You are insane, James! There is no such law. You're an able-bodied man who is only forty-four. No one is going to take care of you. If you insist on doing this, I'll divorce you for adultery."

FINDING BUCKY

It was George's turn to explode as he shouted, "Go ahead! Then what will you do, become a prostitute? You have nothing else but your breasts to earn money."

Ida shrieked, "You are really going to regret saying that. You'll never touch them or any other part of me again! Why you wanted to have an affair with that woman is beyond me. She couldn't hold a candle to me!"

"Because, dear wife, she would satisfy my urges and you wouldn't!" he yelled as spittle left his mouth and landed on Ida's furious face.

Ida boiled with rage as their raucous argument was attracting the attention of many passersby, who were either appalled or titillated, sometimes both.

Finally, Ida put her foot down...literally. She jammed her thick heel into her adulterous husband's right foot. He screeched, and she then turned, reached into the buggy, grabbed the buggy whip and began to lash her hopping husband severely.

A Denver city deputy marshal had been listening to their diatribes almost since it started. When she mashed her husband's foot, he began to get closer to the public display of spousal differences. Then, as she began whipping him, he quickly pushed through the burgeoning audience, but took almost thirty seconds after she had begun to whip James before he could stop it.

He grabbed the whip from her hand and before he could say anything, she did to him what she had done to her husband. She rammed her heel into his foot, breaking two of his long foot bones. He fell over in pain before she realized that she had just attacked a lawman. She quickly boarded the buggy and using the whip she had snatched back from the deputy, snapped it over the horse's rump and was soon flying down the cobbled street, leaving two men with broken feet squirming on the road as the stunned crowed watched her race away.

————

An outsider couldn't tell by watching Stan and Ellie on the morning of their upcoming marriage that it was a special day. Ellie cooked breakfast and bantered with her very-soon-to-be-husband as she had every day since she arrived at the ranch.

Stan was curious what Ellie would wear to the ceremony. She had a bag with her annulment papers and the dress she would wear in a bag on the bed in their room.

"Are you ready, Ellie?" Stan asked after cleaning up after breakfast.

"I'm ready," she replied coming out of the bedroom with her bag.

Stan had already saddled the horses, and Ellie was wearing her riding outfit because they were riding their horses into town, after all.

She did allow Stan to help her board the gelding, though.

They rode into Boulder a little after nine o'clock, stopped at the sheriff's office and went inside.

"John, are you and Laura ready to go to the courthouse?" Stan asked as they entered, finding the new sheriff sitting at the desk.

"She'll be here in a little bit. She had to stop at her room and change out of her waitress outfit."

"How did it go with the ranch?" Stan asked.

"I never did get a chance to go and check it out. It's still there, I'm sure. After three years, what are the odds that it gets sold today?"

"Not very high," Stan replied.

Laura appeared wearing a light blue dress and a big smile on her face.

"You look very pretty, Laura," said John.

"Thank you, John," she smiled.

"Shall we go across to the courthouse and see if Judge Whitaker is available?" asked Stan.

"He'd better be. I told him you and Ellie were coming over and he practically jumped out of his seat."

"Then let's go. Ellie needs to get changed when we get there."

"The judge said she could use his office while he's out front filling out the forms."

"Let's go."

The two couples crossed the street to the courthouse, as both Stan and Ellie suddenly felt the casual demeanor that they had enjoyed all morning vanish as they grew closer. Stan held Ellie's hand as they stepped up to the entrance, and neither noticed that John and Laura were also holding hands.

They entered the courthouse, walked down the main hallway, and turned into Judge Whitaker's office.

"Good morning, Stan," said a smiling Joseph Prince, the judge's clerk.

"Good morning, Joseph. I'd like to introduce you to Ellie."

"Hello, Ellie. I'll let the judge know you're here," he said as he rose.

He turned, rapped twice on the door behind his desk, then stuck his head in.

"Judge, Stan is here."

"I'll be out in a second," his honor replied from inside his office.

Joseph returned to his desk, took his seat and ten seconds later, Judge Whitaker appeared from his office wearing a giant grin.

"So, Stan, this is the young lady you've traveled so far to find. She was obviously worth the journey."

"She was. Your Honor, I'd like you to meet Ellie McCormick."

Ellie smiled and shook the judge's hand, pleased to hear Stan introduce her with her maiden name, which was technically correct now after the annulment.

"I hear you'd like to use my office, Miss McCormick. You go right ahead, and we'll start filling out forms."

Ellie took her bag from Stan, skittered into the judge's office and closed the door.

They only took five minutes to fill out the necessary forms, and the judge didn't even bother looking at the annulment papers. Stan told him what was in the envelope, and that was good enough for him.

FINDING BUCKY

"What do you think she's going to wear, Stan?" asked John, "She has all those really nice gowns."

"If I know my Ellie, and I do. It'll be something pretty but understated, and I think I know what she'll be wearing as an accessory."

"She does have a lot of nice jewelry," said John.

"She does," agreed Stan, but knew she wouldn't be wearing any of the sparkly pieces.

The door opened less than a minute later, and Ellie exited wearing an ivory and pale blue dress that accented her figure very well. But it was her accessory that surprised everyone, everyone but Stan. She had Mary's shawl over her shoulders, and smiled at Stan, knowing that they were the only ones present who understood the significance of the shawl. He held out his hand and she took it gently.

No one said anything as Judge Whitaker led them into the courtroom.

The ceremony was as understated as Ellie's dress. They exchanged vows and rings and completed the ceremony when they kissed for the first time as husband and wife.

After everyone else went to the outer office to finish the paperwork, Ellie used the judge's office again to change back into her riding outfit.

After everyone but Ellie had signed the forms, Stan asked, "We need to stop at the bank for a little bit, John. Why don't you and Laura come by later for dinner?"

John replied, "Stan, it's your wedding day. Don't you and Ellie want some privacy?"

"We're not asking for you to stay the night, John."

John turned to Laura and asked, "Laura can you get the night off?"

"I can. Did you want to walk me down to the diner, so I can let them know?"

"I'd be happy to," he said as he smiled, offering her his arm.

"Around six o'clock, John. We'll see you then," Stan said as they prepared to leave.

John and Laura waved their acknowledgement as they left the outer office.

Ellie exited the judge's office thirty seconds later, allowing Judge Whitaker to return to his desk, then signed the marriage forms making it official.

Stan folded their copy of the marriage certificate, slid it into his vest pocket, then smiled at his new bride and asked, "Well, my beloved wife, did you want to go and start mischief over at the bank?"

She grinned and replied, "Let's."

Stan carried her bag with him as they headed for the bank, and after they entered the bank, they headed for clerk Bob Feldman's desk.

"Morning, Stan. What can I do for you today?" he asked as they approached.

"Bob, Ellie and I were just married, and I need to get her added to my account and we need to transfer the money out of her account with the First Colorado Bank in Denver."

"Well, congratulations to you both, and please have a seat, Mrs. Murray, while I go and get the forms."

Ellie smiled and took a seat as Bob headed for the cashier's window, then smiled at her husband and said, "That sounds really nice, Stan."

"It really does, doesn't it?"

Bob brought the forms back and had Ellie sign in two places, then he had her fill out the account information from her Denver account.

"We should get this transfer by tomorrow. We deal with them a lot."

"Thanks, Bob. We need to see Thaddeus Harkins, too. Is he in?"

"He is. His door is open, and I'm sure you know the way."

Stan shook Bob's hand, then they left his desk, crossed the lobby to Thaddeus Harkins' office, then Stan tapped on the door jamb when they reached it.

The banker waved them inside and stood as they entered.

"Stan, how's that ranch working out for you?" he asked.

"Perfectly. We couldn't be happier, Thad," he replied as he held a chair so Ellie could be seated.

"What can I do for you today?"

"Thad, I'd like you to meet Ellie Murray, my wife of thirty minutes."

"Well, congratulations to you both. So, what do you need today?"

"We'd like to buy another ranch. The Bar L that's over our way."

"Stan, I'd like to sell it to you, but John Bickerstaff is interested in the property. Can you wait until he makes an offer?"

"Nope. That's the point, Thad. Ellie and I plan on buying it, fixing it up and then giving it to John."

Thad broke into an enormous smile as he said, "I'd love to have a good friend like you, Stan."

"It was Ellie's idea. So, how much can you let me have it for without a lot of negotiating. My wife and I would like to return to our own honeymoon ranch."

"I'll let it go for eighteen hundred, and that's really as low as I can go."

"That sounds fair, Thad. Let me write you a draft. When John comes to ask about it, tell him that the original owners have decided to return, and it's off the market. Give us about two weeks to get it all fixed up. If he wants another place, stall him."

"This will be fun, Stan," Thad said with a grin.

"Not for John. At least not until the place is ready."

Stan wrote out the draft and Thad wrote out the sales contract and put John Bickerstaff's name on the deed.

"I need to go to the land office anyway to get Ellie added to our deed, so I'll run this over."

"You made another interesting day for me, Stan."

"Thanks a lot, Thad," he said as he shook the banker's hand.

Ellie smiled at him as she rose, and Thad smiled back, before Stan took her hand and they strolled out of the bank.

Ellie asked, "What next?"

"After the land office, we're off to the construction company. We'll get them to fix up the house and barn and paint it. I need to see about building a good-sized carriage house on our place, too. We need the space."

"That's a marvelous idea. After that, do we order the furniture and things for the house?"

"We can do that. It's more your area, anyway. Never ask a man to decorate a house. They wind up looking like a combination barn and gun shop."

Ellie laughed, but was already excited, as the idea of decorating an entire house appealed to her and already had some ideas for their own house as well.

After their stops at the land office, Miller Construction, Lipton's Furniture, and Brewster's General Store, they still returned to the ranch by two o'clock. After they unsaddled their horses, they walked to the house, entering through the kitchen, but Stan didn't let his wife cook lunch, not now. It was their wedding day and he wanted to make it official in his own way.

He turned her, and pulled her into his arms, saying, "We are going to legally consummate this marriage, Ellie, I don't want you to have an excuse for an annulment this time."

She laughed lightly and kissed him not-so-lightly before they slid down the hallway to their bedroom.

———

An hour later, they were mutually exhausted, yet eating a light snack as they prepared dinner for John and Laura.

"Do you think the repairs and painting will be done before the furniture and kitchenware arrives?" she asked.

"It should. The repairs shouldn't take long and clearing the access road will only take a few hours. Hauling away the old furniture is simple enough and the painting will only take two days, so it should all be done within a week or so."

"That's perfect. And thank you for letting me pick out the paint."

"I think the dark green will look very nice with the white trim."

"I hope they like it."

"They'd better!" he said as he laughed.

"I was surprised they will be able to get our carriage house built so quickly, too."

"It's not a surprise, really. It's a straightforward design, and if you have a full crew doing it, I wouldn't be surprised if they don't get it done even faster than two weeks."

"It'll be fun watching it go up," she said as she chopped an onion.

———

John and Laura arrived a half an hour early, but the food was almost done, so Stan and Ellie joined them in the sitting area.

"Do you know what happened a little while ago?" asked John.

"They fired me!" Laura exclaimed with a laugh, "Can you believe it?"

"So, what are you going to do, Laura?" asked Ellie, already guessing the answer when she laughed about losing her job.

"Oh, I don't know. Maybe spend all my time at the ranch with my husband," she replied as she looked at John and smiled.

Ellie grinned and took both of Laura's hands in hers.

"John?" asked Stan, raising his eyebrows, "Holding out on us, are you?"

John grew sheepish and waved his hands denying any such thing as he said, "I just thought this was your day. I didn't want to spoil it."

"Well, I guess that's as good an excuse as you can come up with, so we'll let it go."

"We did get some bad news, though. The ranch I wanted isn't available any longer. Thaddeus Harkins told me that the original owners will be moving back, so they took it off the market. It seemed like it was perfect for us, too. It would have taken some work to get it fixed up, but I could have done it."

"Are there any others around that you like?"

"Nothing in my price range. They're all too big."

"That's a bad break, John."

"Let's all go and eat. The food's ready," Ellie said to minimize conversation about the ranch.

Everyone stood and walked to the kitchen, where Laura joined Ellie in moving the food to plates.

They sat down and enjoyed a very full dinner that ended with an apple pie and coffee. The dinner conversation had focused mainly on the newlyweds and the soon-to-be newlyweds.

When the pie and coffee were gone, Stan told Ellie that he and John would clean up so she and Laura could spend time going through her gowns and jewelry. She took him up on his offer, promising him a reward for good behavior later.

While John and Stan were washing the dishes and pans, Ellie was displaying her gowns for Laura who was almost exactly the same size, but a bit shapelier than Ellie. Ellie told her how she could modify the gowns to make them just very nice dresses, like the one she wore at the marriage ceremony.

After she mentioned the ceremony, Laura asked her about the shawl.

A slight smile formed on Ellie's lips as she said softly, "Stan received the shawl from a Ute woman that he had saved on the trail, and she told him it had two meanings. One is that it will provide safe passage for the bearer through Ute lands and those of their allies. Then she told him it represents perfect love and will provide passage for the holder to his intended's heart."

"Ellie, I know this is asking a lot, but could I borrow it when we get married?" she asked quietly.

"Yes. But don't put it on until you're almost ready. When Stan first put it over my shoulders, I felt a warmth flow through me, then again when he told me what it meant. I knew that we already had a perfect love and the shawl was almost just a reminder. I don't doubt for a second that he knew that I would wear it when we were wed. It was a symbol, Laura. It was a symbol of what he had gone through to ensure that our perfect love didn't go unshared for the rest of our lives."

Laura was in awe of what Ellie felt for Stan and what he must feel for her.

They sat quietly for a minute and then Laura finally picked out two gowns that she'd modify. She would visit the ranch to do the modifications there rather than in her room. Then Ellie picked up her large jewelry box and opened the lid.

"My goodness! Ellie, this is a lot of jewelry!" she exclaimed as she stared at the box of gold and precious stones.

"Most of it I can't stand, but these three pieces I bought despite Mrs. Rafferty's insistence that they were 'too plebian, my dear'," Ellie said, adding a royal hand flick.

They both giggled at the idea.

"Do you see anything you like?" Ellie asked.

"I like this ruby necklace," Laura said as she touched the red stone.

"Then it's yours. I'll probably take a lot of the rest and have the stones removed and made into more elegant pieces."

"I can have it?" she asked in astonishment.

"Laura, I have no need for any of this or the gowns or furs. I never did. Stan took them out of my room as much to annoy them as anything else."

"You're serious, aren't you. They really don't mean anything to you."

"No, they don't. This ranch, this house and the freedom to be me, those are important. I didn't include Stan because he's all that really matters to me. The ranch, the house and the freedom are all because of him."

Laura held up the simple, elegant ruby necklace and let the sun flash off its surface.

"It's very beautiful."

"Then try it on and see if John notices."

Laura's hands were a bit shaky, but she managed to get the clasp done and Ellie gave her a fancy gold hand mirror with inlaid pearls, another of Stan's acquisitions from her gilded cage.

Laura wore a giant smile as she looked at the necklace on her breast.

"Can we go out to the kitchen?"

"This ought to be interesting," Ellie said as they headed for the bedroom door.

The men were just about finished when Laura and Ellie stepped into the room. John glanced at Laura and saw her bright, smiling visage and saw the reason why she was so pleased at the same time.

"Laura, that necklace looks beautiful on you. But you really didn't need it. You're already beautiful."

"Chalk up ten points for John," Ellie thought.

Laura rewarded John with a kiss and a hug. John repaid the favor and then turned to Stan.

"I think you and Ellie need some private time, so we'll be heading back now. Is that alright, Laura?"

Laura nodded, then gushed, "Thank you for dinner, Ellie and John. It was wonderful."

"You're both welcome," replied Ellie.

"I'll see you later, John," said Stan.

John waved with his left hand as they stepped away, leaving the house with their arms linked.

Stan and Ellie heard their horses' hoofbeats a few minutes later as they left the ranch.

"So, Ellie, who needs the private time more, us or them?"

Ellie laughed and replied, "Right now, it's us because I still owe you for doing the dishes."

As she laughed, Stan looked into that happy face. This is what he dreamed about all those years on the battlefields and on the open plains. He had dreamt that this woman, this perfect, wonderful woman would be his wife and now she was.

Ellie stopped her laugh when she saw his serious face.

"Stan, is something wrong?"

"No, Ellie. Everything is perfect. I spent so many nights dreaming of this exact moment, of having you with me, seeing you laugh, and knowing that you were my wife. I can't ask for anything more, Ellie."

She moved close and kissed him gently.

"You never have to ask, my husband. But I can give you more."

Stan picked up his bride and carried her into their bedroom where she proved true to her word.

CHAPTER 9

The next two weeks proved to be even better than they had hoped. The money transfer was completed the day after they were married, leaving them a balance of over almost forty thousand dollars, an enormous sum.

The new carriage house was completed in eleven days and the horses were moved in, including the four beautiful mares and the gentle Morgan gelding brought to the ranch by George and Geoffrey Rafferty, who were both impressed with the ranch with its spring and horses.

Ellie was flabbergasted by the difference in the two men, who then stayed for lunch before returning to Denver later that afternoon having spent almost six hours with the newlyweds.

But it was the old bar L that underwent the biggest change. It went from a barely surviving ranch to a showplace. The furniture was all in place and Ellie had added her personal touch with curtains, rugs and bedding.

They had to fib a bit when John commented about the repairs ongoing on the nearby ranch and had been told that it was probably the original owners who were having the work done before they moved back in.

John was still beside himself with his inability to find someplace to live with Laura. Their wedding date was set, and he still had no place to live.

They had hired a new deputy, a young man named Gus Jorgenson. Gus had gotten over his fear and felt with both John and Stan there, it was safe. Hiring Gus gave John some well-needed freedom.

It was the day before they were to be married, and a very anxious John was with Laura at the B-P connected for one of their frequent visits as Laura and Ellie had spent hours hemming and stitching Laura's dress.

They had just finished lunch when Stan asked, "Say, do you ladies fancy a ride?"

"We're all done, Stan. Wait until you see the dress, John," Ellie replied.

"I'm sure it'll be every bit as pretty as the one you wore, Ellie," Stan said, "John and I will go and saddle the horses, while you can change into suitable riding attire."

Ellie laughed and said, "Suitable riding attire, Stan? Why don't you just tell me to put on my britches."

"Because, Ellie, you would accuse me of all sorts of nefarious reasons for telling you that."

"I would, and I'd be right, too."

"Well, then go put on your britches," was Stan's parting comment as he and John went outside to saddle the horses.

"Are you really going to wear britches rather than a riding skirt?" asked Laura with raised eyebrows.

"Not just any britches. My lecherous husband had me modify a pair to make them more form fitting. I can't wear them in town, but out here they're quite comfortable. Of course, there are consequences for wearing them."

"I would imagine so. Do you think we could make a pair for me?"

"I'll tell you what. I'll give you a pair of my unadjusted britches and see how you like them. If you do, we'll take care of it after the wedding."

"You know John's really worried about where we'll live. I think he's going to wind up renting an apartment."

"Let's see if something works out."

Stan and John had been talking about the lack of affordable ranches and Stan had been commiserating as they finished saddling the four horses.

When John saw Laura step out of the house wearing pants and a tight shirt, he almost fell over. He and Laura had already shared some serious groping, so he knew she was well-formed, but this was something else.

Stan didn't notice as much, as he was still fixated on his Ellie. She may not have the spectacular equipment like Laura, but her perfect face and still nicely curved figure suited her perfectly, and she was wearing her modified britches, too. He also noticed that she had tightened her blouse a bit as well.

Stan assisted his wife into the saddle as usual and John, seeing Stan's chivalrous action, followed suit and Laura thought this whole tight britches thing might catch on.

"So, where are we going? Out to the spring?" asked John.

"No, I thought we'd head west. I haven't been that far out, and I want to see what it's like."

"That sounds different, Stan. Let's try it," concurred Ellie as she nudged her gelding into a trot.

They all matched her horse's speed, soon leaving the ranch and turning right on the road.

"You know that old Bar L is down this way. I really wanted that place. I can't believe those people moved back," John said loudly over the four sets of hoofbeats.

"I wonder what it looks like now that they fixed it up?" asked Ellie.

"We'll see soon enough. It's coming up," Stan shouted.

As they approached the access road, they all slowed.

"Look at that!" exclaimed John, "They painted it green with white trim. It looks amazing! And the grounds are all cleaned up, too."

"Maybe they're inside, so let's go talk to them and see if they're nice folks," said Stan.

"I don't know, Stan. I'm still a little beat up over losing it," John replied.

"I'm really curious, though. I haven't seen anyone new in town. Have you?"

"No, but maybe they just contracted to have it fixed up and haven't arrived yet."

"Maybe. But I'm going to check it out," said Stan as he kicked his gelding toward the access road.

"Me, too," said Ellie, following Stan.

John looked over at Laura and shrugged before they both followed Stan and Ellie.

Stan rode right up to the house, stepped down, and Ellie followed suit. John was surprised at their behavior and trotted up next to them.

"What are you doing, Stan?" he asked while still mounted.

"Just looking. It seems like it's empty. I'm going inside."

Now John was horrified as was Laura. Both dismounted quickly and chased after their friends who were already at the front door and opening it!

"Wow! This place is really fixed up!" shouted Stan as he looked around at the new furniture and the recently rebuilt fireplace as Ellie stood beside him admiring her choices.

John and Laura went from horrified to amazed.

"This looks like a new house!" said John.

John turned to Ellie. "Ellie, do you remember the name on the deed for this place?"

Ellie looked like she was deep in thought, then replied, "I think so. It was John…something. It sounded so familiar. Oh! Now I remember, John Bickerstaff."

John stared at Ellie and then at Stan with his mouth open. Laura was almost in a state of shock.

Stan pulled out the set of keys and held them out to John as he said, "It may be premature, but congratulations Mr. and Mrs. Bickerstaff. Welcome home."

John accepted the keys but was still somewhat shaken as he asked, "Are you two serious? You bought this place and fixed it up as a wedding gift?"

"We wanted you for our neighbors, John. It was Ellie's idea. It turned out nicely, I think."

"It's absolutely beautiful," sighed Laura.

"John, Ellie and I are going to head back. The larder is full, so you can stay in your house. Don't forget to add Laura's name to the deed after you're married," Stan said as he handed the deed to John.

Laura hugged Ellie while John slapped Stan on the back. Then Laura hugged Stan and gave him a kiss on the cheek. Stan didn't want to admit to Ellie what effect Laura hugging him had. He was sure she knew anyway, and he was already planning on ridding his wife of those tight pants when they got home, if they made it out of the barn.

They left the house and waved as they rode back to their own ranch. The consequences of Ellie's modified britches and Stan's close contact with Laura pushed their horses to a higher than expected rate of speed.

––––––

As they lay on their bed an hour after returning, Ellie sprawled against Stan, half on and half off, with Stan running his fingers over her damp skin as he usually did, Ellie asked, "Stan, do you think they'll be as happy as we are?"

"I have no idea. We had a head start over any married couple I've ever known. I've known some couples that knew each other for a long time and went to school together, but you and I,

FINDING BUCKY

Bucky, we were forged together by all the ugliness that was around us.

'We had no one else but each other, but there was more than that. If you had already been hardened by how you were being treated, then I wouldn't have been able to get close to you. But your soft heart and your tenderness were what allowed me to become your best friend."

Ellie exhaled softly, then said, "You were always much more than that to me, Piggy. When I arrived in school on that first day, and saw everyone staring at me, I tried to cover my mouth. I went to the back of the room where no one could see me, and you were there already.

"I had my hand over my mouth, and do you remember what you said to me? I remember it as clearly as if it had happened ten minutes ago. You looked at me and smiled. You said, 'They call me Piggy. You can too if it makes you feel better. I think you're pretty.'"

Stan picked up the story, saying quietly, "And you took your hand down and smiled at me. Then you asked, 'Do you still think I'm pretty.'"

Ellie smiled softly and said just as softly, "And you said to me, 'You're the prettiest girl I've ever seen.' And then I felt better, Stan. Not because you said I was pretty, but because you told me that you were called Piggy by the others.

"You told me that and you were still so nice. You showed me that you hadn't let it change you into a sad or mean person. Then I knew two things. I knew I could make survive whatever the other kids called me, and I knew at that moment that I would marry you. Even then, on the first day that I talked to you, I knew I loved you, Stan."

"Ellie, when you walked into the classroom, I watched you look around with your hand over your mouth and hoped you'd come and sit with me. I could already see the fear and worry in your eyes. I could never understand anyone else's feelings so easily. I sat and waited for you to join me, so I could tell you that you weren't alone. I was with you that day and will always be with you."

Ellie slid up a bit and kissed Stan gently on the lips.

"Thank you, Piggy. I love you."

Stan stared into Ellie's teary eyes, and whispered, "And I love you, Bucky."

EPILOGUE

John and Laura were married the next day and moved into their ranch, living close to their dear friends, Ellie and Stan.

Ellie told Stan she was carrying his baby a month later, and Laura followed her lead and became pregnant the next month.

Ellie gave birth to a beautiful baby girl on March 4, 1868, and they named her Mary.

Mary would grow up with her father's teeth and her mother's beautiful figure, as would their other three daughters. Ellie began apologizing to Stan after the third daughter, but he wouldn't hear it because he loved all of his little girls.

The ranch thrived and was soon producing dozens of beautiful horses each year. John and Laura also began raising horses, with an assist from Stan and Ellie yet again.

Mrs. McCormick was never heard from again after she rode her buggy out of Denver. The rumor was that she took her husband's final suggestion and became a madam of a large brothel in Pueblo and prospered at the position.

Her husband refused to take the clerk position that George had offered him but took the money from the sale of the house and returned to Michigan where he married Maude Murray, claiming that his wife had died.

George eventually took over the controls of the bank and would go to Boulder often to see his friends.

On the first day that Ellie and Stan took Mary to school, they heard the chants of some boys teasing a first-year student.

"Hey, Fatty! Want to eat some more pig slop so you can get fatter!"

Stan was going to say something when he saw Mary walk up to the boy, smile and say, "Hello, I'm Mary. What's your name?"

The boy smiled at her and said, "My name is Willie Johnson. They call me Fatty, to be mean. You're pretty."

"Well, I think you're nice," Mary said and smiled at Willie.

Willie smiled back, then Mary and the boy walked to the school's steps, sat down and began to chat.

Stan hooked his arm through Ellie's, and said, "Let's go home, Bucky."

FINDING BUCKY

1	Rock Creek	12/26/2016
2	North of Denton	01/02/2017
3	Fort Selden	01/07/2017
4	Scotts Bluff	01/14/2017
5	South of Denver	01/22/2017
6	Miles City	01/28/2017
7	Hopewell	02/04/2017
8	Nueva Luz	02/12/2017
9	The Witch of Dakota	02/19/2017
10	Baker City	03/13/2017
11	The Gun Smith	03/21/2017
12	Gus	03/24/2017
13	Wilmore	04/06/2017
14	Mister Thor	04/20/2017
15	Nora	04/26/2017
16	Max	05/09/2017
17	Hunting Pearl	05/14/2017
18	Bessie	05/25/2017
19	The Last Four	05/29/2017
20	Zack	06/12/2017
21	Finding Bucky	06/21/2017
22	The Debt	06/30/2017
23	The Scalawags	07/11/2017
24	The Stampede	07/20/2017
25	The Wake of the Bertrand	07/31/2017
26	Cole	08/09/2017
27	Luke	09/05/2017
28	The Eclipse	09/21/2017
29	A.J. Smith	10/03/2017
30	Slow John	11/05/2017
31	The Second Star	11/15/2017
32	Tate	12/03/2017
33	Virgil's Herd	12/14/2017
34	Marsh's Valley	01/01/2018
35	Alex Paine	01/18/2018
36	Ben Gray	02/05/2018

37	War Adams	03/05/2018
38	Mac's Cabin	03/21/2018
39	Will Scott	04/13/2018
40	Sheriff Joe	04/22/2018
41	Chance	05/17/2018
42	Doc Holt	06/17/2018
43	Ted Shepard	07/13/2018
44	Haven	07/30/2018
45	Sam's County	08/15/2018
46	Matt Dunne	09/10/2018
47	Conn Jackson	10/05/2018
48	Gabe Owens	10/27/2018
49	Abandoned	11/19/2018
50	Retribution	12/21/2018
51	Inevitable	02/04/2019
52	Scandal in Topeka	03/18/2019
53	Return to Hardeman County	04/10/2019
54	Deception	06/02/2019
55	The Silver Widows	06/27/2019
56	Hitch	08/21/2019
57	Dylan's Journey	09/10/2019
58	Bryn's War	11/06/2019
59	Huw's Legacy	11/30/2019
60	Lynn's Search	12/22/2019
61	Bethan's Choice	02/10/2020
62	Rhody Jones	03/11/2020

Made in the USA
Columbia, SC
30 March 2020

90146123R00178